When Peter Holland married Sarah Wood-ard's dear cousin, she was astonished. After all, contrary to turn-of-the-century convention, the two girlhood companions had vowed they would *never* marry. And when Peter's wife mysteriously passed away, Sarah was convinced the man she'd never met had something to do with it. So she hired herself out as a tutor for Peter's little boy, determined to expose a heartless fiend. But instead, she found a warm, devoted father who arouses in her feelings of forbidden passion. And now that Sarah has learned Peter's ideal high-society marriage was anything but, she must decide whether he is the perfect man for her—or a dangerous deceiver.

"With her trademark blend of wit and sensuality, Tanya Anne Crosby has created a remarkable love story. *Perfect In My Sight* is wonderfully entertaining from the first page to the last."
Lisa Kleypas, nationally bestselling author

"Richly sensual, each tale is magnetic."
Stella Cameron

"Tanya Anne Crosby writes stories that light the darkest corners of history with the warm, glowing beacon of love."
Pamela Morsi

Other Avon Romantic Treasures by
Tanya Anne Crosby

KISSED
LYON'S GIFT
THE MACKINNON'S BRIDE
ONCE UPON A KISS

If You've Enjoyed This Book,
Be Sure to Read These Other
AVON ROMANTIC TREASURES

AFTER THE THUNDER *by Genell Dellin*
BRIGHTER THAN THE SUN *by Julia Quinn*
DEVIL'S BRIDE *by Stephanie Laurens*
THE LAST HELLION *by Loretta Chase*
MY WICKED FANTASY *by Karen Ranney*

Coming Soon

SLEEPING BEAUTY *by Judith Ivory*

TANYA ANNE CROSBY

PERFECT IN MY SIGHT

An Avon Romantic Treasure

AVON BOOKS ◆ NEW YORK

This is a work of fiction. Names, characters, places, and incidents either are the product of the author's imagination or are used fictitiously. Any resemblance to actual events, locales, organizations, or persons, living or dead, is entirely coincidental and beyond the intent of either the author or the publisher.

AVON BOOKS
A division of
The Hearst Corporation
1350 Avenue of the Americas
New York, New York 10019

Copyright © 1998 by Tanya Anne Crosby
Inside cover author photo by Clay Heatley
Published by arrangement with the author
Visit our website at http://www.AvonBooks.com
Library of Congress Catalog Card Number: 97-94322
ISBN: 0-380-78572-2

First Avon Books Printing: May 1998

AVON TRADEMARK REG. U.S. PAT. OFF. AND IN OTHER COUNTRIES, MARCA REGISTRADA, HECHO EN U.S.A.

Printed in the U.S.A.

WCD   10   9   8   7   6   5   4   3   2   1

PERFECT IN MY SIGHT

Prologue

"**Y**ou are the *only* one I would let read this, Sarah—not even Papa has seen it!"

Dressed in their pajamas and ready for bed, both girls lay upon their bellies on the bed in the room they shared, staring down at the little book that lay between them.

Sarah Woodard gazed down at her cousin's neat penmanship and relived through her cousin's words the events of the day. The wedding had been an elaborate affair, though hardly something Sarah ever cared to experience. At seventeen, she didn't feel particularly keen upon the notion of abandoning her goals and dreams simply to serve a man—not any man! If Diana Halloway wished to give away her freedom and her life to that end, far be it from Sarah to condemn her for it.

She and Mary, however, would never be so small-minded!

Placing a finger at the center of the page, upon a particular passage, Sarah agreed, "That was so very

1

funny. I cannot believe he sneezed in the middle of their vows!''

Mary giggled, and Sarah did as well, remembering the moment with her best friend and confidante, her cousin Mary, by her side.

''I thought Diana would swoon!'' Mary exclaimed. ''Did you see the look upon her face when the pastor asked him a third time and he sneezed yet again rather than say 'I do?' How horrifying!''

Sarah's giggles intensified. ''How dreadfully embarrassing,'' she said, and rolled upon her back. She reached out and seized a pillow, clutching it to her breast, laughing.

Mary did too, leaving the diary on the bed between them. ''Gawd!'' she said, and ceased laughing abruptly, reaching up to plug her nose, imitating the pastor. ''Do you, Donald Alfred Salinger, take this woman, Diana Marie Halloway, to be your lawful wedded wife . . .''

Sarah giggled and clutched the pillow tighter, answering, ''Achoo!''

Mary pursed her lips, trying not to laugh as she continued with her imitation. ''To have and to hold,'' she persisted, as seriously as she was able, ''to love and to cherish, for better or for worse, until death do you part?''

''Achoo!'' Sarah replied, and burst into even more giggles.

Mary's imitation erupted into laughter. ''How terribly funny!'' she exclaimed. ''How dreadfully embarrassing, but how funny. Good Lord, I should never ever, ever wish to marry at all.''

"Me either," Sarah agreed.

The two cousins shared a look.

Sarah didn't know what she'd do without her cousin and her uncle. They were all she had in life. Her own mother and father had died too young to leave her even with memories. When she had been orphaned, her uncle Frank had taken her in hand and had raised her as his own, despite the fact that she had not been a blood relation. Her mother and Mary's mother had been cousins, but Mary's mother had long been dead, and Mary's father had upon his own decided to take Sarah into his home and his heart. He'd taught both girls to be strong. He'd inspired in them a love for academia, and he'd encouraged them to follow their dreams and to cow before no man. Sarah and Mary both had embraced his ideals and his teachings with a grateful heart.

"Promise you'll not," Sarah said.

"I do," Mary swore, and then demanded, "You swear it too, Sarah. Swear you will never marry."

"Ugh!" Sarah exclaimed. "Why should I desire to give up my life to a man who only wishes to use me for a breeding vessel? Please!"

"Why, indeed?" Mary affirmed.

"Silly creatures," Sarah muttered beneath her breath in reference to the male gender. She peered at Mary. "Except for Uncle, of course."

Mary smiled. "Papa is so wonderful. Did you hear what he said to Mrs. Brighton, when she inquired with *concern* over our *lack of marital prospects*?"

Sarah grinned and flipped over upon her belly

once more, an expression of glee upon her face. "He told her we were not allowed to marry a man unless he cooked and cleaned and bore children as well."

"How scandalous!" Mary declared, applauding her father.

Sarah did as well. "Did you see her face?" she asked, grinning. "I thought Mrs. Brighton would die of apoplexy."

"She has no sense of humor at all," Mary agreed.

"I don't ever wish to be like that," Sarah countered. "I want so much else in life . . . I want to paint, and I want to visit Paris. I want to visit the Louvre someday."

Mary turned on her side, reaching out to caress her journal reverently, as she spoke of her own dreams. "Yes, and I want to be a news reporter, I think," she revealed, somewhat hesitantly. "I know it seems a lowly job, Sarah, but I should love to write about people. I love to watch them, don't you know."

"You would make a fine reporter, Mary," Sarah assured, watching her cousin's uncertain expression. "I would proudly tell everyone I know."

"Would you?" Mary asked her, lifting her brows in surprise.

"Of course! And Uncle would too."

Mary smiled softly, reassured. Her eyes shone over the prospect. "He has always, always said we should do what makes us happy inside."

"Yes, he has," Sarah agreed. "We are the luckiest women."

Mary nodded.

"You're my very best friend, Mary. I don't know what I would do without you."

"And you are mine," Mary swore, "and it shall always be so."

"I will never leave you," Sarah stated.

"Let us make a vow, then," Mary proposed. "No man shall ever come between us—not ever!"

"Never," Sarah promised fervently. "We shall grow old together." She grinned. "And we shall be the two happiest old women upon the face of the earth, doing whatever we please."

"Yes we will," Mary agreed. "And don't you dare go and fall in love, Sarah Woodard!" she demanded.

Sarah grimaced. "Don't be silly. I shall never. It would be you first, Mary."

"Not I!" Mary denied adamantly. "And just to be certain . . . we should seal this vow somehow."

"How?"

"I don't know . . ."

"I know. What would you most regret losing?" Sarah asked her.

"That's easy, my hands, lest I am unable to write," Mary answered.

Sarah cast her a glance. "I cannot lop off your hands," she told her cousin. "That's no good. It will not do."

Mary giggled. "No, I don't suppose you can. I should need my hands for more than to write with."

"What besides that?" Sarah prompted.

"How about my hair? It is my one true vanity, I fear."

Sarah gave her cousin a nod and a knowing smile. "Your hair, then . . . If you marry, then you must cut off your hair."

Mary shrieked, her hand going to her hair. "Gawd! I shall truly never wed, then. Not ever!"

Sarah giggled. "Good."

"And you?" Mary prodded. "What shall you give up?"

Sarah had to think about it a long while. There was only one thing she held at such high value and she never wished to lose that ever in her life—her family, her uncle and her cousin. Besides that, little compared. "How about . . . my painting," she proposed. "If I marry, then I shall never again lift up another brush to paint."

"Then we've a bargain?"

Sarah smiled. "That we do."

"But we needn't worry," Mary added, "because we have each other. We don't need some silly husband to lock himself away with his fellows in some stuffy library and smoke cigars until he goes bald."

Sarah grinned at Mary's unflattering description. "Yeah . . . who needs them!" she exclaimed, giggling.

"Not I!" Mary declared once more, and both girls fell again into fits of giggles, swearing upon their very souls that nothing would ever, ever keep them apart.

They laughed until they cried, and then grew sleepy.

"It's been a very, very long day," Sarah said wearily, and Mary agreed, closing her eyes.

Sarah reached out and clasped her cousin's hand. "You're my very best friend," she said again, and sighed.

"And you are mine," Mary replied, reaching out to place a hand upon her journal. "G'nite, Sarah," she mumbled sleepily.

"G'nite, Mary," Sarah replied.

They fell asleep together, holding hands.

Chapter 1

~~~⌒◯⌒~~~

New York City, 1886

Somehow the daily never seemed to arrive as expected.

Sarah's pique was only magnified by the condescending attitudes of those men who'd stood ogling her rudely while she'd procured her paper from the corner boy—something she should never have to do, mind you, as her daily was scheduled to be delivered into her hands each day. Confound it all, despite the fact that she paid her own bills and kept her own house, *someone* had obviously taken it upon himself to decide her reading material for her. Well, she was *not* the sort to sit at her embroidery like some good little maid, and she would certainly read whatever she chose!

Despotic men, all of them!

Flinging off her coat, she hung it upon the rack to dry, swiping her hand down the length of it in annoyance. Another cold, drizzly March morn, and

8

the filth of the city hung upon the air like a black mood. Good grief! A body could freeze to death simply walking down the street. Frowning at the trace of ash that remained upon her fingers, she shook her head and made her way into the study. All those smoking chimneys could make a person ill.

"Shall I bring you tea, Miss Woodard?"

Sarah started at the voice, halting abruptly, turning. She slid the paper to her side, hiding it behind her skirts. "Yes, thank you, please," she answered.

Somehow he always managed to appear, even when she thought she entered as quietly as a church mouse. She smiled as she watched him pivot and go, wondering if he employed little spies to inform him. For a butler, he wasn't particularly amiable either— not at all, to her experience. Not at all. Perhaps he was that way because she was a woman alone in the city. That thought particularly peeved her. In fact, not many approved of her status; no doubt it was expected that she flaunt her wares at some idiotic soiree, instead, trying to snare herself a wealthy man to *care for her*. That, of course, would be so much more acceptable than enjoying one's own company and minding one's own affairs.

Good lord, but the very notion outraged her.

Only her cousin Mary had shared her convictions. Her uncle Frank had taught his daughter better. Poor sweet Mary.

Cradling the morning edition of the *Times* beneath her arm, Sarah closed the door to her study and made her way to her favorite chair. Opening the paper first, as always, to the society page, she assured herself as she did so that most of what she would read there would be absolute drivel. Only one name interested her.

Peter Holland.

Mary's husband.

Was he her murderer, as well?

Sarah had to know. And someday she bloody well would. If she spent her dying breath in pursuit of the truth, then so be it. Mary's son, whom she had never set eyes upon as yet, deserved better than to be raised by a murdering papa. If Sarah discovered that Peter Holland was in truth responsible for Mary's death, well! Sarah knew one thing for certain; she would *not* leave Christopher in the care of a man who could have his wife murdered for the sake of her money.

Money was evil, Sarah believed, but not as evil as Peter Holland if the rumors were true.

It was said that his wife's death was entirely too coincidental. It was said he'd been on the brink of financial ruin before her death. And then miraculously, he'd recovered after.

A bit too miraculously.

The papers speculated it was Mary's money that had saved him. Unfortunately, only Mary knew the truth of the matter, and Mary had died that night protecting her son while her *loving* husband had sat in a drunken stupor at the other end of the house.

How could he not have heard the intruder? Why hadn't he been there to protect his wife and son?

Sarah wanted to know these things and more. And Mary might yet be able to tell her the answers: Her cousin had kept a journal from the time she'd learned to scribble her first words. It had been Mary's passion: her writing. And her prose had stirred both Sarah's heart and mind. After the murder, much of her writing had been leaked to and exploited by the press, at whose prompting, Sarah had no idea. But the unhappy details of her cousin's life had been printed in excerpts by thoughtless idiots more concerned with selling papers than respecting a dead woman's memories. The journal entries, however, had ended abruptly about three months before her death, and no one had been able to produce the final three months of her life.

Without Mary's journals, Sarah only knew what the papers had reported . . . that poor Christopher, not more than six months old that awful night, had been blinded by the glass breaking in the window above his crib.

The intruder had entered, the *Times* had said, *startling the sleeping mother from her bed. The screaming infant, he'd abandoned as he'd escaped through the broken window, leaving the mother lying in a pool of her own blood.*

The very thought of it left Sarah ill.

She hadn't been able to sleep for months afterward, thinking of Mary, wondering if she had suffered much and regretting forevermore her own behavior toward her beloved cousin.

Sarah's eyes stung with tears. So angry had she been over her cousin's *betrayal,* she'd not even attended Mary's wedding. In retrospect, Sarah knew she was the one at fault. She understood that now. She should have stood by Mary's decision—whether it be right or wrong. Good grief, it had been Mary's right to decide. Such foolishness!

And yet . . . it had bereaved Sarah so to see her cousin, her best friend, married to a man who admittedly wed her only for the heir she could produce for his name and fortune. Such a notion was positively medieval, though she knew it to be common still. Sarah had been abroad at the time, otherwise she might have, in her outraged youth, gone and dragged Mary away from the altar by her hair! Peter Holland hadn't loved her cousin; he'd been forthright about that, at least. And still Mary had been willing to wed him, because her foolish heart had lost its way. Sarah thanked God she wasn't so inclined!

And yet . . . she had been wrong to turn away from one of the two people in her life who had stood beside her.

Sarah had gone to France with her uncle to study painting, and Mary had remained, intending to join them later. She'd never arrived to meet them, instead had sent a messenger to her papa with her profession of love for this man who had not cared a whit for her. Her uncle had taken the news quite well. With his good and kind heart he had stood behind Mary and had returned dutifully to watch his daughter take her vows. Sarah had not been so benevolent. She'd refused to watch her cousin throw her life away and had remained in France.

She'd lived to regret it.

For more reasons than one. Her uncle had fallen ill a year after Mary's nuptials, and he'd passed away so quickly that Sarah had received the news of his illness only days before the news of his death. She'd written to Mary with her wishes to join her, but Mary's response had been full of anger and bitterness. In a return note, she'd informed Sarah that she was no longer welcome in her home. And so Sarah had remained in France to grieve alone. Less than six months later came the news of Mary's death. She'd not even learned of Christopher's birth until she'd read the report in the papers.

Sitting blindly with the paper clutched in hand, Sarah relived the anguish of those moments. Even now, all these years later, she could hardly dispel the incredible sense of regret. Lord only knew, there were so many things she would do differently if only she could.

So much she would change . . .

The knock upon the door startled her.

Good Lord, she'd completely forgotten about her tea.

"Come in," she said, a bit unsettled as the door opened.

"Your tea, Miss Woodard."

Sarah straightened. "Yes, thank you, Hopkins."

He entered, bearing his tray, and she ignored the slight raise of his brows as he glanced down his nose at the paper in her hand. She held her tongue, resenting in herself the need to explain. Why should she be forced to? What man felt obliged to explain himself when caught with a paper in his hand? One he'd paid for twice at that! Having scarcely read a word of it, she refused to set it aside, just on principle. Her tea could wait.

"Thank you, Hopkins," she said again, dismissing him, and didn't bother to wait until he left to continue her perusal of the morning edition. With Hopkins dismissed and her morose thoughts chased away, she began to scan the articles in earnest, finding little of interest . . .

She perused an article about some new headache and hangover remedy:

Coca-Cola goes on sale May 8 at Jacob's Pharmacy in Atlanta, where local pharmacist John S. Pemberton has formulated his esteemed Brain Tonic and Intellectual Beverage from ingredients which include dried leaves from the South American coca shrub . . .

She flipped the page. What a thing to call a hangover remedy: Esteemed Brain Tonic and Intellectual Beverage!

A model Bloomingdale's department store to open on Third Avenue at Fifty-ninth Street . . .

And then . . . there it was . . .
His name in bold print, as it so often was.
Peter Holland's personal life was fodder for gossip, and his business dealings carefully scrutinized by his peers and the press, but rarely was there a

single word spoken of the one person Sarah most
wanted to know about. Christopher. And here it was
at last, though indirectly.

And more.

*Wanted. Personal instructor familiar with the
systems of Louis Braille and William B. Waite.
Must be willing to work and reside in house,
and must deal well with children. Generous
pay with benefits. Willing to employ the blind.
Send résumé directly to Peter Holland at corner of University Place and Twelfth Street. Applicants will be personally selected and
interviewed.*

Sarah inhaled a breath, and her hands began to
tremble. She was forced to set the paper aside. Good
Lord . . . this was precisely the opportunity she had
been hoping for . . . waiting for . . . for six long
years . . .

"Miss Woodard?"

It couldn't have presented itself more propitiously.

"Miss Woodard?"

Shivering away her thoughts, she peered up to find
Hopkins standing at the doorway still, the knob in
hand, but he was frozen in his stance, staring at her.
Waiting for her response.

She blinked, her thoughts still upon the article,
and its import. Her mind raced with unmade plans.
"Yes?"

"Are you quite all right? You appear as though
you've taken a sudden malaise."

''Oh yes,'' Sarah declared, ''I'm fine, thank you.'' Never better, in truth! Despite that she had hoped and prayed for such an opportunity—prepared for it even!—she simply hadn't expected to find it *this* dreary morn, not when she'd checked the paper literally hundreds of mornings before to no avail.

She peered up from the paper, placing it upon the table beside her. ''I'm quite well indeed. That will be all, Hopkins, thank you.'' Intrusive man. And this time she waited for him to leave her before rising from the chair and going to her desk. There was so much yet to be done! And so little time! But no matter what it took, no matter what the risk, she was going to do this—she wanted Mary's journals. She *needed* to know the truth. Mary's journals had all been discovered and dissected by the police and the press, but for one—the one that held the accounts of her days until the date of her death. Sarah wanted *that* diary. All her carefully laid plans would not go to waste, and Peter Holland was going to pay the consequences of his actions.

Sarah was determined to see it so.

She was going to find that missing journal!

Opening her desk drawer, she plucked up a sheet of paper and reached for her quill. She scribbled a brief note and then called for Hopkins, instructing him to hire a messenger to deliver her message to an address on Twelfth Street. That done, she returned to the desk and plucked out another sheet. Wholly absorbed now with the task at hand, she sat down to pen her résumé.

Inadvertently, with his very own ad, Peter Holland

had given her the most ingenious idea how to search his house free of suspicion.

Who would ever suspect a blind instructor for the blind?

Chapter 2

Most six-year-old boys might have entered a room with a boisterous shout and a slide to his knees, particularly in the case of this room, which was situated at the rear end of a long, wide corridor with bare wood floors, floors that were buffed to a brilliant, blinding shine. His son entered quietly with a smile that shone more brightly than any wood floors possibly could. His steps were cautious and yet unerring, his bearing straight and dignified.

Pride filled him.

"Daddy?"

Peter Holland swallowed the knot that rose in his throat.

Christopher couldn't know that his father's eyes had been trained upon him from his first glimpse of movement at the far end of the long hall. Even before Christopher had spoken, Peter's attention had been fully riveted on his only son. It pained him that Christopher might scent his presence, hear his every

18

movement even, but his son could never perceive the stillness of a loving stare.

"Here, son," he said, and his voice wavered a bit.

Christopher's smile brightened. "I knew that, Daddy," he boasted, and spoiled the prideful boyish response with a statement that sounded entirely too mature. "I can smell your port."

Peter chuckled, but his gaze fell to the glass that remained ever before him upon his desk, never touched, never acknowledged, except by his child who couldn't possibly understand its meaning. He turned away from it, his gaze returning to Christopher, but the sweet scent of the liquid lingered. He closed his eyes and took the scent into his lungs . . . a soft, sweet burn upon the air.

But how much of the burn was remembered and how much was real?

Did his son smell it the same way?

Would he describe it as such when he had never felt the sweet, numbing heat slide down his throat?

He refrained from asking; some things, he just couldn't.

"Are you working, Daddy? Am I botherin' you?"

"Never," Peter answered without hesitation. "Come in, son."

His steps were less cautious now, as Peter had never placed obstacles between his desk and his door. By design, the room was almost sterile in its decor, as was the rest of the house. And yet Chris did not run into his arms as Peter craved. His son had never done so. There seemed to be imaginary walls between Christopher's black world and the universe beyond, barriers that barred far more than color and light. It was as though his blindness robbed him of confidence, as well.

But this moment, Christopher's expression was eager, and something more. "I couldn't wait, Daddy! May I stay?"

To listen to the interview, he meant. "Christopher," Peter protested.

"I'll be quiet, Daddy. I promise! I promise!"

Peter had never a doubt. His son's deportment had never been anything less than upright. Christ, he was an old man at the ripe age of six.

"It's not that," Peter said. "I just can't imagine why you'd wish to. We don't even know if this will be the one, Christopher." Neither was he entirely certain he wished his son to hear some of the answers the applicants gave. They angered him enough with their lack of regard for his son's condition.

Then again, admittedly, much of what angered Peter failed even to register with his patient young son. Certainly Christopher was wise beyond his years, but perhaps, as a father, he was a bit overprotective.

"If you wish," he relented.

Christopher beamed. "Where may I sit, Daddy?"

"How about in my lap?"

"No!" Christopher declared at once, and halted in his step. He crossed his arms with stubborn little-boy pride, and exclaimed, "They'll think I'm a baby if I do."

Peter chuckled at his son's alarmed expression. "Impossible, sport. You forgot to be a baby. Everyone knows that."

And it was true.

His son was brilliant, his mind unparalleled in its thirst for knowledge. Peter had rarely seen such a grasp of the English language in a child so young, nor had he ever witnessed such a profound sense of logic. Were Christopher not blind, Peter would have labeled his mind photographic. Even from as early as the age of three, Christopher had been able to recite a tale, word for word, after the first time it was read to him. Christopher had graduated from his crib to a mountaintop, from his baby squeals to the gentle words of a sage. Peter had no reason to believe he should wait before introducing him to Braille.

"How about you sit at my desk," Peter suggested, "and I'll sit upon the divan?"

Apparently that satisfied him, because Christopher came forward once more and Peter opened up his arms to embrace his son. "I think I'll just sneak myself a hug," he said playfully, and Christopher squealed with embarrassed delight as Peter lifted him onto his lap.

"Who's coming today?" his son demanded to know.

"Someone better than yesterday, I hope."

Yesterday's applicant had come near to leaving with a bloodied nose when he'd dared to suggest that Christopher wear dark spectacles in his presence always. It seemed the man was uncomfortable with *the stare*. Without warning, Peter had bolted from his seat and the man had leapt from his own, taking his leave at once. He'd been fortunate. Had Peter set hands upon him, he might not have walked out the door at all.

The day before that he'd interviewed an older woman who had never had the first contact with Braille but had *cared for her blind mother until her death*. The poor woman seemed to have missed the point entirely. If he'd wished to hire an escort for Christopher, he'd have done so long ago. Christopher didn't need a bloody chaperon. He had Peter and he had his aunt for that. What he needed was to begin to learn to manage his own affairs—and the first step toward that end was to instill in him a sense of confidence that he could accomplish anything he set out to do. Matters of intellect did not seem to intimidate his son, so the next order of business was to empower Christopher with the tools he would need to achieve his goals.

Blindness was a disadvantage certainly, but not an insurmountable obstacle. Peter refused to see it as such.

His son would succeed despite it. Peter intended to make certain of the fact.

"Whatsis name, Daddy?"

"Not *him*, son. *Her*." He lifted his brows. It was something he had great reservations about, to be quite honest. He hadn't wished to grant yesterday's interview with the old woman either, but he never left a stone unturned—not that he was opposed to hiring a woman, but most were simply not so well lettered. "Her name is Sarah . . ." He leaned forward to peer over his son's shoulder at the file upon his desk. "Sarah Hopkins. But you should call her Miss Hopkins."

"All right," his son replied.

The tin sound of a distant bell rang, and the echo of footsteps pursued it into the foyer, heavy but distinct footfalls upon solid wood. A knock upon the door at the far end of the hall followed and then the door was opened, the caller greeted.

Because their visitor had been expected, Gunther escorted their guest in without announcement.

Peter stood, with his son in his arms, and peered down the hall to find not one, but two women being escorted down the corridor to his office.

He lifted a brow at the sight of them.

"We are being invaded," he jested to his son. And then whispered, "There are two of them."

His son giggled while Peter settled him at his desk.

"What do they look like?" Christopher asked.

Peter understood his question. "Not too awful scary," he answered.

His son covered his ears and whispered, "She sounds like Aunt Ruth!"

Peter watched as they entered the room. The taller of the two overshadowed the other. Boisterous in her demeanor, she prattled on to Gunther, who dutifully ignored her snippy tone and answered her questions with a *yes madame, no madame*.

"She rather does at that," Peter agreed, peering over his shoulder at Christopher.

Though he couldn't quite hear their discourse, he thought her rather confident in her bearing, a positive trait in one who would teach, and an indication to Peter that she knew her position and was well at ease with her abilities. The other woman, he could not see entirely, as the boisterous one managed to shield her from his view. He moved forward to greet them.

She—they—were hardly what he had expected.

Both were lovely, and some bit younger than he had imagined. The boisterous one appeared to be in her early forties, he surmised, while the other couldn't be more than thirty.

"Mel Frank," said the boisterous one, extending her hand in greeting.

Peter stepped forward to accept it, and was about to bring it to his lips for a gentlemanly peck, but she wrapped her fingers about his hand and, with the grip of a deadly boa constrictor, shook it fiercely.

Her boldness took him aback so that he failed at first to note the name.

Mel Frank.

She looked him squarely in the face, and with her piercing blue eyes staring back at him, the realization struck him first that she was not blind.

She was not his applicant.

His attention turned at once to the woman who stood behind her. He blinked then, and entirely dismissed Mel Frank.

He forgot, even, to breathe.

Good God, she wasn't just lovely.

She was damned well beautiful.

With delicate brows that arched over dark spectacles and a princess nose, she exuded a sort of little-girl charm. Deep golden strands escaped her otherwise neat coiffure, and framed her face with gentle highlights that contrasted with her rich brown hair. But it was her lips that caught his attention, and held it—full lips that seemed formed to suit a man's pleasures. Not those of a child at all.

Did she know how to use them? The thought stirred his loins.

"Mr. Holland," Miss Frank said, drawing his attention once more. "May I introduce to you my employer, Miss Sarah Hopkins."

Miss Hopkins stepped forward, and Peter held his breath. His heart began to hammer.

"How do you do?" she replied at once, and extended her hand, as Mel had done. Only her gesture wasn't nearly as bold. He was so stunned by the sight of her that his hand remained at his side.

He couldn't remember the last time he had been so instantly taken with a woman.

Breaking free of his stupor, he took her hand but refrained from kissing it, merely shook it. He had the indication from both women's demeanors that a gentleman's kiss would be an entirely unwelcome gesture. Though Sarah's manner was not nearly as forward as Miss Frank's, her carriage was filled with the same haughty defiance, despite her obvious handicap; she couldn't see him.

Peter's first thought was that he wished she would remove her dark spectacles so he could see the color of her eyes. The mischievous shape of her brows intrigued him and he found himself peeking down over the rim of her spectacles, trying to get a glimpse. And then his focus shifted to the spectacles.

Blind, she was blind.

He was ashamed to admit that the notion left him slightly unnerved. His gaze fell once more to her lips, not quite able to meet her eyes, despite that she couldn't spy his.

And yet, to his stupefaction, and despite her disadvantage, for the first time in so long, surrounded by such disparate female company, Peter found himself at a loss for words.

"Do come in," he managed, still not quite able to tear his gaze from her lovely lips.

Slightly pouty.

Unpainted.

They looked so soft . . . he longed to brush a finger across them. Like the velvet blush of a rose petal . . . they begged to be touched.

Hardly by design, he held her hand a bit longer than was appropriate.

Chapter 3

Her hands were trembling.

Sarah prayed he wouldn't notice.

Confound it all, this wasn't going to work.

How did one pretend to be blind in the face of such masculine beauty.

Good Lord! This, of course, was the man who had turned her cousin's heart. Of course he would be beautiful. For him, Mary had cast away all her values. For him, she had thrown away her life!

Sarah tried to remember as she stared into his eyes—deep blue, and piercing in a way she'd never experienced before. In that instant she was grateful that her own eyes were shielded, for she doubted she could have hidden the thoughts that were going through her mind.

There was something slightly wicked in the way he gazed at her . . . something slightly thrilling about the way his eyes lowered to her mouth . . . lingered there.

It gave her a delicious but unwelcome shiver.

Resisting the urge to turn away, she reminded herself that a *blind woman* could not be cowed by what she could not see. And she tried to appear oblivious, tried to appear blissfully unaware of his lips, which parted once more to speak.

Sensual lips that promised a lover's gentle kisses . . . Another shiver raced down her spine.

She closed her eyes.

He was Mary's murderer, she reminded herself—a heartless wretch.

"My son, Christopher," he said, introducing the boy who sat behind the desk with a wave of his hand—a gesture she wasn't supposed to see.

She could scarce hide her gasp of surprise at his introduction.

How could she have failed to notice the very face she most wished to see?

Swallowing the lump that rose in her throat, she resisted the urge to turn to him fully, to drink in the sight of Christopher Holland with her eyes. So long she'd waited for this moment! She tried to focus on Mel's advice, and instead tilted her head toward the sound of his voice when he spoke, *seeing* him first through the sound of his little-boy voice.

"Hello," he said quietly, and the single word was the sweetest greeting Sarah had ever heard. It was the dulcet voice of a six-year-old angel.

Peter Holland's brows lifted. "Forgive me," he said, "I certainly didn't intend to startle you with his presence, but . . . you see . . . my son wishes to personally . . . er . . . *conduct* this interview."

He smiled a devastating smile that Sarah wasn't

supposed to react to. Because she wasn't supposed to spy it. A reflex, she was quite certain. He probably couldn't help himself, she thought sourly. He was probably quite used to stealing hearts and charming young women to death.

And still her heart quickened its pace.

Murderer.

"Have you objections to his presence?"

Sarah resisted the urge to turn and stare at her cousin's child. "Not at all!" she replied, and tried not to sound overeager for his presence. "He's the one I most need to impress, is he not?"

Peter chuckled at her question. "After all he is at that," he agreed, and seemed to relax a bit in his stance. He turned to his son. "Ready, sport?"

"Yes, sir," the boy replied.

In the meek sound of his voice, there was little evidence of his tempestuous mother, and the realization filled Sarah with grief.

And yet, she determined, how could there be anything of Mary in him at all when Mary had had so little influence upon his life?

"Very well," Peter continued, dismissing his butler with a nod. He turned to Mel, motioning toward the facing chair. "My apologies," he said, "but as you see, I've only the one. I was expecting Miss Hopkins alone, I'm afraid—though I should have anticipated perhaps. If you will see her to her seat, you are welcome to the divan yourself." And with that he dismissed Mel and sat on the corner of his desk.

Mel, bless her heart, suddenly took a servile role,

quite unlike their entrance, which was anything but deferential and caused Sarah to wince. Taking Sarah gently by the arm, she led her to the chair as though Sarah were indeed unable to find the black leather monstrosity on her own. Sarah did her part to appear awkward though not entirely helpless—she couldn't quite manage helpless.

Mel bent to whisper in her ear. "Eyes closed," she demanded.

Sarah closed them at once. And suddenly it was all she could do not to run screaming from the room. All that kept her focused and calm was the strength of her purpose . . . and the little boy sitting not more than five feet from her.

Christopher was the reason she was here, she reminded herself.

Opening her eyes, she sat facing the enormous desk, trying not to weep with joy at the sight of the six-year-old child seated behind the hulking piece of furniture, his little face barely visible above the papers stacked there. She tried to keep a blank expression. And yet she dared not look away, dared not twitch a brow at the sight of him. She could scarce keep her hands from trembling as she sat inspecting her cousin's child for the first time, her emotions in melee.

Her uncle would have been overjoyed to see him this moment.

He looked so like Mary, with his tawny hair and his upturned little nose. It saddened Sarah that her uncle had not lived to set eyes upon his only grandson—her sweet uncle who had sworn *his two girls were all that any papa should need.* She could almost hear him speak the words as though he were standing over her shoulder, and the sensation choked her breath away.

"If I recall correctly . . ."

Peter Holland, too, had been gazing at his son, and shifted his attention suddenly, crossing his arms as he turned to assess her. Sarah spied him from the corner of her eye, but dared not acknowledge his renewed regard. She continued to stare at the desk, at Christopher, repressing her emotions.

"Your résumé states you studied at the Institution Nationale des Jeunes Aveugles in Paris? Quite a feat for someone so young, much less . . ."

"A *blind woman*?" she finished for him, recognizing the tone and wholly offended by it. She lifted her chin, tilting her head, though kept her calm, taking Christopher's presence into consideration, recalling her purpose. It wouldn't suit to begin railing over the iniquities of male supremacy, though it galled her nevertheless. "You need not finish, Mr. Holland," she told him. "I hear it in your tone. Do you not believe a woman capable of academics?"

"I did not say that, Miss Hopkins."

Sarah was certain she heard amusement in his voice now. A note that only further provoked her.

"It is *Miss* Hopkins, is it not?"

"Yes, it is, *Mr. Holland.* And you need not have said a thing, sir. Pardon my speaking so plainly, but I am blind, *not* deaf, nor am I stupid."

He had the audacity to chuckle at that. "No, you are not, I see."

Sarah didn't quite appreciate his good humor.

"My apologies once again," he offered, and managed to sound quite sincere, despite the laughter that tinged his voice.

"In any case," Sarah continued, bolstered now by a renewed sense of injustice for the plight of her gender, "*I* did not study Braille at the Institute. You misunderstood my letter of credits. My late tutor was a retired professor there."

"I see," he said. "And how long have you been using the Braille code, may I ask?"

"Five years," Sarah lied, prepared for his question. She was well rehearsed. "Long enough to lament the fact that there is too little published as yet."

"Yes, I tend to agree," he said. "But I shall remedy that for my son's sake, I assure you."

Sarah swallowed and forced her reply. "He is quite a fortunate child to have such a caring father."

The praise sat like acid within her belly, burning with her anger.

Murderer.

He glanced at Mel. Sarah refrained. She didn't dare look at Mel, didn't dare give herself away.

"And in what capacity does Miss Frank *serve* you?" he asked her then.

"She is both my friend and my aid. She sometimes assists with instructions, as well." A greater understatement, Sarah had never uttered. Mel's knowledge of the Modified Braille code and her work with the sightless would be the key to effecting this plan. Though Sarah had anticipated having to teach Christopher someday, hoped to at least, Sarah only knew the minimal. Without Mel, she'd never have been able to complete this ruse.

He seemed to be studying her. "I have but a few more questions, if you might indulge me."

Sarah braced herself. "Certainly."

He lifted up her résumé, scanning it.

Sarah's gut turned as he read over her lies.

"Your credentials are excellent. I've no reason to doubt them, but it's essential I understand your commitment . . ."

He sounded all the world like a loving, caring father, but Sarah knew better. "Of course," she replied.

"Why Braille? Why not the New York Point System?"

"Well," she began, "I must confess that my résumé is a bit misleading as it stands." She took a deep breath—*it was more than a bit misleading!* "Braille is in fact the system I was primarily taught, but I am also familiar with the New York Point System. My preference, however, is a rather new code, the Modified Braille."

His brows lifted. "Modified Braille? I'm afraid I am not familiar with that one."

"Yes, well, it has yet to be accepted by the British Braille authorities—though it has been used with some success at the Perkin's Institute in Boston. It is very similar to Louis Braille's system, but the new code's key feature is that the most frequently recurring letters are represented by the smallest number of dots. Therefore, it may be written and read more quickly.'' She glanced at Mel out of the corner of her eye and saw that she was nodding her approval. ''The New York Point System, on the other hand,'' she continued, encouraged, ''though at present it receives much favor, is a bulky and confusing system. I wouldn't recommend it at all.''

''And so you would propose to teach my son this Modified Braille?''

Sarah shook her head. ''The choice is solely at your discretion, of course, Mr. Holland. I am merely giving you my humble opinion. I am quite capable of instructing him in any of the codes we've discussed, but yes, I do have strong leanings toward the Modified Braille. And yet . . . I should caution you to consider that most of what is published already is published in accordance with the British Braille authorities. That does not mean, however, that it will always be so. The debate is quite heated at the moment, and there is a diversity of opinion as to which code is actually the better. There are strong advocates for both the New York Point System as well as the Modified, but as yet, as I said, the British Braille authorities do not recognize either.''

''You certainly seem to know your work, Miss Hopkins.''

Sarah felt nearly dizzy with relief at his approval. Not that she gave a blast what he thought of her truly. She was merely relieved that he had accepted her story.

''Now I would like to know why it is you are applying for this position.''

Because she wanted to catch a murderer!

The directness of his question startled her only an instant.

She took a deep breath. "Because I was not always blind, Mr. Holland," she replied, repeating the story she and Mel had rehearsed.

She came aware of the sound of footsteps, and tilted her head toward the newcomer, not daring to turn and acknowledge the person with her glance. It wasn't easy to catch herself at every gesture, but she *must* do her absolute best. It was crucial she not give herself away. She closed her eyes now, and kept them closed, forcing herself to see the room only through the confines of her mind.

"I had a friend, you see, when I most desperately needed one," she continued passionately, and silently berated herself for not considering acting as a career. "My tutor . . . he inspired me when I thought nothing might. He taught me that my blindness was not a death sentence, Mr. Holland, and that I need not waste myself with self-pity and lamentations. Someone cared enough to give all that to me, and I only wish to give it back."

The room remained silent.

She heard his intake of breath and knew he was moved by her words.

"That is certainly commendable," he said after a contemplative moment.

"You see," she continued, encouraged, "there *must* be a reason under the sun for everything, Mr. Holland. And I refuse to allow my own *accident* to pass in vain."

"You are quite a remarkable woman," he said with meaning.

Sarah opened her eyes.

The sincerity in his tone was disarming.

The way he was looking at her was even more so. It was a look she wasn't supposed to spy behind her dark glasses, and yet she did.

Her heart hammered a strange beat against her breast.

She had to will herself to breathe.

It was dangerous to believe him capable of even human compassion, she reminded herself. Any man who could murder his wife so coldly had a heart as black as coal.

Peter Holland was a dangerous man—more so because he bore the face of an angel. He wasn't an angel, but a heartless killer.

"Thank you," Sarah answered, a little breathlessly.

What the devil was wrong with her?

"Well, then . . ." He turned to look at Christopher. "Are you ready to conduct the interview, sport?"

Sarah could scarce see the little face that lit with excitement behind the massive desk. She was grateful for the sudden turn of Peter's attention.

"I really can do it, Daddy?" Christopher asked, bubbling over with enthusiasm. And yet he didn't rise up on his knees as Sarah expected most boys would have done. He didn't vie for a better view of her. He didn't look her in the face. He merely sat within his father's chair, glowing with excitement.

"Of course," his father replied. "She's all yours, son."

Sarah smiled despite herself at his choice of words.

"What should I ask her, Daddy?" he whispered anxiously, and seemed to think, perhaps, that no one but his father could hear.

"Ask whatever you wish," Sarah answered. "What may I tell you that will convince you to give me employ?"

"Ummm," he replied a little uncertainly, and placed a finger to his head, as though to touch upon the answer in his brain. "Do you . . . umm, keep taffy in your dress coat?" he asked.

Sarah smiled, forgetting her darker thoughts in the face of such sweet innocence. "Why, yes, I do!" she confessed, and resolved to do so, "though sometimes, I fear, I sneak them for myself. But shhh," she urged him. "Don't tell anyone."

He giggled, and Sarah had to restrain herself from peering over the desk to better see his expression. He had his mother's laughter, she thought—that impish little giggle that made one want to giggle, too, even when one wasn't certain what the laughter was about.

"Next question?" she prompted him, and was very much aware that his father was watching them carefully . . . and someone else was watching too.

Sarah sensed the scrutiny upon her and yet dared not turn to see who it was that watched from the doorway behind her.

"Ummm," he said again, and paused awhile to

think. He cast his head back, as though to gaze up at the ceiling in contemplation. Sarah tried to remain sober at the sight of him. "Do you have a little boy of your own?" he asked next, surprising her with the question.

Sarah smiled again. "Why, no, I don't. Nor a little girl, though I wish very much that I did," she confessed.

"Then why don't you get one?" he suggested with the innocence of a child.

Sarah laughed at that. "Well, it is not quite so simple as all that, I'm afraid."

"Why not?" he persisted, and Sarah caught herself before she could glance up into his father's face.

She wasn't even certain why she was compelled to, and the realization perturbed her.

She frowned. "Because I don't wish to marry, is why."

"Oh," he replied, and seemed to ponder that an instant, before asking, "Why not?"

"*Christopher,*" came a woman's voice from behind them, her tone full of censure.

Sarah started at the sound of it.

Christopher quieted for a moment and then asked, "Do you smell?"

Sarah's brows collided. "Do I smell?"

Peter Holland covered his mouth with his hand and tried not to laugh, Sarah noted. "I think he is wondering if you wear perfume," he clarified.

Oh! Good Lord, but they begin so young. "Just a bit," she answered. And it was her turn now to ask, "Why, Christopher?"

" 'Cause I don't like it!" he answered fervently.

"I see." Sarah bit her lip. She certainly was not going to laugh at his disclosure, even though she wished to.

"That is because you are much too young to appreciate it," the woman at the door announced somewhat defensively.

Sarah was plagued with curiosity now. Christopher seemed reluctant to speak again. Nor did she fail to note the uneasy silence that had fallen over the room.

Until Peter Holland's deep baritone spoke to breach it.

"Miss Hopkins," he said, "please make the acquaintance of my sister . . . Miss Ruth Holland."

Sarah didn't dare search out the woman's visage. She lifted her chin, closed her eyes, and listened for her voice.

"Very good to meet you, Miss Hopkins."

Sarah blinked at the tone of her voice: cold disapproval. But why?

Why the instant dislike?

"Au contraire," Sarah answered, smiling, "the pleasure is all mine."

"Yes, well . . . I shall leave you to your interview. Please forgive the interruption. Peter," she said, dismissing Sarah rudely, "I shall see you at dinner. I should love to hear about the remaining applicants."

Peter said nothing in the uneasy silence, but then he replied, "I shall be out this evening, Ruth. Dinner engagement . . . business, so it will simply be you and Christopher tonight."

"I see," Ruth answered, her tone clipped and cool. "Very well, then. Perhaps tomorrow."

And then Sarah heard her departure, soft footsteps for one with such a bold presence. She waited for them to ebb completely.

"Did I do something wrong?" she asked then. "I've the impression she has dismissed me already." Sarah didn't have to pretend disappointment. If Peter Holland turned her away now . . . her chance to discover the truth would be gone forever. The thought aggrieved her enormously.

"Not at all," Peter assured. "My sister does not run my household, Miss Hopkins."

Sarah sensed in the pause that ensued that he would have liked to say more on the subject, but he refrained.

"In fact," he continued, "I think you are precisely the candidate I am seeking. If it suits you, the position is yours."

Her stomach lurched. She was both thrilled and terrified at once.

Sarah wasn't certain she could do this, and yet she must—every word, every action, she would have to scrutinize, but the end would be worth the means.

She straightened her spine. "It most certainly *does* suit me, Mr. Holland!"

"Then it's settled. The position is yours."

Sarah suddenly wasn't certain whether to thank him for the opportunity or to weep. Behind her dark glasses, she dared to look up into Peter Holland's eyes.

Innocent?

Guilty?

He was one or the other, and she had the sickening sensation she was about to find out which.

Chapter 4

The interview couldn't have gone more successfully.

Preparations couldn't have gone more smoothly.

So why did Sarah suddenly feel like crawling under the bed and never coming out?

All arrangements were complete now, and there was no turning back. All that remained to be done was to call a hansom and return to the corner of University Place and Twelfth Street.

Mel watched her from the divan, her legs drawn up upon the gold damask. "Lord, your pacing is making me dizzy, Sarah!" she complained.

"I cannot help it, Mellie!"

The two of them had been inseparable since Sarah had sought her out three years before. She'd gone to Mel hoping for instruction in dealing with the teaching and rearing of blind children, and had been stunned to find that Mel Frank was in fact *Melissa* Frank. Sarah had been horrified at her own discrimination, especially since she loathed it in others.

She'd been so mortified to have made such an error of judgment based on the biases of society that she'd apologized to Mel until Mel had been driven to shush her. The two of them had laughed so hard after, and Sarah had left the Institute with a new best friend.

"What time are we scheduled to arrive?"

"Two P.M.," Sarah replied.

"Try to calm yourself," Mel advised her. "It won't do you any good to make yourself ill with worry."

"What if I cannot act the part?" Sarah fretted. "What if he discovers my ruse?"

Mel watched her nervous strides with a patience Sarah had come to admire. "Yes," she dared to agree, "what if he does?"

It was a question Sarah had not permitted herself to ponder long—perhaps because the answer terrified her.

"What is the worst that could happen?" Mel asked her, forcing her to consider the consequences.

Sarah cast her friend a disbelieving glance at the question.

"Come now, Sarah . . . indulge me. At worst . . ."

Sarah didn't have to think about the answer. "If he killed the mother of his own son—" she began, and couldn't continue.

"Then he could most certainly do away with you easily enough?" Mel said, daring to finish her thought.

"Well, yes!" Sarah clasped her hands together, wringing them.

A genuine look of concern reentered Mel's eyes. "But are you willing to walk away, Sarah? Can you do that?"

"No."

There was no question of that at all.

Sarah would never be able to live with herself were she to walk away now that she finally had the opportunity to learn the truth.

"I cannot, Mel. You know that."

"Well, then . . . you've really no choice in the matter, have you?"

Sarah shook her head in answer. She truly didn't. "If Mary's journal remains in that house, I will find it, Mellie, I swear to God I will!"

"I have every faith you will," Mel assured, her blue eyes twinkling with something like admiration. Sarah cringed at the sight of it. She didn't deserve any such esteem. She'd bloody well failed Mary when Mary had most needed her. Had Sarah been there, had she been at Mary's side, her cousin might well be alive today.

If Mary had only had someone to talk to . . . to confide in . . . If she hadn't felt so isolated, with nowhere to turn . . .

Now was the time to make amends.

"Always wear your spectacles," Mel suggested, her voice firm. "You need not remove them save to sleep," she persisted. "And try not to hold anyone's gaze directly."

"I'll not," Sarah assured her.

Her expression grew resolute. "And keep your eyes closed, Sarah, as much as possible, unless you are absolutely certain you are alone and need not be on your guard. It is easier to be blind when you cannot see," she suggested, and winked to add a bit of levity to the soberness of the discussion.

Sarah nodded, storing the advice, trying to remember everything. Her nerves were at their ends.

"And use your cane as I have shown you. Make your way by it even when you think you need not."

The last-minute flood of advice infused her with a sense of panic. She froze in her step and peered up at the woman sitting so calmly upon the divan.

"Blast, Mellie!" she said. "You've not changed your mind, have you? You'll be coming with me, right?"

"Of course, Sarah. But I cannot be at your side every instant, else he will never believe I am simply your aide. That is why I told you to ask him whether I might make use of his servants' quarters. God only knows I have never aspired to such a thing, but there you have it—a servant must act as a servant, as you have already pointed out."

"Yes," Sarah agreed, nodding, her thoughts racing. "Yes. You are right, of course. I just cannot think straight now."

"I can well imagine."

Sarah chewed nervously upon her bottom lip, trying to recall if she had indeed remembered to ask for a room in the servants' quarters. She certainly hoped so.

"Anyway, I know you'll take good care of me," Mel said, with a laugh. "I cannot live long without *some* of life's little luxuries. Take pity on me and sneak me something sweet once in a while. I shall be content enough then.''

Sarah peered up at her, and Mel winked once more.

She could scarce wait to see Christopher again, to spend time with him alone, to get to know him.

''Braille is not such a difficult code, Sarah, so don't worry. I shall only caution you once more that when you practice them, do not practice them by sight.''

''I have not once done so,'' Sarah assured.

''Very good.''

''If I can only remember to keep my head.''

''You will,'' Mel replied, without hesitation.

''I've no choice,'' Sarah agreed.

''No, you don't, Sarah.'' The two of them shared an anxious glance. ''Not unless you care to find your toes cocked up—and mine as well,'' she added with nervous laughter.

Sarah felt a renewed sense of gratitude for Mel's friendship and help. ''I shall never be able to thank you enough for making this cause your own, Mel.''

Mel smiled. ''Yes, you will . . . by discovering the truth and doing what is right for that precious little boy.''

Sarah returned the smile. ''He is precious, isn't he?''

''Quite,'' Mel agreed.

''You know I intend to do the best for him.''

''I've no doubt,'' Mel said, and then asked the dreaded question, ''Are you ready to go, Sarah?''

Sarah took a deep breath and steeled herself. "Ready as I ever shall be."

Mel gave her an approving nod and rose at once from the divan. "That's my girl!" she said. "I'll send for a cab, then. Wish us luck," she suggested.

"Luck!" Sarah replied with resolve. "But not for us . . ." She laughed a bit, her stomach turning with anticipation of the ominous task before them. "For the unfortunate person who is bound to try to steal our hansom . . . because I know he's like to find himself flat upon his back and your umbrella up his nose!"

Mel returned a chuckle. "How true," she agreed, throwing her hands up as she went. "These rude city men think they were born with the right. I shall show them all, I think!"

Sarah chuckled as she watched Mel go, considering how very much like her cousin Mel was. And she suddenly missed Mary fiercely.

"I will *not* fail you, Mary," she whispered. "I swear to God I will not!"

If there was a journal to be found, Sarah would find it. And if Peter Holland was a murderer . . . he would pay dearly.

Sarah intended to see to it.

"Peter James Holland!"

Peter cringed at his sister's use of his full name. He loathed when she did that, but it was a habit she might never break.

"Good God! I cannot believe you would bring a strange woman into this house. You do not even know her! What sort of example do you think it will set for your son?''

Peter rolled his eyes but didn't halt his stride. ''Damn it, Ruth,'' he answered, ''she is not my lover, she's my son's bloody instructor!''

Ruth's fury was unmistakable. She followed him down the hall as he made his way toward his office, all the while shrieking her protests at his back. Christ, but that voice of hers enlightened him as to why some men did murder their wives—though he had a twinge of malaise at that thought.

''Don't you think it rather strange that the majority of your applicants were men,'' she continued to rail, ''and yet you hire the *young beautiful woman*?''

Damn, but Sarah *was* lovely, he allowed himself to acknowledge. Lovelier than any woman had a right to be. And vaguely familiar, too, he thought . . . as though he knew her somehow . . . and yet he'd never set eyes upon that face before.

He would have remembered.

He entered his office and made his way to his desk, refusing to address his sister's question.

''Were there no qualified men, Peter?''

She'd not been blind forever, she had said. What sort of accident had robbed her of her sight? Curiosity needled him.

He sighed at his sister's tirade. ''It seems I'm damned if I do, damned if I don't, Ruth. Had I hired a man, you would have blasted me to Hades for that, as well.''

''What was wrong with the older woman?'' his sister demanded to know.

"She was a bitch," Peter answered without mincing words and without compunction. "Christopher doesn't need a goddamned attendant!"

Ruth gasped in outrage, at his language, he knew. "You are such a crude man, Peter! Just like your mother!"

He peered up from the papers he had begun to sort, and raised a brow at her accusation. The two of them had shared the same father, but not the same mother. Ruth was the older by far at thirty-nine to his twenty-eight years, and was as yet unwed—it had never been difficult for him to understand why. He had long ago ceased to allow her to bait him about his mother—a fact that particularly seemed to nettle her. "If you mean plainspoken, yes, my mother was quite so."

Ruth narrowed her eyes at him, but didn't dare continue in the current vein. It had always been clear Ruth disliked his mother. His mother had been beautiful and vibrant, and Ruth seemed resentful of the fact that their father had doted upon her. And yet despite her feelings toward his mother, she had never taken them out upon Peter directly. If anything, she had mothered him fiercely, and though he had despised her controlling demeanor, he appreciated her devotion to him and to Christopher, nonetheless.

After Mary's death, Ruth had moved onto the estate with them and had, at once, taken over the rearing of his son. He'd been grateful for her presence, particularly so in the first years after Mary's death. He hadn't quite been able to function well enough. And he trusted Ruth fully. He did not, however, appreciate her manipulations, as he was no longer a child in need of direction.

He set his papers aside. "Ruth," he began patiently. "Not that I need to justify my decision to you, in any case, but she *was* the best applicant by far. She simply happens to have a pretty face, as well. Leave off!"

"That remains to be seen," Ruth persisted. "All she has presented to you thus far is that pretty face."

"Not true," Peter countered. "You should have seen the way she spoke with Christopher. Christopher was comfortable with her, and that counts for much."

"I did see her with Christopher!" Ruth shrieked with renewed vigor. "And what I saw was a woman shamelessly using her wiles to snare a little boy. Disgusting display if you ask me."

Peter shook his head. "I don't care how she got him to speak. How often do you see Christopher so at ease with strangers? You know that was one of my greatest concerns over hiring an instructor. As I see it, Ruth, Sarah Hopkins is perfect for the position, and it is my wish that you will make her feel at home during her interval with us."

"Humph! Well, I shall, of course, but I do not like this. I am opposed to it, Peter, and have been from the outset."

"I know," Peter said simply, sensing the turn in their conversation, and bracing himself once more.

"What point is there in teaching him to read? He is blind, Peter! Why can you not accept that?"

Peter tensed, restraining his temper. "Because my

son is blind, Ruth,'' he said with forced patience. ''He is *not* crippled nor maimed—nor is he stupid. His mind is bright and he is willing to learn. Someday, given the proper resources, he *will* be perfectly capable of running this business.''

Her hands went to her breasts in supplication. ''*I* am here to care for him,'' she reminded him.

Peter clenched his jaw. ''And will you always be?'' he asked his sister, weary with this particular topic.

''You push too hard, Peter. You want too much,'' she accused him once more, and Peter felt a stab of guilt.

Did he? How could he be certain?

Did he push his son too hard?

''I don't believe that,'' he denied adamantly.

The door chime rang, saving him from their discussion.

Dismissing his sister, he rose from his seat. ''In any case,'' he told her, ''it's too late. That would be Miss Hopkins, and I would appreciate it if you would go and fetch *my* son.''

One thing Ruth was not, was obedient to his every command.

''I shall not go and *fetch* your son!'' she returned angrily. ''I will take *no* part in this charade at all, Peter. You do this against my greater advice, brother mine, and I shall not be a part of it.''

Peter heard the door open and listened as Gunther ushered in their new guest. ''Suit yourself,'' he told her. ''But you *shall* be courteous at *all* times,'' he demanded of her.

Ruth glowered at him, shivering. She rubbed her arms. "I have a terrible premonition about this, Peter. Something about this woman disturbs me. You will sorely regret this," she warned, and then turned and left him to follow her into the hall. She hurried away from the front hall, but not in the direction of Christopher's room.

"Fetch your son yourself!" she said.

Shaking his head as he watched her go, he shrugged away whatever doubts his sister had managed to instill in him and went to greet the woman who had somehow managed to turn his household upside down after having scarcely set foot inside his door.

And perhaps his sister was just a little bit right ... because something like butterflies took flight within his breast at the mere thought of seeing her again.

Chapter 5

As they entered the foyer, Sarah's second impression of the Holland estate was no less ominous than her first.

She'd been far too nervous the first time to notice much of anything at all, but the gloominess struck her once more as she entered. Dark, rich woods adorned the floors and banisters, and the paper upon the wall was far from cheery, with its deep midnight blues, burgundies, and a touch of rich gold.

The sight of Peter Holland at the end of the long corridor turned her legs to water.

His expression was as dark and ominous as the decor of his house.

And yet . . . there was something about him . . .

Something that had snared Mary and had turned her from everything and everyone she had loved.

And God help her . . . something that appealed to Sarah as well, if she could be honest with herself . . . even knowing who he was . . . what he might be . . . her heart turned somersaults against her ribs.

She watched him approach and tried not to swoon with trepidation over the monumental task she had set before herself, and so she tried to focus, instead, on the good things that would come of it. Seeing and spending time with Christopher, even if she failed to find those journals and prove Peter an unfit father, would make it all worthwhile.

Now that she had seen her cousin's child, she could no more walk away than she had been able to forgive Mary for abandoning her all those years ago.

Peter walked toward them, wearing a smile now that was meant to disarm—instinctive perhaps—but Sarah refused to allow it. She needed every strap of her armor to keep her wits about her. Somewhere deep within, she knew that.

The man was a rake and ruthless at the very least, a murderer at worst.

"Miss Hopkins," he said in greeting. "I trust your preparations went well?"

"Quite," Sarah replied without meeting his gaze. She kept a blind stare upon the corridor's end, upon the distant glow of the lamp within his office.

However was she going to do this?

"I shall see them in, Gunther," he said to his butler, and sent the man ahead with their luggage to ensconce within their rooms.

"When shall you bring the rest?" he asked Sarah.

"The rest?" His very proximity made her head swim. "The rest of what?" She could scarce think.

Too many emotions vied within her: Anger, too much that had never been dealt with. Sadness, that she was such a stranger in her cousin's home—Mary had had an entire life Sarah had never been a part of. And something else. Lord, she could deny it if she wished to but what good would it do her? Sarah prided herself on being a realist. Peter Holland had been born with a face and presence that made women's hearts pound—and not entirely with fear.

"The remainder of your luggage," he said, and gently took her by the arm to lead her. She followed as he urged her, wincing at the warmth of his hand as it remained upon her arm.

"Oh! Silly me. Of course."

Good lord, his touch was unnerving her.

She wished to God he would release her, but didn't dare ask. It wasn't supposed to disturb her so, she reminded herself. As a blind woman, she should be more than accustomed to the guidance of others. And yet . . . this was Peter Holland's hand upon her, not just anyone's.

"This will be all, I'm afraid, as I don't find the need for much, Mr. Holland. It is a failing of mine, I'm certain, but it is not so easy to remember to adorn myself for others when I cannot see it myself." She didn't dare look at him, and hoped she *sounded blind.* She had no idea where the remark had come from, but it made sense to her.

"I understand," he replied. "Forgive me?"

When the sky fell, she would!

"Of course," Sarah replied sweetly. "How could you know I would feel so?"

"Because it makes perfect sense," he said, and tightened his grip upon her arm. He drew her around a corner. "I hope your quarters will suit you. I thought to settle you near the nursery. Christopher no longer uses the room, but it will be perfect for your lessons, and there is also a room adjoined to it with full amenities. It is one of the few as yet equipped with facilities. My wife saw it so, as she used it regularly. She planned to update the other rooms as well, but only this one and the master chambers were completed before she passed away. I've not had the time or the inclination to see to them myself, and my sister has had her hands full with my son. I'm sorry.''

He was going to ensconce her where Mary had slept?

Where she had died as well?

A shudder passed through her. The notion both terrified and pleased her at once. She shuddered again, hoping he wouldn't acknowledge it, and said quietly, ''It is more than I am accustomed to, I'm certain.''

She felt his gaze boring into her, and the corridor, good Lord, seemed to grow darker the closer they got to their destination. It was her imagination, certainly, as the decor had scarce changed, but for the richly woven carpets that stretched beneath their feet now, softening their footfalls. Over the thundering of her heart, she could barely hear Mel as she followed quietly behind them.

He pointed out the nursery as they passed it, then stopped at the very next door.

It had been left ajar for them, and within Sarah could see the few pieces of her own luggage that Gunther had carried ahead. Gunther, however, was nowhere to be seen. As they entered, she saw that the door to the nursery, too, had been left ajar, and then she heard a hall door open and close once more. Gunther, she thought. He'd departed through the nursery, and she made a mental note that her room was accessible through the nursery as well.

"You should find the room easy enough to navigate," he reassured her. "For Christopher's sake, we keep our decor rather sparse here."

It was true, he did. There was very little excess furniture about to tumble over—in her room, only a bed, a small nightstand, and a wardrobe upon the far wall.

Was this the room, then, where Mary had slept?

Upon the left wall there was a small window. Sarah stared at it, wondering, fearing it might be the window through which the intruder had entered. It wouldn't behoove her, however, to ask, and she blinked away the thoughts entirely, reminding herself that the papers had said the intruder had come in through the nursery itself, shattering the glass window above the crib. No crib here. This was not the nursery . . . and yet . . . this had to be where Mary had slept . . . where she had been awakened from her slumber that night . . .

The images tormented her.

She shoved them resolutely aside.

"How would you like to proceed?" he asked her, bringing her back to their present discussion. "Do you wish me to give you some time to settle before meeting with Christopher or shall I lead you there directly?"

Sarah's first inclination was to go to Christopher, but her hands were shaking, and her thoughts were entirely too scattered. "I think I would appreciate a few moments to settle," she said. "That might be better, so I may spend the time with your son free of that task later."

"I understand," he said, and proposed, "Perhaps we should wait, then, and see you at dinner?"

The suggestion surprised her. "Christopher shares your evening meals?"

He smiled down at her. "Of course."

"You must be very close, then? The two of you . . ."

"We are," he answered without hesitation. "He is my son, Miss Hopkins."

"Yes, of course. I didn't mean to imply . . ."

"I know," he said, dismissing the subject once and for all, and turned to address Mel, who had stood quietly in the doorway, listening to their discourse. "I suppose I shall leave you, then . . . to settle . . . and I'll lead Miss Frank to the servants' quarters."

Mel said nothing, and Sarah felt a twinge of panic at the prospect of a separation. "Yes," she answered anyway. And added, "Thank you." She dared to meet Mel's gaze only briefly through her dark glasses. Mel's expression, ever calm, eased her.

"Till tonight," he suggested, and ushered Mel away, closing the door behind them, leaving Sarah for the first time alone.

*   *   *

Why did he feel he knew her?

Something in Sarah Hopkins's manner was entirely too familiar, and Peter found himself experiencing a strange sense of déjà vu.

He peered down at the woman who had accompanied her into his home. "How long have you been working for Miss Hopkins?"

She hesitated before answering. "Oh, about three years."

"She seems quite a remarkable woman," Peter proposed, watching her curiously.

Miss Frank was a strange paradox of a woman; nothing about her seemed remotely subservient, not from their first introduction. He supposed it was a trait necessary in a blind woman's aide. He was certain it was nothing at all the same position as it would be to work for the seeing. Sarah needed guidance, and it was Miss Frank's duty to give it.

"She is," Miss Frank replied.

"I'm curious. How did you come to work for her?"

"My husband was blind," she replied. "I suppose I chose this career for the same reason Miss Hopkins chose to enter the teaching profession. It was a fine way of turning a bad experience to some greater good."

"That is quite commendable."

She smiled up at him, her blue eyes twinkling. "Not at all, Mr. Holland. Some of us deal with unfortunate circumstances by accepting a sort of premature death. Others use them to live by."

Sage words. Peter digested them, and said, "I

think we shall get along quite well, Miss Frank.''

She peered up at him and surprised him with a wink. "If not, then I can always find my way to the door, Mr. Holland. Can't I?''

Her reply brought a smile to Peter's lips. Saucy woman. Remembering Sarah's tart replies to him during her interview, he was not the least surprised that the two of them got along so famously.

For himself, he seemed quite partial to strong women—they intrigued him.

The last who had spoken to him so defiantly . . . he'd ended up marrying; he was going to have to continue to remind himself what a disaster that had turned out to be.

Peter knew he was prying, but couldn't seem to help himself. While he wouldn't consider broaching such a tender subject with Sarah, he hardly saw the harm in asking Mel. The worst she could do was to tell him to mind his own affairs.

Still, he hesitated. "You wouldn't happen to know . . . how Miss Hopkins lost her sight?''

She peered up at him and gave him a look that warned him it was, indeed, a delicate topic. "Terrible accident,'' she replied, and shook her head. "I wouldn't bring it up, were I you. She lost a fiancé in that accident, along with her sight.''

"Fiancé?'' Peter's brows lifted. Why did that knowledge disturb him? It was not as though it should concern him. She was hardly a child, nor was her personal life any of his affair. Nor should he be surprised that someone so lovely would have found herself attached.

"Any more than that," Mel added, dismissing the topic, "and you shall have to ask Sarah, I'm afraid."

Peter fully intended to—not that he had any right to know, but when had that ever stopped him before?

No, Sarah Hopkins was quite an interesting woman, and he found himself intrigued.

He hadn't left her with a light, but Sarah supposed he hadn't thought she'd need one. What need had a blind woman for a light to see by? No, she would simply have to make do.

Her room was not large, but hardly was it small. And yet it seemed cavernous with its notable lack of furnishings. Bathed in shadows as it was, the room seemed permeated by something dark, almost sinister. Sarah inspected every nook and every cranny with keen eyes.

If Mary had used this room, little remained as evidence to the fact. There were no portraits upon the walls or furnishings, nothing at all of Mary's taste to remind her, and yet . . . something of Mary was here . . . or perhaps it was merely Sarah's imagination. Perhaps it was due to the fact that she knew the room's history. No matter, she liked to think she and Mary still had some connection of sorts.

Silly, perhaps, but somehow she liked to think Mary would guide her now.

The bed was a small one, occupying a corner of the room almost inconspicuously. The bed coverings themselves were nondescript and blended with the shadows. And the view from the single window was obscured by shades that were drawn.

Sarah made her way to the window, lifting the shade to peer outside. It slipped from her grasp and sprang open, letting in daylight and scattering dust motes.

A group of small children played upon the street, batting at rocks with sticks.

They must be about Christopher's age, she thought . . . perhaps a year or two older. But Christopher would never join them.

She wondered if he knew what he was missing. Was he happy? He certainly seemed it, and yet . . . how could he truly be happy with a murdering father? And his aunt . . . Sarah had little more than a name and a voice to go by as yet, but the voice had hardly been warm.

Turning from the window, she mustered her courage and ventured to the door that joined her room to the nursery. She took the knob in hand and drew it a bit wider, peering within.

This room was far more cheery in its decor.

Light and airy blue draperies adorned the full-length French windows, letting in the brilliant afternoon sunlight. The other three walls were vividly decorated with the images of a carousel. Designed to appear as though the room in its entirety were a carousel in motion, horses and unicorns and bears and zebras leapt about playfully. The domed ceiling, too, was adorned, completing the illusion, and a vibrant blue and white circular carpet was spread upon the nursery floor.

The crib itself sat still before the windows, a grim reminder of that horrible night. Terrible images accosted Sarah as her gaze fell upon it, and she winced in pain at what her cousin must have suffered at the hands of a killer.

Morbid curiosity drew her farther into the room.

Leaving the door ajar behind her, she ventured toward the crib.

It was bare . . . as though it had been stripped that night so long ago and never again remade. Sunlight pierced the window panes and fell across the wood, highlighting the rich maple grain. It continued across the floor and lit upon the face of a blue unicorn on the far wall with its icicle horn and vivid violet eyes.

It was a child's fantasy, this room, a feast for the senses, with its display of colors and parade of exotic toys. Little wooden toy soldiers lined one shelf, and colorfully painted blocks, another. Every sort of toy, from a red and white painted drum set to an enormous hand-carved rocking horse with a lamb's-wool mane and black onyx eyes, lay about in careful precision, untouched, it seemed, by raucous little-boy hands.

The sight of it all saddened her, left her feeling a keen sense of loss.

How ironic that such a stunning room should be painted for a little boy who would never see it.

In a strange way, it was almost as though no child had been born to Mary at all, because the little boy Sarah had spied a week before in his father's office had been a somber little child, with the soul of an adult.

Contemplating that, Sarah abandoned the nursery

and returned to her room. The door closed with a scrape, but no click. No latch.

Later she would return, when all were asleep and the house was quiet and there was no chance of discovery.

Later when her heart was not bleeding and her head was not pounding with thoughts of Peter Holland.

She didn't want to think of him this way.

Didn't want to think of him at all!

Whatever was the matter with her that she couldn't seem to forget the brilliance of his smile?

He was *not* some dandy beau, and neither was she some naive schoolgirl waiting to be charmed.

He was a murderer.

And she was the woman who intended to bring him to justice.

Chapter 6

Entering his office, Peter made his way directly to where he kept his port, and contemplating the day's events, poured himself a glass.

Christ, but he didn't even like to venture near those rooms.

That was the reason he hadn't lingered, despite that he hadn't wished to leave Sarah so quickly. But even now, so many years later, the sight of those rooms disturbed him in a way that he could not quite handle.

That he'd not closed off the wing entirely was something of a wonder.

That he'd ensconced his *guest* there was a matter of necessity.

In the years since his wife's death, the Holland estate had entertained few guests. Polite society had little enough to do with a second-generation American responsible for his own fortunes, and less with one suspected of murdering his own wife. Even if Peter were inclined to give a damn at this late hour, he didn't think he could simply ignore the fact that they had all been so quick to judge him. It had been a brutal reminder to him that he was an outsider—and always would be. No matter that they were cowed by him, no matter that they threw their money at him to invest for them—or that he had more money than the bloody lot of them together—he would never be one of them.

Well, it didn't matter.

His priority was his son.

Taking the glass with him, he sat within his chair at his desk, setting the glass down just out of reach as he contemplated his *guest*.

Something about Sarah Hopkins . . . something he couldn't quite put his finger on . . . something disturbed him, as well as intrigued him.

She was lovely, yes . . . and she was quick and intelligent, too. He heard it in her words as she spoke . . . recognized it in her wit, as well. And despite that he seemed to set her teeth on edge, she was caring, too—he'd heard that in her voice. He'd believed in the sincerity and genuine concern for his son reflected in her voice. Even more than the fact that he'd wished to remind his sister who ruled in his home, that had been the deciding factor in his decision to hire her.

And yet there was something more . . .

He stared at his glass of port, seeing it, though not seeing it, but rather peering through it.

It was his penance . . . to see it, to smell it, but not to touch it.

It troubled him that he craved it still, that he

would, if he allowed himself, lift up the bloody glass and suck it down to the last swallow.

He was weak.

In body and mind, he was weak.

He squeezed his eyes shut as images of that night came back to plague him. Shame overwhelmed him once again. A woman's laughter tinkled in his ear . . . sweat and the taste of female skin manifested upon his tongue and mingled with the sweet burn of port . . . a tumble to the floor . . . And then the dreams . . . dreams that had not been dreams at all— fearful shrieks of a woman in terror, screams that had reverberated down every hall, shattering glass, a babe's incessant wailing . . . wails that had sounded within his brain for years afterward . . . like the guilty dong of a Sunday morning church bell to a man who'd forsworn his faith.

The wails he sometimes still heard in his nightmares.

It was the first time he'd strayed from his vows . . . or rather he'd nearly done so. Were it not for the fact that he'd passed out cold upon the floor, he would have become an adulterer that night as well.

But it didn't matter . . .

He was guilty as hell.

His face twisted with self-disgust.

He *would* have betrayed her that night, he had no doubt. His body had been hungry and his bed too long cold. His anger had been a balm for his injured pride, but he hadn't wished her dead . . . and more, he'd cherished her for the way she'd loved their son. As much as she'd loathed him toward the end, she'd loved their child fiercely. Christopher had felt the warmth of her arms and the glow of her love, and Peter had often snuck into the nursery to find them arm in arm, mother and son. He'd envied his son those nights. God, how he'd envied Christopher!

Mary had even moved her bed within the nursery itself at one point, and had often fallen asleep with Christopher at her breast. The image haunted him still. She had been so beautiful with her golden hair and dark skin ... and those blue eyes that had glowed with warmth.

He hadn't loved her, hadn't thought himself capable of it, but he'd respected the hell out of her and he'd liked her immensely. She had been pleasant company and lovely besides, and he'd found himself, upon meeting her, yearning for something more than an empty bed.

It wasn't long after they had married that things had begun to fall apart, and he faulted himself for it.

Honesty be damned!

Why had he felt compelled to be so brutal with the truth?

Had he simply refrained from telling her that he cared for her but didn't love her, she never would have felt so rejected when he'd begun to spend so much time with his business affairs. She had tried so hard to be all that he'd needed, to give him the family and wife he'd craved—tried so hard to make him love her.

And perhaps he might have, but they hadn't had the time.

They'd been married less than six months before his business had begun to fail and he'd had to spend long hours trying to salvage it. By the time Christopher had been born, she'd withdrawn from him completely, safeguarding her heart with emotional and physical distance. And Peter had allowed it, thinking in his youth and pride that they would have the opportunity later to mend it . . . that there would be time enough to woo her back once his business was settled . . . time enough to convince her that if he didn't love her, per se, he cared for her deeply and would strive with all his might and heart to make her happy.

But time had slipped away, and not so silently at that.

His gaze lowered to the glass of port.

Goddamn bloody rotten drink.

His father had been inclined to imbibe, but he damned well hadn't forced Peter to follow in his footsteps.

How many times had he listened to his father bemoan his own weakness? How many times had his father pleaded with him, even inebriated, never to fall prey to its influence?

And still Peter had turned to it.

It had been his own choice to pour that first drink.

And it had been his own decision to run to it each time thereafter, like a lovesick man into the arms of his mistress.

When his business had faltered, he'd taken comfort in his drink rather than in the arms of his wife, and she had responded by withdrawing from him completely. Peter couldn't blame her. He'd never been the least affectionate with her, never given her reassurances. She had been much too young to understand that his emotional distance hadn't had a thing to do with her at all, and he had been too self-absorbed to see that he'd wounded her each time he'd walked away from her heartfelt attempts to comfort him.

When Mary had begun to sleep in the nursery not long after Christopher's birth, Peter had begun to feel like a failure in all aspects of his life.

And yet it had been that decision of Mary's that had propelled him back into his business affairs with a vengeance. He had applied himself with vigor to his work and *had* salvaged it, though *not* with Mary's inheritance as he was well aware people were so willing to believe. Mary's inheritance remained untouched to this day, and would continue to be so. She'd intended it for their son, and Peter had every intention of honoring her wishes.

It was the least he could do, as he'd failed her in every other way . . .

A knock sounded upon his door, drawing his attention. "This came for you, sir, while you were seeing Miss Hopkins to her room."

Peter glanced up to find Gunther standing in the doorway, holding a folded note in his hand. As he brought it nearer, the handwriting became familiar. Cile Morgan.

Heir to the Morgan estate, she was not only one of his biggest investors, but a confidante, and sometimes lover. During the worst time after his wife's death, Cile had stood by him. She had been the first to reinvest funds with his firm—and hardly a pittance. Her own husband had died a mere three months before Mary had, and the two of them had naturally banded together. In thanks for his support and friendship, Cile had brought him some of her dearest friends and his biggest clients. For his part, it felt a little like whoring at times, but Cile was hardly a child at thirty-two, and Peter was hardly a saint. The two of them seemed to feed well off each other. Nor was it as though they weren't friends in truth, because they were. All in all, as friends went, she was probably his closest—though what that said about his personal state of affairs, he wasn't entirely certain.

He shook his head as Gunther handed him the note. "Who brought it?"

"A carrier, sir. I don't know."

"Thank you, Gunther," Peter said, dismissing him as he unfolded the note.

Darling, it said, *drinks this afternoon at Delmonico's. I've something yummy for you. Four P.M. sharp. Don't be late!*

The something yummy was no doubt an introduction to a new client.

Anything else would have been presented to him over dinner or even a nightcap. Cile wasn't the sort to dally.

He had no choice but to go, and felt a stab of regret that his own dinner plans were to be preempted. He had been quite looking forward to dinner with Sarah Hopkins. He drew a watch from his pocket. Half past three.

If he hurried, perhaps he could make drinks with Cile and still return before dinner was over . . .

He hoped Sarah wasn't one to retire early.

And with that in mind, he set out to meet Cile.

His thoughts, however, remained somewhere in the vicinity of the nursery at the corner of University Place and Twelfth Street.

From the journals of Mary Holland:
December 20, 1880

I think he must be having an affair.

He has ignored all of our guests tonight . . . all except Cile. And he ensconced himself within his office . . . with her . . . and I wanted so much to go and see . . . but didn't dare. What reason would I have given? What should I have said: Excuse me, Cile, but are you sleeping with my husband?

I can't seem to stop crying tonight. What a child I am! It's not as though he ever lied to me, is it? It's not as though he promised me his heart. How I wish I could speak with Sarah! How I wish I would not love him so much!

Why must he turn to Cile instead of me? I know something is going on, and yet I cannot put my finger upon it. Ruth has implied so much. I know what I am going to do. It is my last chance, I think, to win him back. If he sees that I have withdrawn . . . if he loves me just a bit . . . he will urge me to come back. Won't he?

I'm going to move into—

"Am I disturbing you?"

Sarah started at the voice, tucking the timeworn newspaper clipping into the pocket of her skirt at once. Thank God her dark glasses shielded her surprise at the unannounced intrusion. "Not at all," she said, her heart hammering.

The woman standing at her door was not so much unattractive as she was dour. Her dark eyes were narrowed on Sarah, assessing, and her spectacles fell low upon the bridge of a nose that seemed too large for the thin face she bore. It might have been an attractive feature, Sarah thought, on a man, but on her it was less than appealing. Her rich blue-black hair was caught back a bit too severely, and she stood tall, almost as tall as Peter Holland.

"I'm Ruth Holland," the woman said, and suddenly the voice was familiar. "We met briefly at your interview."

As with their first meeting, her tone was disapproving.

"Yes, I remember," Sarah replied, and Ruth entered the room without invitation, looking idly about, though her stride seemed to hold a particular purpose. She circled Sarah, hardly sparing her a glance, her attention drawn about the room.

Sarah felt a bit like a hare being stalked by a hungry wolf.

"It has been quite some time since I've stepped

foot into this room. It still manages to make me ill,'' she said finally, though without emotion.

"This room?'' Sarah replied, trying to seem oblivious to her meaning. She was not, however, and her heart began to beat a little faster.

Peter had spoken briefly of Mary, but Sarah hadn't dared to ask intrusive questions so soon. She was eager now for every little bit of information she could glean.

"Yes," Ruth answered. "This is *the* room, I'm afraid."

"What room?" Sarah persisted. "I'm certain I don't understand."

Ruth cocked her head a little in disbelief. "Do you not read the papers?" she began, and then at once reprimanded herself. "Oh, silly me! What a goose I am! You wouldn't be able to read them now, would you?"

Her tiny smirk, the one Sarah wasn't supposed to see, provoked her ire.

"Forgive me," she said, studying Sarah.

Her obvious condemnation, and her lack of regard for Sarah's supposed condition, were shocking. Was this how she treated her nephew, then?

Or was there another reason she seemed so determined to prick Sarah's temper?

Watching Peter's sister out of the corner of her eye, Sarah braced herself. Her hands fell to her sides and she consciously flattened them upon her skirt, willing her annoyance to ease. It wouldn't do to become angered, she knew. This was Ruth Holland's home, not hers. She was the guest with the precarious position. If Ruth didn't want her about, Sarah was certain she had some say in the matter.

"In any case," Ruth continued, "this room leaves me ill at ease." She was watching Sarah carefully. "You did know that Christopher's mother was murdered here, did you not?"

Interesting choice of words, Sarah thought. Christopher's mother? Not Peter's wife?

It was as though she denied Mary that rightful title. Had she not liked Mary, then?

"I wasn't aware," Sarah said. "Murdered?"

"Yes. Nasty business, that. The papers accused my brother," she disclosed and didn't elaborate. Sarah wondered that she did not at once defend her brother.

Was he guilty, then?

Did Ruth know the truth?

"She was discovered just about where you are standing, in fact."

What a morbid fact to impart to a guest!

Again she seemed to be watching Sarah's reaction carefully. What was it precisely that she was after with this discourse?

Sarah restrained herself from peering down where she stood . . . at the floor where her cousin's body had lain . . .

"That is not, however," Ruth went on to announce, "why I came to speak to you."

Sarah tried to compose herself, tried not to think of Mary's final moments. She blinked, and shook her head, and then forced herself to ask, "Why . . . why did you?"

"I came to tell you that if you have the least decency at all, Miss Hopkins, you will leave this house at once and leave that poor child alone. He has suffered enough in this, and I shall not stand by to see him hurt anymore."

The attack came so suddenly that it took Sarah aback. "I beg your pardon!" she exclaimed. "I am *not* here to harm that child. In fact, it is my fervent wish that I might be able to help him!"

And God help her, if it was the last thing she did, she would indeed. How dare she be accused without reason. Thinking Ruth must surely be expressing doubts concerning the legitimacy of the Braille system, Sarah tried to reassure her. "It is true that Braille is not so widely supported as yet, but it is a valid and effective system, Miss Holland. If you need reassurances, I would be most pleased to provide—"

"This has absolutely nothing to do with your silly alphabet!" Ruth exploded.

Sarah blinked behind her spectacles, taken aback by the woman's vehemence.

"It has everything to do with Christopher," she continued angrily. "That child is merely six years old," she pointed out, "and I am deeply troubled to see him treated as though he were an adult. He is not—he is but six years old!"

Sarah had been so eager to use this opportunity that she'd never even considered the things Ruth was suddenly spouting at her.

"Why can he not be allowed to be a child? Why must he become a man so soon?"

Sarah didn't have the answers to her questions, but she suddenly felt conscience-stricken for the accusations thrown at her.

Ruth seemed to realize her words were registering, because she calmed and said, "As I said, Miss Hopkins, if you have any decency at all, you will leave here at once. You will hand my brother your notice and you will leave that poor child in peace."

Sarah shook her head. She couldn't. She just couldn't leave without finding out the truth. She couldn't simply walk out the door—and even less now that such an implication had been made concerning Christopher.

If what Ruth said was true, then Christopher *needed* her.

She straightened. "I am quite sorry if you disagree with your brother's decision, Miss Holland, but no, I cannot agree to leave here. And furthermore," Sarah pointed out, "If I do go, who is to say your brother will not hire someone else to take my place?"

"And why need that concern you?" Ruth Holland asked bitterly.

Sarah refused to be cowed by threats or intimidation, no matter the validity of her reasoning.

"This is *not* something I chose to do, Miss Holland. This profession chose me. If I can help that child, then my own loss is not so great. I suppose you might say I am doing this for me, as well." *And for Mary,* she wanted to shout.

Ruth's face paled with anger. Her lips thinned, and her hands shook at her side. "I am *not* powerless in this, you realize. I am *not*! And so understand me when I tell you, Miss Hopkins, that if I feel you are a threat . . . to that child . . . I swear to God you will be removed from this house at once!"

Sarah stood there, her own anger fading in the face of Ruth's fury. She had nothing to say in response. Ruth Holland clearly loved her nephew and would protect him at all cost. And knowing that, how could Sarah truly be angry? She wanted so much suddenly to reassure Ruth, but dared not, and so she simply stood there.

"If you have a complaint with the way I perform my duties," Sarah replied finally, "I suggest you take it up with your brother."

"I *shall* be watching you," she apprised Sarah, her eyes narrowing with open condemnation.

"I understand."

"My brother will not be available for the evening meal, Miss Hopkins. I suggest you order dinner served in your room."

And with that, she spun on her heels and left the room, her message perfectly clear:

Sarah was not welcome in her home.

She had no allies here, but she hadn't expected any. She had Mel, and she had justice behind her—and she wasn't going to leave until she learned the truth.

Peter and Ruth Holland be damned!

Chapter 7

Cile Morgan was accustomed to things going her way.

The fact that Peter had attempted to excuse himself at least three times since their client had departed didn't seem to be fazing her in the least.

And despite the fact that she hadn't made a single attempt to *seduce him* before he'd called it a night, she was suddenly adamant that he stay with her.

"Since when do you rush home?" she asked, and gave him that little half smile that promised rewards if only he played her way.

And he always did; he knew which buttons to push, knew how to tease her.

"Christopher has long been in bed, darling."

It was true, normally he didn't find himself in a hurry. But tonight was different. Tonight he *was* anxious. "It's been a long day, Cile," he said, and reached into his pocket, withdrawing his watch. He checked the time: 8:20 P.M. He wondered if Sarah was already abed.

Was she an early riser?

Did she awake full of energy?

Or was she slow to stir . . . her body stretching lazily against the sheets . . . her hair spilling upon her pillow . . .

His body stirred at the images that came to mind.

Cile protested with a familiar whine, a low, throaty purr that normally managed to tighten his loins and make him hungry for a more fleshly sort of dessert. Tonight, however, it only managed to annoy him.

Her ice blue eyes narrowed slightly and her beautifully painted lips formed a sensual pout. "You are no fun tonight," she complained. "Whatever has gotten into you? You have been sitting there the entire eve looking for all the world as though you were ready to leap up any moment and fly." A few strands of the hair in her coif came free and fell into her face. She blew them away, and turned her expectant gaze upon Peter once more.

The truth was, Peter had no blasted notion what had gotten into him. His thoughts kept returning to his houseguest.

Something about Sarah struck him as odd.

Something about her attracted the hell out of him as well.

He stared at his glass of wine and then returned his attention to his companion, meeting her sultry gaze. Cile's eyes were quite beautiful, and yet they lacked the warmth Mary's had had when first he'd met her. Cile was hardly the sort one imagined rocking a baby to sleep. Nor could he envision her lying upon the floor surrounded with toy soldiers and blocks.

Damn, he'd let so much slip away.

Reaching out, he fingered the glass of wine, and wondered what color Sarah Hopkins's eyes were.

His mind embraced a picture of his wife, his lover, the two of them gazing into one another's eyes . . . and it was Sarah he saw.

He had been able to see into Mary's heart when he'd looked into her eyes. He had recognized both her love and then her hate for him, and though her withdrawal had been painful, he'd never had to guess at her feelings. That was the problem with Cile; he had never guessed at *any* of her thoughts. Her beautiful eyes were rarely a window into her heart, merely a reflection of her mood.

And yet Cile had never done anything but look after his best interest; if she had anything other than genuine concern for him, he wouldn't know it. He didn't sense in her any sort of agenda. She had money enough, and he doubted she even wanted a new husband in her life. If she had any selfish motive at all, it was simply that she was greedy for his company. She didn't seem to appreciate his taking an interest in other women.

Until now, that hadn't been a problem.

He lifted the glass of merlot and tilted it toward him, swirling the fragrant liquid until it eddied against the fine crystal, but he didn't lift it to his lips.

What was it about Sarah that drew him?

"I appreciate the introduction tonight," he told

Cile. "An account with August Belmont is nothing to sneeze at."

Her disappointment was palpable. She retreated a bit, sitting straighter in her chair. "Of course, Peter," she said, and sighed. "I know you do, and it was my pleasure to introduce you. At any rate, he has entirely too much money to invest with one firm, and I have every faith you will serve him well. He knows it, too, or I'd never have talked him into this meeting tonight. I really didn't do you any favors, you know."

"You do me entirely too many," Peter countered. "I shall never be able to repay you."

Cile cocked her head with an expression of annoyance and leaned all the way back in her chair. "I have never asked you to . . . have I?"

It was true.

She never had.

And yet he'd never been able to get beyond a sense of indebtedness to her. He stared at her a moment, and then looked away.

"Good lord!" she exclaimed when he didn't reply. "I don't think I like what I am sensing!"

He hadn't meant to offend her with his silence. He stopped swirling the glass's contents a bit too abruptly and spilled a deep red droplet upon the table. It soaked into the white cloth until only a deep shade of mauve remained.

"What in blazes is wrong with you?"

Peter shook his head. "Not a thing," he assured, and scratched at the spot upon the tablecloth. "I've merely a few things on my mind."

"Oh? And what is her name?" Cile demanded at once.

Startled by the question, Peter looked into her eyes. "Her?"

"I am not stupid, Peter!"

"I hardly said you were, Cile."

"I cannot remember a time when you have seemed less interested," she said, pouting. "You sat here even with Mr. Belmont and seemed wholly lost in your own thoughts, and I cannot imagine anything that should capture a man's attention so fully but another woman."

Peter didn't know what to say.

"Who is she, Peter?"

He glanced once more at his watch, and then shoved it into his pocket. "You are being ridiculous, Cile."

"Am I?"

"I'm merely tired," he assured her, and made to rise. "It's been quite a long day. I'll see you home now, I think."

"Humph!" she said, and rose from her chair. "We shall see, shall we not?" She gave him a narrow-eyed glare and reached across the table to seize his glass of wine. Without a word, she drank it down and then clunked the glass upon the table, giving him a pointed glance. "No need to waste good wine. And no need to see me home, darling. I'll go just the way I came. I'll call myself a cab."

She'd left angry.

Of that particular fact, Sarah had little doubt.

Sarah sat upon the small bed and contemplated the things Ruth Holland had revealed to her. It was true that Christopher was entirely too young, in relation to his peers, to begin to learn how to read. Most children his age were hardly contemplating school at all, much less reading. And yet she remembered the spark of intelligence in his eyes and couldn't say she had been struck first by his youth. She hadn't even considered it at all, in fact, but neither had she before she'd met him. Her mind had been focused primarily upon her goal.

The missing journal.

She slid off the bed and began to pace the room. Where would it be?

Giving the room a cursory search, she considered the possibility that it might be here in this room where Mary had slept, though she doubted it. It had been more than six years since Mary's death, and even had Mary kept them here, Sarah doubted they had been overlooked all this time.

Besides, there were too few places to hide something of that nature, especially when all of the New York City police force and a guilty husband might be searching for it.

Keeping that thought in mind, Sarah made her way to the wardrobe. Opening its smooth mahogany doors, she expected to find nothing. She wasn't disappointed; it was empty, but for a very ornately designed hatbox.

Stooping to reach it, she lifted it up, testing its weight. She then set it back down. There was something within, but she couldn't imagine what it could be. It was too noisy to be a hat, and too light to be Mary's journal. Then, of course, she hardly expected to find it so soon, and out in the open as this was. She opened the box and sifted through the pale tissue, searching for the object she had heard rattle across the bottom of the box. It was nothing of any substantial size, that much was certain. Her fingers skimmed the bottom of the box until she felt the object. She drew it out and blinked at the sight of it. It was a small golden key, tiny like a charm from a bracelet. In fact, attached to it was a tiny golden loop that appeared as though it had been pried apart. Perhaps it was a charm, but it was nothing Sarah recognized. Like Sarah, Mary had not been one to wear jewelry. She stared at it, admiring it, and then dropped the small trinket back into the box, replaced the lid, and returned it. Rising, she closed the wardrobe doors. That done, she moved down to the only drawer in the wardrobe, a long, thin one at the foot of the hefty piece of furniture.

Opening the drawer revealed a folded soft blue cloth. Sarah lifted up the blanket and let it unfold into her lap. A baby blanket, solid blue with the beginnings of an embroidery in its center. A closer inspection revealed a threaded needle still embedded within its folds, and a strand of dark blue thread. The embroidery appeared to be a set of initials. She could make out the *C* quite clearly, but the next initial was unclear . . . perhaps a *J*?

She sat down upon the wood floor and reverently traced the embroidery with a finger. She had never known Mary to embroider; but she was quite certain it was Mary's effort. The stitches were far from perfect, but lovingly done. Had she been stitching the blanket just before she'd died? Or had she given it her best effort and found her patience lacking and set it aside?

Knowing Mary, and Sarah liked to think she did despite that they'd parted ways so long before her death, she had decided to embroider, and embroider she did, and hadn't set it aside at all. No . . . Sarah was near certain she would have finished the task she'd set herself, and if the blanket was for Christopher, she hardly would have lost the passion for it.

The initials . . . *C* . . . Christopher. But the *J*?

With a sigh of disgust, she realized she didn't know Christopher's middle name. John? Jack? God! Life was unfair. She hugged the blanket to her breast and allowed herself to grieve once more. For Mary . . . Her throat closed. Her cousin had been her closest friend. Her sister, for all purposes. They had been confidantes, had shared everything together, and here was such an enormous portion of Mary's life that Sarah knew *nothing* about.

She couldn't help herself. She began to weep silently.

She sat on the floor in this room where Mary had died, hugging a blanket Mary had been sewing for the child Sarah had never known, and tears spilled down her cheeks.

Who was this man who had taken everything from her?

Who was Peter Holland *really*?

And why had Mary thrown away so much to be with him? How could she face Mary's husband in the morning after sleeping in this room where Mary had died? Burying her face in the blanket, she wept quietly . . . lest someone overhear her.

She *would* face Peter Holland because she *must*.

There were no choices to be made here.

Mary hadn't been given one, and neither had Christopher, and she owed it to both of them to make things right.

Peter Holland might have the face of an angel, she reminded herself, but he had the heart of a jackal.

Sarah was determined to see him pay.

Someone must.

It wasn't Peter's idea of a warm welcome.

He'd insisted upon seeing Cile home only because he didn't particularly like the thought of leaving her to fend for herself on New York's streets at night. Cile Morgan rather liked to think herself a match for any man, but the truth was that she would be little more than dessert for some of the city's seedier sort.

He lived already with one woman's death on his conscience.

He certainly didn't intend to add another.

His sister greeted him at the door in a fit of temper unlike anything he had ever witnessed in her before. The best he could make from her rambling was that she'd had words with Sarah Hopkins, and that their guest had eschewed dinner with her new pupil. Christopher had been heartily disappointed, and to say Ruth was angry was an understatement.

He left Ruth, promising to speak to their guest, and ignoring her protests that he should do precisely the contrary—that if Miss Hopkins didn't care enough to make the effort, he must be wrong about her character. Peter didn't think so. One did not fake the sincerity he'd heard in her voice when she'd spoken to his son. He didn't know how to explain it, but his gut told him that Sarah Hopkins was good for Christopher.

Pausing at her door, he started to knock and then halted abruptly at the faint sound of weeping coming from within. Something about the way she sobbed took him back . . . evoked memories that made his chest wrench.

Startled by the sounds that came from the room, he listened for a moment, confused, his hand poised to knock.

This was *not* his wife, he reminded himself. She was a stranger to him still.

A beautiful stranger, but a stranger nonetheless.

She would *not* appreciate his interruption, he told himself . . . and what he had to speak to her about could certainly wait until the morning.

He shrugged free of the stupor that held him. Straightening, he pushed away from the door, then turned and walked away.

His chance to knock upon this door . . . to go to his wife and heal her sorrow, was long past.

The time to reassure was gone.

She wasn't here anymore, and he had long since ceased to mourn her.

God only knew . . . it wasn't so simple a task to forgive himself. He may have dealt with his grief, but he hadn't the slightest notion how to let go of his guilt.

It stayed with him, snarling at his soul like a rabid beast.

Chapter 8

"These servants are all a bunch of gossips,"
Mel swore, bursting into Sarah's room,
brimming with energy and excitement. "And thank
God!"

Startled by the unexpected intrusion, Sarah sat up
in the bed. "Good Lord, Mellie! You nearly scared
the life out of me!"

"Poppycock!" Mel said. "Guess what I discovered," she persisted, sitting on the bed at Sarah's
feet.

Somehow Mel's enthusiasm both buoyed and
frightened her at once. She didn't wish her dear
friend to forget the risks they were taking. This was
hardly a game, and the stakes were too high to be
taken lightly.

"That you don't wish to do this and you want to
go home?" Sarah said warily.

Mel waved a hand at her, dismissing her sarcasm.

Sarah frowned. "You are beginning to enjoy this
far too much, I think."

Mel laughed softly. "Perhaps I am at that, but it is rather exciting to play at being a Pinkerton."

"Just remember that this is *not* play," Sarah advised her. "It struck me again last night how dangerous a venture this is. It is not easy at all to play a blind woman, Mel. I find myself reacting instinctively and have to catch myself at every turn."

"But you are doing so well," Mel assured her. "Sarah, I have spent time among the blind all my life, and you are convincing enough even for me. You are doing very well, and if you were not, I would put an end to this at once."

"You truly feel so?" Sarah lifted her thumb to her lips, and gnawed it absently.

Mel gave her an admonishing glance. "When have you *ever* known me to mince words? Of course I mean it, or I'd not say it. I'd be nagging you instead—no, I would be dragging you out by your hair like some Neanderthal man."

Sarah had to chuckle at the images that came to mind. "You would, at that, I think."

"Of course I would." Mel cocked her head. "Now . . . do you wish to know what I discovered, or not?"

"Yes already!" Sarah exclaimed. "Tell me!"

"Very well, then," Mel said, "but I'll not tell you while you are lying in that bed. I cannot believe you are sleeping so late," she scolded, and then demanded, "Get up!"

Sarah flushed guiltily. "I spent quite a bad night in this room," she confessed.

Mel gave her a quizzical glance. "Wish to talk about it?"

"No," Sarah answered at once, and then explained, "it is just this room."

"This room?"

"Yes," Sarah answered. "This is where *it* happened." She gave Mel a meaningful nod at the floor. "There."

"Oh, dear . . ." Mel's expression softened at once. "I'm so sorry, Sarah. I know you loved her dearly. But together," she assured, "we are going to make everything right. You believe that, don't you?"

Sarah shrugged. "I received a visit from Ruth last night. She had little enough to say to me, but none of it was benevolent, I assure you."

Mel nodded. "She's a regular battle-ax, they say."

Sarah lifted her brows. "Battle-ax?"

"So they say. It seems she rules the nest here, and Peter Holland either does not seem to care or is afraid of her as well."

"Afraid!" Sarah exclaimed. "Peter Holland? One look at that man tells me he is afraid of nothing."

"I rather thought so as well," Mel agreed. "And yet . . . I am only telling you what I have gleaned thus far. Most of the servants here seem quite close-mouthed, but for a few."

"How did they welcome you?" Sarah asked with genuine concern.

"Most of them not at all, to tell you the truth. They are all quite self-involved, I think. Not overly friendly, but neither are they cold. As best as I can tell, this is not some medieval household where they are forced into familiarity by necessity. But for a few, they all go home to their families at night, and mind their own affairs while they are here. But for a few," she reiterated. "I did have an interesting discussion with the housekeeper . . ."

"Well, tell me," Sarah prompted.

Mel smiled. "Get out of bed first. It unsettles me to see you lying there looking like a convalescent."

Sarah rolled her eyes, but she couldn't contain her wry smile. She climbed out of the bed and went to the wardrobe, opening the doors.

She'd had herself a good cry last night, and then had passed the time thinking while she'd unpacked. "If they ask, I shall tell them you unpacked my bags," she said, as she rummaged through her dresses . . . all of them dark in color. She hadn't noticed that detail until this moment, and had to wonder if the choices had been dictated by her subconscious. She had long since ceased to wear mourning, but somehow her choices were all somber. For today, she chose a deep burgundy wool dress and her simplest bustle—something she wished had never come back into style as she much preferred the long, slim lines. They *had* come back, however, and while she disdained having to follow someone else's code of style, she wasn't quite willing to draw the sort of attention she might were she to completely eschew the dictates of polite society. So she opted for the smallest petticoats and bustles, and cursed the man who first created such a ridiculous concoction of ruffles and frills.

"Shall I help you?"

Sarah cast Mel a wry smile. "Let us not, and say you did."

Mel giggled.

Sarah glowered at her. "I am only playing a blind woman, remember? I have been dressing myself for years; I hardly think I need help now."

Mel smiled in answer, and then wrinkled her nose. "You are playing a widow, too, it seems, judging by your choice of dress."

"Well, it hardly seemed appropriate," Sarah told her, "that I should adorn myself as though I could see."

"Is that what you think you are doing? *Dressing* the part of a blind woman?"

"I suppose so," Sarah answered, "though I hardly realized it until just now. As carefully as I planned, I certainly did not consciously choose."

Mel rose from the bed and came to help her with the petticoat. "Well, I am sorry to tell you, but that particular effort is wholly wasted." She eyed Sarah with some disappointment. "The blind, as I'm certain you realize, do not shop to appear blind, Sarah. They hardly know what they are wearing. Those that are fortunate to have someone choose for them are dressed by silly individuals who make an exceptional effort to be certain they fit in. Those who are not so fortunate, well, they wear whatever is available to them, as would anyone else. Make an effort to note what Christopher will wear today," she advised. "You will see, I'm certain, that he is dressed as any other little boy of his means."

Remembering her conversation with Peter Holland, Sarah frowned. "How silly of me," she said, and was embarrassed.

"No need to worry," Mel reassured. "You shall simply tell them that I do your shopping and that I am a dour old woman at heart." She laughed. "For myself, I brought only the most conservative attire. Because, like you," she said, "I was concerned with dressing the part."

"But I did not consciously choose," Sarah protested.

"It makes no difference—just as it makes no difference what you wear . . . Peter Holland will still look at you with those love-struck eyes." She peered up from the laces to gauge Sarah's expression.

Sarah blinked. "I beg your pardon?"

"You are a silly goose not to see it!" She raised a brow and stepped away to inspect the petticoat's fastenings. "He looks at you quite appreciatively, I think. And you would be a fool not to use it."

"I hardly think so," Sarah denied hotly. "He's a blackhearted murderer!"

Mel gave her an amused smile. "Even blackhearted murderers suffer lust, my dear. Do not fool yourself. Peter Holland is definitely in lust with you."

The very notion horrified Sarah. "But I'm blind!"

Mel frowned at her. "That's a ridiculous statement, if ever I've heard one. So does that turn you suddenly into a toad?"

Sarah's cheeks heated. It *was* a ridiculous statement, for certain, but it had just popped out of her mouth. She hadn't the first notion what else to say, because she refused to contemplate the possibility that Peter Holland *might* be attracted to her.

She refused even to consider why it should bother her.

It was an entirely unthinkable notion!

Never mind that she was having a difficult time not being attracted in return.

God, but he *was* a beautiful man.

Sarah cast Mel an irritated glance. "So are you going to tell me what you discovered, or are you not?"

"Good Lord!" Mel exclaimed. "I very nearly forgot! It seems Peter Holland's alibi for that dreadful night lives right here in his house."

"Here?" Sarah had entirely forgotten he'd even had an alibi. So little had been reported about it. In fact, considering the gravity of the situation, very little had been reported in that vein at all. Peter Holland's name was bandied about in the worst light. And yet she did recall mention of an alibi . . . a certain maid . . . "Did you chance to speak with her?"

"No," Mel said. "But she remains in his employ, and I did speak to the housekeeper. The girl's name is Caitlin. She's apparently a very quiet sort. Six years ago, however, she was not. She was a giddy young girl in love with her employer."

"Do you think she will speak to us?"

"I'm not certain," Mel said. "It seems Peter gave her employ when she was hungry—an Irish immigrant with no place to go and no family to speak of.

She is quite loyal to Peter, as I understand.'' Mel winked at her. ''But leave it to me. I shall have her story in no time.''

''You are a gem, Mellie!'' Sarah declared. ''Whatever would I do without you?''

''Bite your tongue,'' Mel said. ''I assure you, you shall never have to find out!''

Christopher Holland was a brilliant child; that much was evident within the first hour of their lessons. Dressed as a darling little replica of his father, in trousers and formal shirt, he sat before her, dutifully listening to her every word.

Ruth had brought him to the nursery, practically by the collar of his shirt, as it had appeared to Sarah. Every moment she thought of it, she grew more furious with his father. In the somewhat fearful glance he'd given his aunt, it was apparent that the child was unwilling to accompany Ruth to the nursery. And yet . . . that was not the impression Sarah had received that first day during her interview. He had seemed excited by the prospect of her instruction, in fact.

Something wasn't right here.

Something didn't ring true.

Ruth hadn't remained long after delivering the boy to Sarah. She'd left them alone practically at once, and Sarah had thought it rather odd. Were she as concerned for Christopher as she claimed to be, she might have stayed to see that Sarah would not push him too hard on this first day of their lessons. She hadn't, however, and in fact, seemed eager to leave. Sarah sat puzzling now over Ruth's contradictory behavior.

Having spent the better part of their hour simply talking, so she might better gauge where to begin teaching Christopher, Sarah found herself with the most incredible urge to take him out of doors, to let him experience the heat of the sun upon his face. The park would be nice, a stroll together. The child knew entirely too much for a boy of his age. But they sat together instead, in a splendid nursery he had never seen, both of them seated at a miniature table with miniature chairs, and surrounded by toys it appeared he'd never played with.

Frowning, Sarah pushed a block at him, one of a set she had purchased long ago with Christopher in mind. She had spied them in a novelty shoppe. It was claimed they had once belonged to Louis Braille, though Sarah highly doubted it.

It had been these blocks that had first given her the notion she could make a difference in Christopher's life. And it was afterward she had sought out Mel. They would be useful, though it wasn't precisely the code she planned to teach him.

"The letters of the code shall always be two dots in width by three dots in height . . . Do you understand, Christopher?"

"Yes, ma'am," he answered much too shyly.

"Give me your hand," she urged him. He seemed reluctant to comply, and she said, "I wish to show you by feel, Christopher."

He offered his little hand, and Sarah couldn't contain her smile as she reached out and took it. She guided it over the block and closed her eyes, trying to feel the block first with her own hand. After a moment she released his hand, and began to feel the raised dots more earnestly.

Confound it all, she couldn't do this so easily.

It was difficult to tell where the starting point and the ending point were. She grew frustrated and opened her eyes, peeking at the block. Closing them again, she said, "All right, Christopher, let us try this once more."

Guiding his hand back to the block, she took his index finger and placed it over the first and largest dot. "I am showing you this, but I'll not tell you what the letter is, I think, because it is not the code I plan to teach you. This one is quite a bit more complicated, though all six dots are in formation, and I wish you to know how they will feel when they are all together."

She released him, letting him rub his finger over the raised spots, without any direction. Sarah seized his hand once more, though gently, and guided his finger, setting it firmly upon the first raised dot. "This is the first. Feel it?"

"Yes, Miss Hopkins," he answered softly.

Sarah frowned at the hesitant way he spoke her name. "No need for such formalities, Christopher," she admonished him. "You may call me Sarah, please."

"Yes, Miss Hop—"

"Uh-uh-uh," she scolded, and laughed.

He giggled—thank God!—and said, "Yes, Miss Sarah."

Sarah smiled at him indulgently. "Do you feel most comfortable calling me Miss?"

"Yes, Miss Sarah," he answered once more.

Sarah smiled. "Then Miss Sarah is quite all right with me, I think."

He beamed at that and announced, "My aunt Ruth says I must be respectful."

Good Lord, he didn't even speak like a six-year-old, Sarah thought.

"Oh, but you are so very respectful," she assured him. "But she is quite right, Christopher. Children must mind their elders, though I cannot imagine you misbehaving at all. Now . . ." She moved his finger slightly to the right, thinking it best they not discuss his rearing in her present mood. "Do you feel another dot here?"

"Yes," he answered, and she moved his finger once more.

"There?"

"No, ma'am."

"That's because it will always be no more than two dots in width," she reminded him, and then shifted his finger once more to the left, and then down. "Now?"

"Yes, ma'am." And then down again. "Yes," he said, before she could ask him.

"Very good, Christopher. Two dots in width," she repeated, "by three dots in height. The Braille code will always be no more than that." She gave his fingers a gentle squeeze. "Very, very good," she repeated, and he smiled up at her. Unable to bring herself to release his tiny hand, she took the block away and set it aside with her free hand. "I think we shall be fast friends," she whispered to him, and was pleased to see his smile deepen. "My goodness, you are such a smart little boy! I wonder, however did you get to be so?"

His smile widened to such a degree that Sarah thought it would split his face. "My daddy says I am just like my mommy!"

Sarah blinked in surprise, taken aback by the disclosure. He *did* look like Mary, and Mary *was* quite intelligent, this much was true, but this mild little boy was nothing like the woman Sarah recalled. Mary had been vibrant and charming, and boisterous and headstrong. Meekness had not been her way at all. And yet he said it so enthusiastically, and it was quite a generous thing that Peter should give his dead wife such credit in her little boy's eyes . . .

She frowned at that thought, and felt a growing confusion over her perceptions of Peter Holland.

No. She couldn't allow herself to lose focus, she reminded herself.

She'd read all the accounts of Mary's life as Peter's wife—just as had everyone else who'd followed the *Post.*

At the very least, he'd made her cousin miserable.

At worst . . . well . . . she couldn't think about that again just now . . . or she would burst into tears as she had last night.

Christopher's little nose began to sniff, and he looked so like a little bunny that Sarah chuckled. "I smell something sweet!" he said abruptly.

"Oh! Do you now?"

Sarah laughed.

The sound of it sent a quiver down Peter's spine.

He stood in the doorway to the nursery, watching the two of them together, his son and this stranger, who seemed less and less a stranger every instant that passed.

Why was that? he wondered. Why did she seem so familiar?

"I wonder what it might be," she said, and laughed again.

The sound of it warmed the blood in his veins more potently than any liquor could have.

"Well, perhaps you do, at that," she teased, and reached down into her dress pocket. "You, Christopher Holland, have a very, very keen nose! Did you get that from your mother as well?" she asked him.

His son giggled, and Sarah reached across the table, finding his hand still nestled within her own. She pressed a sweet into it and wrapped his little fingers about it.

"There now," she said to him. "You have done quite well today, but we've such a long way to go. Ready to go on?"

Christopher greedily unwrapped his treat and then shoved it into his mouth.

Sarah smiled, and her reaction took Peter aback for an instant.

He frowned, contemplating . . .

Sarah Hopkins was a lovely woman, that much was certain.

Even her dark, ugly spectacles could not detract

from the delicate beauty of her face. She wore an equally unappealing dress, but that did not conceal from his greedy eyes the artful lift of her breasts.

His pulse quickened.

God, he had gone to bed last night with her image in his mind, and he was beginning to feel that perhaps Cile was right.

The bloody truth was that he had not for two consecutive moments managed to remove her from his thoughts.

He told himself it was for his son's sake, but the fact that he was preoccupied just now with the image of her breasts made that rationale highly questionable.

How long had it been since he'd been so taken with a woman?

God, had he ever been?

He didn't think so.

Even Mary had not invaded his thoughts so thoroughly. He'd adored Mary, thought her charming and sweet and kind. He'd been infected with her enthusiasm for life, and invigorated by her spirit. He'd been challenged by her wit and impressed with her thirst for knowledge, but he hadn't been in love with her. And he had never, except at the end when he'd been wracked by guilt, been obsessed with thoughts of her.

What was it about Sarah that attracted him so?

Perhaps he simply admired her determination in the face of such a disabling condition. Perhaps it was that she didn't *act* blind. There was little about her, save for those dark glasses, that reminded him of her disability. No, Sarah Hopkins was a strong woman whose presence was undeniable—certainly undeniable in his thoughts, because he couldn't seem to eradicate her from them.

"Are we working too hard for a walk in the park?" Peter asked suddenly, startling himself with the question.

Christ, what the devil was he doing? He was paying her to instruct his son, not to take bloody walks in the park!

Sarah's head popped up, though she didn't turn in his direction. "Mr. Holland!" she exclaimed.

"Daddy!" Christopher shrieked through a mouthful of chewy sweets, but he didn't rise from his seat at the table. His face, however, reflected his pleasure, and Peter took joy in that expression so filled with love.

With his gaze fixed not upon his son, but upon the woman seated before him, Peter stepped into the room. She sat still at the little table, her posture straight and her previous good humor seeming to have vanished with his sudden appearance.

"Good morning, Miss Hopkins," he said.

"We have only just begun, Mr. Holland," she replied, ignoring his greeting.

He got the immediate impression she was dismissing him, and Peter suddenly refused to take no for an answer.

"A walk in the park will clear our minds, and do us much good," he suggested.

"A clear mind, at this point, is not what we need," she countered.

"Perhaps, but I should like to speak with you,"

Peter said, and his tone brooked no argument. "Your lessons may continue this afternoon."

She lifted her chin, and Peter watched her, uncertain what it was about her that left him ill at ease, besides.

"You wish to speak to me?"

"I do," he said.

"Very well," she relented, her annoyance quite clear in her tone. "A walk in the park would be *lovely*," she said, and rose from the table, bending first to seize her cane from the floor.

Chapter 9

L *ovely* was hardly the word for their afternoon.
It hadn't been Sarah's dislike for the man that
had made her reluctant to accept his invitation, but
fear, if the truth be known. She scarce knew how to
act around Christopher. Naturally, she was uncomfortable under his father's careful scrutiny.

And she wasn't certain which was harder to tol-
erate, the brisk March winds or the scalding warmth
of Peter's hand on her arm as he *guided* her through
the park.

Blast, but must he touch her so solicitously?

She wanted nothing more than to free herself from
his mindful grip. She didn't need his bloody atten-
tions, nor did she appreciate his guidance. She felt
a little, in fact, as though he kept her upon a leash.

Sarah walked along beside him, tapping her cane
and listening to father and son's discourse with a
sense of growing hysteria. The two of them were
discussing the content of the morning's lessons, and
Sarah was surprised to hear Christopher recite nearly

every word she had uttered to him. He certainly was a prodigy, and yet, as she watched him, it was also quite apparent he had never been allowed to be a child at all. Christopher Holland was a little wizened man, and Sarah was uncertain whether to be proud of him or furious with his father.

She tapped her cane a little viciously at the thought.

"And Miss Sarah says Mr. Braille was in an accident like me."

"Was he?" Peter asked with some interest. Sarah was entirely too aware of his gaze upon her. It was making her quite ill at ease.

"Yes, sir! And he went to school and they even made him a teacher! And he made up the whole code all by himself!"

"Not quite by himself," Sarah interjected, trying to hide her discomfort. "He had a bit of inspiration from a man named Barbier," she explained. "Mr Barbier was an officer of artillery who was interested in the blind and did what he could to promote their education. It was he who first suggested embossing by means of a point method. Mr. Braille simply restructured the code so it would be easier to use."

She felt Peter's gaze bore into her, and her heart skipped a beat.

Naturally, she told herself, it was fear that made her react so—fear of discovery.

She certainly didn't care one whit whether he was attracted to her or not.

Was he?

Mel had to be wrong. He couldn't possibly be attracted to her.

Nor did she want him to be!

"Miss Sarah is quite knowledgeable, is she not?" Peter said.

"Yes, sir!" Christopher agreed. "And she smells good too, I think!"

"Does she?" Peter leaned closer, and Sarah's heart tripped. He was so close now that she could swear she felt the heat of his breath upon her face. "She does smell rather nice, doesn't she?" His grip upon her arm seemed to tighten a bit. Sarah could scarce breathe as she heard his intake of breath. He held it, and then released it, blowing softly upon her cheek.

The feel of it sent electric tingles down her spine.

What the devil was wrong with her body? Didn't it seem to care anything at all for what her brain was saying? She couldn't be attracted to him. Shouldn't . . .

Christopher responded with a hearty, "Yes sir!"

Sarah forced herself to breathe.

She hadn't realized she'd been holding her breath until she went dizzy upon her feet. Her heartbeat, however, was another matter entirely. It began to thump mercilessly, and she couldn't seem to slow it at all.

Forcing her attention upon Christopher, she doubled her efforts to ignore the man walking at her side.

Unlike other children, Christopher did not run ahead of them, kicking at rocks and climbing atop the tiny hillocks that composed Central Park. Nor did he beg to climb the winter-bared trees or to run and play with his friends. He remained by their side, tapping at the walkway with his cane, and Sarah's heart ached for him.

She wanted to reach out and scoop him into her arms. She wanted to hold him and tell him that everything would be all right. She wanted to spirit him away and shelter him from harm.

She wanted to beat some bloody sense into his father with her blasted cane.

Her conversation with Ruth plagued her immensely.

"Tell me, Mr. Holland," she began, her tone quite perturbed, though she tried not to show her ire.

"Peter," he suggested, his tone warm and gentle in contrast, entirely too charming. It irked her. "Please call me Peter."

On a cold day in bloody hell!

Is this the way he had spoken to Mary?

Had he wooed her with his wit and charm?

Well, Sarah was very well aware of where it had gotten Mary, and she didn't intend to fall prey to it as well.

She swallowed her anger, and said, "Peter, it is, then." Taking a deep breath, she willed her nerves to calm. "Tell me . . . Peter . . . why did you not simply enroll Christopher in New York's Institute for the Blind? Why hire me, or anyone for that matter, when you have at your disposal one of the finer schools for the blind in the entire country?"

He peered down at her; strange how she could

sense his gaze so keenly, even when she dared not look at him. "The most obvious reason, his age, Sarah . . . May I call you Sarah?" he asked her abruptly.

Sarah bristled at the question. Some part of her sensed danger keenly in his familiarity. She *wasn't* going to end like Mary. She wasn't! She swallowed the tart reply that came to her lips and said instead, "Certainly," and couldn't help herself—she swung her cane and smacked him squarely in the shin.

Blackguard!

"Ouch!" he cried.

"Oh, dear!" she pretended to fret. "Was that you?"

"It was," he said, and hopped along beside her an instant, massaging his leg. She could sense his frown even though she didn't dare look at him.

"Please do forgive me," she said, her tone as dulcet as she could manage, and tried not to smile, because the vicious act did indeed make her feel better. Her uncle was right, she feared; she *was* a termagant.

"Not a problem," he replied, though she could still hear the frown in his tone. "You have quite a healthy grip on that cane, Miss Holland." And then he continued, "At any rate, they would hardly embrace my son as a pupil at so early an age."

Sarah tightened her grip on her cane. "Have you considered that there might perchance be good reason for that?"

"With most children perhaps," he countered, "but I'm quite certain you've realized by now that Christopher is *different* from other children."

"Yes, he is," Sarah agreed, her tone carefully subdued, lest she reveal her infamous temper. If Mary had been spirited, Sarah had been labeled temperamental, and rightly so. God help her, but she felt herself ready to explode even now. Her face heated with anger. "I'm uncertain, however, whether it is justifiable to exploit his talents at such an early age."

"Exploit?" There was genuine surprise in his voice at her veiled accusation. "That is a rather harsh view, Miss Hopkins. As I recall, you did not voice such an opinion at your interview. Why now?"

Sarah was unsure how much to say about her discussion with his sister. She wasn't even certain whether to reveal it at all. Ruth was hardly her ally in this, and yet she couldn't blame the woman for trying to protect an innocent child. Sarah had gone to great lengths for just the same purpose.

Then, too, she wasn't entirely certain she could afford to make this an issue. If she dared to, and he released her from her duties, what then would she do? She had no proof of anything as yet, and if she went complaining to the authorities that Peter forced his son to study . . . who would champion her? Nobody! They would applaud him in truth. At least Ruth, no matter that she did not seem to like Sarah, was looking out for Christopher's best interests.

His father was an overbearing oaf who expected too much of his son.

"I should ask," Sarah ventured, "*why* do you wish him to begin his studies so young?" It was a sensible enough question, Sarah thought, and she waited expectantly for his answer, certain that he could not have a very reasonable one.

"I smell taffy!" Christopher exclaimed all at once, averting their attention. "May we get some, Daddy? May we? May we?"

Peter chuckled at his son's enthusiasm. "I should have known you'd smell a vendor at ten paces. Why not?" he relented. "Wait here."

He left them standing beneath an old oak that was bearing its first leaves, just the two of them, and hurried after Christopher's treat.

"Are you having a good time, Christopher?" Sarah asked him, as she watched his father, for the first time unheeded. His back was to them as he drew out some coins from his pocket, handing them to the vendor. He was quite a handsome man, she had to admit. He drew attention from women without even seeming aware of it. Sarah hadn't missed the appreciative stares they'd received as they'd passed other female strollers in the park—even those hanging on the arms of their lovers.

"Yes, ma'am!" Christopher answered.

Sarah laughed. There was little doubt as to his enthusiasm by the expression on his face and the tone of his voice. "I suppose this is rather exciting," Sarah agreed. "Much better than being locked away indoors all day long."

"Yes, ma'am!" Christopher answered, and thrust his little hand into his pocket. He turned his face up to the sky, and appeared to be scenting the wind, his expression quite blissful.

"How would you feel about bringing our lessons

to the park sometime?'' she asked him.

He grinned.

''Would you like that, Christopher?''

He nodded. ''Yes, ma'am!''

He was so quiet—except around his father—so well mannered. Had he not recited her words almost verbatim to his father, she might have wondered that he'd listened to her at all, because he scarce gave a response unless prodded for it. ''I suppose you don't get out very much?'' Sarah asked in an attempt to draw him out.

''Oh, yes, ma'am!'' he answered. ''My daddy brings me to the park every Saturday, and sometimes on Sunday too.'' He smiled at that, looking rather proud. It was obvious he had great admiration for his father.

Her surprise was evident in her tone. ''He does?''

''Oh, yes, ma'am!''

''Good Lord, Christopher!'' Sarah exclaimed, laughter tinting her voice. ''Don't you ever say anything besides 'Yes, ma'am'?''

Her question seemed to amuse him. ''Uh, yes, ma'am,'' he replied, and burst into giggles. Unable to help herself, Sarah giggled along with him. The two of them, she realized, stood there, giggling, looking and sounding like a pair of loons. She wondered how others perceived them—she with her dark spectacles, Christopher with his sightless stare, both with their canes, and both laughing hysterically at nothing apparent. Passersby probably thought them mad.

Well, she didn't care.

It felt wonderful to be in Christopher's company.

Too bad his father chose that moment to return, albeit bearing taffy and flowers. When she saw the flowers, Sarah's heart began to thump once more. Her laughter died abruptly as he handed the taffy to his son. Christopher tore into the confection with unmistakable fervor.

"Your second today," his father reminded him. "Enjoy it, son. It will be your last, or we'll both find ourselves bearing long faces at dinner."

Sarah suddenly felt like an intruder in their midst.

It must be a wonderful feeling to have a family, to share meals together, and laughter . . . and hugs.

She had to remind herself this was not a regular family, although at the moment, they certainly seemed it—despite their lack of a mother . . . and wife.

"Aunt Ruth will be mad!" Christopher predicted, but didn't seem the least bit concerned.

Peter patted his son's head. "I'll not tell if you'll not tell," he said.

"All right, Daddy. I won't tell if you won't tell," Christopher returned, smiling, as his father smoothed the hair down over his forehead.

"And . . ." He turned to Sarah. Sarah pretended obliviousness to the offer he held in his hand. "I've a bribe to ensure Miss Hopkins won't tell either."

"Flowers?" Christopher said matter-of-factly, tearing off a generous portion of his taffy with his teeth. "Figures."

Sarah marveled at his keen sense of smell. "Oh, my!" she exclaimed. "I thought I smelled them, too.

Lilacs?'' she asked, taking Christopher's example, though she could see very well what they were.

''Very good,'' Peter said, and pressed them into her hand, smiling down at her.

Sarah's throat closed a bit. His gesture left her at a loss for words, but she refused to be moved by it. It was a smooth maneuver, to be sure, by a man who was accustomed to giving flattery to get what he wanted. He'd managed to win Mary's heart, though Mary had sworn she'd never be wooed. He wasn't going to win hers so easily. Not that it was his intention, she realized . . .

What did he want?

''They   are . . . absolutely . . . beautiful,''   she stammered, and brought them closer to inhale their delicate scent.

He seemed to go suddenly still at her declaration. He was looking at her curiously, and Sarah's heart slammed against her breast when she realized what she'd said.

''The scent of them,'' she amended quickly, hoping to divert him. Her heart hammered. ''They smell so beautiful. Thank you!''

He was still staring at her, she was aware, though Sarah dared not look at him. In fact, he was studying her quite intently and it made her skin prickle with gooseflesh.

''I don't think I remember *ever* getting flowers,'' Sarah added uncomfortably.

''Never?''

Sarah shook her head.

He bent closer, and whispered. "Not even from your fiancé?"

Sarah blinked at his question. "Fiancé?" Whatever was he talking about?

"The man with whom you were engaged to be married . . ."

Her brows lifted as she belatedly recalled the story she and Mel had concocted. "Yes . . . of course," she said after a moment, a bit provoked by his sarcasm, "but no . . ." When had he the occasion to ask Mel about her personal affairs? "He never did," Sarah continued, deliberating the answer to her own question. "He wasn't the sort to bring me flowers, I'm afraid."

He fell silent, and Sarah knew he was contemplating how best to ask her about her accident. If Mel had told him about her *fiancé*, then certainly he must have asked about her *accident* itself. And yet there was no story to tell, because she and Mel had agreed that their web of lies was best kept modest. They had agreed only to give the most cursory details and to refuse further inquiries. It wasn't as though Peter needed to know the cause of her blindness to give her employ, was it?

She refused to elaborate.

"It isn't the most pleasant subject for me," she told him, dismissing it once and for all.

"I'm sorry," Peter said, and let it go, though reluctantly.

It was clear by her tone and her body language that she would not appreciate his prying. And yet curiosity needled him.

What sort of man had she loved? And why had he never brought her flowers?

Had they an arrangement as he'd had with Mary? Or were they to marry for love?

Standing there, staring down at her, he could scarce imagine any man maintaining any measure of distance from her. How could any man look at those lips and not crave them? How could he see the pleasure in her face as she inhaled the fragrance of those lilacs, and not wish to bring her flowers every damned day? How could he spy the flush of her cheeks and not yearn to place fingers to her warm, soft skin?

It must be soft—it seemed to Peter she had the most perfectly luminous complexion he had ever laid eyes on.

What color were her eyes?

He longed to see them.

He had to stop himself from reaching out to remove her spectacles from her face, from looking into her eyes.

"Sarah," he said.

"Yes?" She lifted her face from the lilacs, and it was all Peter could do not to bend and kiss those lovely lips.

Damn, but he craved the taste of her more than he had craved anything in so bloody long—more, even, than he craved the sweet numbing liquor against his tongue.

He reached out and touched her cheek, couldn't help himself. She startled at the touch, and he dropped his hand.

"*You* are beautiful," he said low, and watched her breast rise with her intake of breath.

What would she do if he kissed her now?

He didn't dare.

That didn't stop him from imagining . . . the feel of her lips upon his mouth . . .

"You won't tell, will you?" Christopher asked suddenly.

Sarah started at Christopher's question, as though she'd somehow forgotten his son's presence. "Tell?" she asked, sounding confused. "Tell who?" It was obvious to Peter that she was flustered, and that, for some reason, pleased him immensely.

"Aunt Ruth," Christopher replied with a scrunch of his nose.

"Oh, that. I think not!" she assured his son rather passionately. "If your father says you may have taffy, then who am I to say you may not?"

Peter bent low, and said for her ears alone, "A very, *very* intriguing woman, Miss Hopkins, that's who you are." She buried her nose in the lilacs he'd brought her, and he added, not entirely benevolently, "I shall look forward to getting to know you better, Sarah."

The afternoon had left him with more questions than answers, and answers were what he wanted now.

Chapter 10

"**N**o need to bother, Gunther," a woman's voice echoed from the hall. "I'll see myself in."

"But, ma'dame!" Gunther protested. Their hurried footsteps echoed from the hall. "Mrs. Morgan!" he declared a little louder, and it sounded more a desperate warning. Peter glanced up from the papers strewn upon his desk to see Cile approaching his office, her expression furious.

Their gazes met. Her blue eyes glittered angrily. "Didn't you get my message?" she asked him as she stalked into his office.

Peter pushed aside his papers. "What message?"

She came directly to his desk and leaned on it, looking straight into his eyes. "The one I sent telling you to meet me at August's home!"

"I did not," Peter assured her.

"Damn you, Peter! Whatever has gotten into you? Do you know how embarrassing it was to wait there for you and have you never show up?"

"Cile," he repeated. "I did *not* receive it."

She straightened and peered down at him, giving him that familiar pout. "I heard you were at the park today," she said.

Christ, news traveled fast in this town. "No doubt you did," he told her, and suddenly understood the nature of her visit. In fact, he doubted she'd sent a message at all. It was hardly unlike Cile to use such a tack. The last thing he needed was Cile on the warpath, and he decided to soothe her temper rather than call her on it. "In any case," he said, "I didn't get your message. But now that you're here, why don't you join us for dinner?"

She suddenly had that all-too-familiar gleam in her eyes. "Are you certain you wish me to?"

Peter gave her a wry smile, wondering what it was she was up to. "Of course, Cile."

"Well . . . I *did* wish to meet your . . . guest," she confessed, and Peter lifted a brow.

So that was what this was about, he thought, and resigned himself to an uncomfortable evening under Cile's watchful eye.

Sarah wasn't certain what it was that woke her, but she thought perhaps it was the click of a door as it closed.

She opened her eyes to the faint light of a candle flickering by the window and an empty room, and closed them once more, so tired she could scarce remain conscious.

God, she was so tired . . . having stayed awake so late the night before, weeping over Mary. She'd thought herself long past mourning, but evidently it wasn't so. Being here, in this room, was not easy.

Exhausted, she drifted back into a troubled sleep.

Today in the park ... she had been so confused ...

Peter's actions and her perceptions of him were becoming muddled.

She remembered what her cousin had written in her journals; she had saved every last printed excerpt. But the man in her company today had not been the same man her cousin had written about. He had not been selfish or cold or thoughtless. He had treated his son with respect and warmth, and he had been more than considerate of her, despite that she had been so mean with her cane. But good Lord, it had felt good to vent in such a manner! And still ... how had he rewarded her? He'd brought her flowers, and though she was not quite repentant, Sarah's conscience pricked her just a little.

The scent of lilacs permeated the air ...

He'd had a vase brought to her room, and then had the flowers arranged at her bedside while she'd finished up with Christopher's lessons. They'd been waiting for her upon her return, and Sarah had felt torn between wanting to throw the bloody vase at the door, and ... well ...

No man had ever given her flowers.

She supposed her attitude was hardly conducive to it. She was well aware she came across as cold and even a bit combative at times. She hadn't joined Peter and his guest for dinner, hadn't dared. The afternoon had taken an emotional toll on her, and she hadn't been able to bear the thought of sitting before him, enduring his scrutiny.

Sarah hadn't been hungry at any rate. Though she'd ordered dinner brought to her room, she hadn't had much of an appetite. She'd had perhaps a few bites of bread and drunk her tea. And then she'd grown sooooo tired afterward . . .

Lilacs.

She wasn't supposed to *see* the flowers, but she couldn't miss their scent so near her bed.

Lilacs . . . and another stronger floral scent . . . Sickeningly sweet . . .

The perception confused her.

She could scarce smell anything else . . . except . . .

The smell of smoke jarred her awake.

Sarah opened her eyes to the flicker, not of candlelight, but of a flame.

The curtains were on fire!

A scream caught in her throat.

Her heart leapt within her breast as she tripped from the bed. The room spun before her. The nearest thing to grab was the small blanket she had found in the wardrobe. Mary's last efforts. Snatching it from the chair where she'd left it, she used it to slap at the tiny flames that licked upward upon the curtains.

Smoke began to choke her.

She slapped furiously at the flames, jerking down the curtains and beating at them in growing panic.

In the space of seconds, the room exploded around her.

Her lungs filled with smoke as she pounded desperately . . . until she realized it was a lost effort, and then with the charred baby blanket in hand, she raced for the door, tripping. She fell to her knees. God, it was a bad dream! It had to be a nightmare! Everything seemed so distorted. Crawling the rest of the way upon her hands and knees, she clawed her way up the door and threw it open, collapsing into the corridor.

She screamed at the top of her lungs.

It was the past revisited.

Somewhere in Peter's sleep-drugged mind, the screams registered. His eyes flew open. He leapt out of his bed and bounded into the hall, trying to gain his bearings.

The hysterical shrieks were coming from the direction of the nursery, and he lunged toward the noise, running as fast as his legs would carry him. In the darkness he tripped over a table and vase. The vase smashed in his wake as he regained his balance and turned the corner in the hall.

The far end of the corridor glowed red. He could see the silhouette of a woman standing in the flickering shadows.

Sarah!

Her room was on fire.

He began to shout for help at the top of his lungs. His first thought as he reached her and lifted her into his arms was for Christopher's safety. Christopher's room, thankfully, was near his own, and as long as they worked with haste, they could contain the flames.

They must contain the flames!

Sarah was barely conscious, her arms falling limply down his back. God, he didn't know what to do. Take her and Christopher outside? Or leave them here?

He carried Sarah without a word to his son's bedroom, knowing there wasn't time to dally, and dropped her upon the bed, waking Christopher from his slumber. "Stay with him," he commanded her. "Do *not* leave this room!"

There was no time to waste.

Even as he turned and raced away, leaving Sarah to deal with his frightened child, he knew time was of the essence.

Containing it wasn't simply a matter of saving their own lives. In this city, where rooftops merged one with another, fire was their worst enemy.

Sarah tried to shake off her stupor.

Even in the darkness, the room spun before her.

God! But she hadn't known what to do.

She'd been frozen with fear, but she was regaining her senses. Comforting the whimpering child, she urged him out of the bed and into her arms.

"Hurry!" she pleaded with him.

"Where are we going?" the child whined.

"Everything will be all right," Sarah assured him. "We are going to wait outside for your father." Even in her state, she understood the dangers of remaining inside. The sensation of burning lungs remained with her, and the fear of it propelled her to her feet.

"Why?" he cried, as Sarah started out the door.

God . . . it seemed the corridor swayed beneath her, unbalancing her like a rug pulled out from beneath her feet.

"Where's my daddy?"

Sarah would be damned if they would simply wait here in this room to meet their deaths! For all she knew, Peter Holland had set the fire. She wasn't simply going to wait here to die. No bloody way! And neither was Christopher. Ignoring Christopher's questions and sleepy protests, she found her way through the darkness and hurried toward the front hall, bouncing off of walls as she made her way out. There wasn't any smoke, only darkness, but she couldn't seem to see the way before her. When she reached the foyer at last, with moonlight piercing the sidelights, she followed it, and nearly cried with relief as she unlatched the front door and threw it open.

Tears coursed down her cheeks as she carried her cousin's child into the frigid night air. Once outside, she snuggled him within the charred baby blanket as curious onlookers began to congregate.

A few ran screaming, "Fire!" as Sarah crumpled to the street with Christopher in her arms.

At the far end of the house, a window glowed in the darkness as though it were a demon's eye. Smoke seeped into the brisk night air, dark, sinister wisps against the cloudless night sky.

Sarah held Christopher tight, rocking him.

He whined, "I want my daddy."

"I promise everything will be fine," she whispered to him, and tried with all her might to stay awake. Somehow she couldn't seem to. It was as though she'd been drugged . . .

Someone had drugged her.

The realization smacked her across the brain before a wave of blackness hit.

Someone had started the fire, too, she realized suddenly, and without doubt.

Someone didn't want her around.

Why?

She had only just begun; they couldn't possibly have suspected her so soon. And yet . . . someone did perceive her as a threat.

Who?

The answer, she knew, lay with whoever had drugged her tea.

Chapter 11

S mothering the fire was not the easiest task, but they did it eventually. The last flame was extinguished in the wee hours of the morning.

When Peter stood examining the damage in the eeriness of twilight, he saw the curtains had been completely consumed. The interior of the room was completely charred, the wood floors burned, the windows shattered by the heat. Even the bedclothes were singed. Had the flames licked a little higher, the ceiling would have begun to burn as well, but as it was, it was only thickly layered with soot. The curtain rods were torn from the brackets on one side and it was obvious that they had been wrenched from the wall. It appeared to him that Sarah had tried to put out the flame and she had very likely saved them all. Peter hadn't had to deal with a fire on the ceiling, merely a potential inferno.

By the time the fire department had responded, the fire had been contained.

Peter walked away with lungs burning and soot

covering him from head to toe. Weary as he was, his first thoughts were for his son . . . and for Sarah.

He'd abandoned them in Christopher's room, only because it was so near to the front of the house. If his efforts had failed, he would have retreated to get them at once, and then carried them to safety. It was only now, however, as he walked away from the night's blaze, that he realized how deadly his decision might have been.

As he contemplated the possible outcomes, he felt his stomach churn.

His head began to race with thoughts of *what if* . . .

What if he had not been able to put the blaze out?

What if he had endangered himself by going into the burning room, and somehow mortally injured himself? No one other than Sarah had known his son's whereabouts.

And Sarah . . . what the hell had she been doing with a lit candle in her room? What need had she for light?

Weariness settled into his brain.

Perhaps someone had brought it in—Mel—and had forgotten it. But who would have been so bloody stupid to set a candle so close to the curtains?

He'd found the brass candleholder on the windowsill. The window had been left only slightly ajar . . . enough so that the updraft had blown the flame toward the curtains, catching it afire.

Whatever had possessed someone to do such a thing?

Someone had endangered them all with their carelessness tonight, and he had quite a few questions to ask of his guest and her aide.

First, however, he wished to see to their comfort, and to make certain Sarah hadn't been injured by the fire—thank God she'd awakened in time! He shuddered to think what might have happened.

He entered his son's room and his heart jolted to a stop.

It was empty.

He'd left them both here to wait—where had they gone? It wasn't so much a sense of immediate danger that made him suddenly sick to his stomach, but the realization that had he needed to usher them to safety, he wouldn't have been able to find them.

Where the hell were they?

He hurried into the hall. "Sarah!" he shouted.

There were strange people walking through his house now. The volunteer fire department, and police as well. They peered at him through suspicious eyes, but at the moment he didn't give a bloody damn. He hurried outside, into the morning light, and sucked in a sigh of relief to see his son with Sarah, the two of them huddled together.

Ignoring the press who were already gathering like hyenas after a kill—intrusive bastards—he made his way toward them, shoving aside one man who approached him.

Sarah's eyes were closed, and she was rocking Christopher in her arms, soothing him. There were a few reporters gathered around her already, asking questions she didn't seem able or willing to answer.

"Sarah," he whispered, not wishing to startle her.

"Sarah?" She didn't open her eyes, but turned her face up to the sound of his voice.

"Peter?" she said.

He reached out and took her into his arms, drawing her against him, and Christ help him, his body reacted at once as she fell into his embrace. "I'm here," he told her, confused by his untimely physical reaction. His heart began to hammer with something other than fear.

Something about the embrace triggered a longing deep within him.

Sarah held his son while he held her, and something inside him responded to that communion.

God, it felt bloody damned good to hold them, to protect them.

To protect somebody.

To know he hadn't failed . . . again.

She seemed unable to speak, and he didn't know what else to say. She looked so like a dirty little waif sitting there in her blackened nightgown and soot-begrimed face. Her expression was one of bewilderment.

Without her dark glasses, he could see her face more clearly, and it was lovely despite the filth. The only thing that possibly detracted from her perfection was her blindness. And yet, did it truly? If he allowed that to influence his feelings, was he any better than those who judged his son? Did he love his son any less for his disability?

The answer was no.

"Daddy?" Christopher whined sleepily.

"Yes, son," Peter answered, and reached out to

take him from Sarah's arms. "Everything is all right," he assured Christopher. His son latched his little arms about his neck as the newshounds began to gather en masse. He shook Sarah. "Come, Sarah."

"Mr. Holland . . . William Neil with—"

"No comment!" Peter snapped out, and urged Sarah up, dragging her gently to her feet. It wouldn't look good to the press for him to throw her over his shoulder like some medieval savage with his stolen bride, but he wasn't about to stand about answering questions for a bunch of reporters with their own bloody priorities. They hadn't had the least compunction about ruining his reputation once before, nor had they given a second thought to dragging his dead wife's name through the proverbial mud. "Sarah," he urged her once more, and she followed his lead as though she were in some hypnotic state.

He led her into the house.

"T-tea," she stammered.

"How did you get outside?" he asked her.

"It was the t-tea," she repeated, and swayed a bit on her feet, scarce able to stand. If Peter didn't know better, he would suspect her drunk or drugged. Perhaps she was drugged? Some women, he knew, were quite fond of laudanum as a remedy for all ailments. His sister was. But Sarah Hopkins somehow didn't seem the type.

Ruth met them at the front hall. "Good God!" she exclaimed. "What is that child doing outside?"

"I don't know how they got there," Peter answered. "Take Christopher to his room and stay with him while I see to Miss Hopkins. She doesn't seem well.''

''Certainly,'' Ruth replied at once, and pried Christopher out of his arms. ''And fetch Miss Frank as well,'' he directed her. ''Send her to Mary's room.''

''Mary's room!''

''Where else?'' he snapped, and with his son in good hands, he lifted Sarah into his arms and carried her to his suite. ''And bring some tea,'' he added. ''She seems to be asking for it.''

''No . . . my head . . . aches,'' she said. As they entered the master's suite, Sarah moaned softly, lifting her hand to her head.

Good Lord . . . her lungs ached as well.

They no longer burned but were sore, and she felt as though the chill of the night air had crept into her very bones.

''Everything is fine,'' he assured her once more.

Sarah was aware enough not to look him in the eyes. She closed her eyes tight, trying to regain her bearings, trying to think. She had to think.

The entire night had been like a terrible dream, and still she had yet to awaken.

She clung to Peter as he laid her down in the bed, afraid to release him. He appeased her by kneeling at the bedside and allowing her to retain the sleeve of his nightshirt in her fist.

''Sarah,'' he said. ''How did you get outside?''

''I went . . . with Christopher,'' she explained, her thoughts still too fragmented to construct sentences.

''I know. But how?''

"Led the way," she explained. "Was . . . afraid."

His tone was firm, but not harsh. "Do you realize how dangerous that was?" he asked her.

Sarah didn't answer. She hadn't been thinking straight . . . but neither had he. The least dangerous place for them to be had been outside.

She had known that at least.

"Was afraid . . . Christopher," she told him. "Safer out there . . ."

He couldn't argue that point and didn't—thank God, because Sarah couldn't think clearly enough to defend herself. Raw fear had set her in motion last night, but whatever she had been drugged with worked with sheer fatigue now to bring her to the edge of oblivion.

She needed to sleep. Exhaustion held her firmly in its grip.

She peered up into his face. "Need to," she pleaded with him, "sleep . . ."

He was staring down at her, frowning. Maybe angry? She didn't know what she had done, but she couldn't think about it right now. She turned away. "Need to sleep."

"Very well," he relented. "Sleep, then, Sarah." He pulled the bedsheets out from beneath her and drew them up to cover her. "We'll talk later," he whispered softly against her cheek as he tucked her beneath the covers.

Sarah was vaguely aware that he had to pry her fingers loose from his nightshirt.

And then he was gone and she fell at once into a dreamless slumber.

Chapter 12

Her eyes were blue.

And she wasn't blind.

The second revelation had come close on the heels of the first.

Drugged though she appeared to be, when she had turned to look at him, begging him to let her sleep . . . he had been struck first with the vivid clarity of her eyes—blue like the pale blue of a cloudless summer sky.

And then he had been stunned to find her eyes beseeching him.

Damn, he'd had no choice but to let her sleep, knowing she was hardly in any condition to answer his questions. But she was bloody well going to! And soon.

Then again, he wasn't entirely certain how to handle this. *Sarah Hopkins* was here for a reason. She'd gone through so much effort for *some* goal. Peter wanted to know what the hell it was.

Who was she?

What the devil was she after?

Could he afford to let her play her little game?

Could he afford not to?

He thought over his options: She was hardly going to come clean and tell him if he asked outright. No, his best recourse was to let her go on, to let her play her little charade, and to watch her.

There had been something about her from the very first, something he had not been able to place, but even despite this incident, he would have figured it out before long. He lived with his blind son, for Christ's sake, knew his every mannerism by heart. Sarah Hopkins—if that was indeed her real name— couldn't have fooled him much longer. Dark spectacles alone were not enough to convince a man with his experience.

He thought back to the morning . . . during Christopher's lessons . . . She had smiled when his son had smiled. Peter hadn't missed her reaction, though at that instant he hadn't been certain what it was about her mirrored response that had troubled him. Now he knew. And then this afternoon at the park . . . her reference to the flowers . . . that they were *beautiful*. That had struck him as odd as well.

And now that he understood, everything made sense.

Almost everything . . .

He couldn't fathom who the hell she might be— a mole for the reporters? for the police? after all this time? He doubted it. Whoever she was, she was good—just not good enough.

And he was going to give her just enough room in her noose to hang herself.

"Mellie, I swear you are a godsend!"

"As soon as I heard, and knew all was well, I went back to your home and gathered a few items."

"Thank you," Sarah said.

"I also took the liberty of purchasing another pair of spectacles for you," Mel continued. "They wouldn't let me in the room to retrieve anything." She reached into her coat and withdrew a pair of spectacles that were nearly identical to the ones Sarah had been wearing. She placed them upon Sarah's face. "I swear to God, you are the only woman I know who can carry those spectacles off as though it were the very fashion."

"You are such a sweet fibber!" Sarah laughed weakly. "Whatever would I do without you?"

"Shush!" Mel said, her expression one of horror. "Quit saying such things!"

Sarah gave her a concerned glance. "They didn't follow you, did they?"

"Whyever would they? Have you given them reason to suspect you?"

Sarah shook her head. "Not that I am aware."

"Well, then . . . why would they even consider sending someone to follow your aide, whom they have no interest in at all? Besides, they are much too busy with cleaning up after the fire to concern themselves even with you, it seems. You have been sleeping undisturbed for some time, and I have been with you at least an hour without the first head popping in to check on you.''

She still felt groggy and out of sorts, almost as though she could go back to bed and sleep for a thousand years. ''I suppose I needed the rest,'' Sarah replied, frowning. ''Mel?''

Mel's brows lifted. ''Yes, dear?''

''I think someone drugged me last night.''

Mel's brows collided. ''Drugged!''

Sarah hesitated to say, and yet the evidence was pounding away in her head. ''Well . . . I didn't bring a candle into my room last night. Did you?''

Mel shook her head. ''I don't believe I am following you, Sarah.''

Sarah tried to focus, to think more clearly. ''Did you come into my room after I fell asleep and leave a candle there?''

''Of course not!'' Mel exclaimed. ''I mean . . . I might have come. I thought about it, even—and had I found you asleep, yes, I might have left again. But I didn't, Sarah, and had I done so, I certainly would never have abandoned a lit candle.''

''Mel . . . I have not used any light at all in that room for fear that I would be discovered, and yet I awoke once and there *was* a lit candle by the window. I saw it, but was entirely too sleepy to understand what it meant. I remember, too, waking and feeling as though someone had been in my room, and yet when I'd opened my eyes, the room had been empty, and once again I had been too tired to pursue it. I fell asleep again without giving either detail a second thought.''

Mel frowned down at her. "You must have been terribly exhausted."

Sarah sat up a little straighter and tossed the covers from her. "I was. Still am. And that is hardly like me, you know."

"No, it's not," Mel agreed.

"I feel like a slug."

Mel's expression was one of concern now. "All right, Sarah . . . let us think about this. What did you eat last night?"

"I skipped dinner," Sarah answered at once. "I was so preoccupied and tired already that I could scarce bear the thought of joining them. I just couldn't undergo their scrutiny over an entire evening meal—felt I'd borne enough of it for one day already."

Mel cocked her head, her face screwing in confusion. "So you ate nothing at all? How could they possibly have drugged you, then?" she reasoned.

Sarah sat up a little straighter, her hand going to her head. "Well . . . but I ordered dinner brought to my room," she explained. "I didn't eat much from it, just a bite or two of my bread . . . but I did drink my tea."

Mel's lips twisted as she speculated. "The tea, then," she said. "Who brought it, Sarah?"

"How the devil should I know, Mellie? You know the servants better than I. Some woman. Caitlin, maybe?"

Mel raised a brow at that, and Sarah felt at once contrite for her snappish tone.

"I'm sorry," she relented, "I am simply a bit confused."

"I understand, Sarah. But it just doesn't make sense to me at all. Peter Holland hired you to tutor his son. Why in blazes would he wish you out of the way so soon? You only just got here. What possible reason could he have to resort to such measures as drugging you and roasting you alive? It just doesn't make sense to me." She continued to shake her head.

Sarah had to agree. "No, it doesn't." Her brows knit as she contemplated the puzzle.

There was silence between them, both deliberating possible motives.

"Unless he's mad," Sarah announced, frustrated by the turn of events. "A madman who lures innocent women to his home and murders them." She frowned. "I'll bet he hides the bodies in his wine cellar," she added viciously, and knew at once that it was a ridiculous notion.

She couldn't imagine that the man who had dragged her from the inferno of her room and then held her so lovingly on the street was any sort of villain at all.

It was dangerous to soften toward him, Sarah reminded herself. Hers and Mel's lives might well depend upon her remaining strong. But he was somehow tearing away her armor, leaving her with doubts and more questions than answers.

Mel tilted her head a little in reproach. "I hardly think he is a madman. He might be a greedy dastard, and perhaps even a murderer as well, but mad . . . I do not think so. In fact, he seems quite deliberate to me.''

Sarah's brow furrowed. ''Well, neither do I. But these thoughts do enter my head. Particularly this morning. Perhaps he knows who I am. Are you certain you were not followed?''

''Absolutely,'' Mel replied, without reservation. ''I was very careful. No one even knew I had gone, until I'd returned.''

Sarah was quiet a long moment, digesting the information. ''But someone doesn't want us here, Mellie.''

Mel nodded. ''I agree.''

Sarah shivered, recalling the blaze in her room. This morning it had held a certain dream quality that was terrifying in itself. God, what if she hadn't awakened? What if she had not smelled the smoke?

''The question is who?''

''That I don't know,'' Sarah replied, ''but I've a feeling we've not heard the last from them.''

Mel sucked in a breath at that. ''I've that notion, too.''

Sarah reached out to pat her friend's hand. She laid her own gently down upon it. ''Mellie . . . you needn't stay, you realize. If you wish to go, I shall understand. I do not wish to put you at risk.''

Mel turned her hand to grasp Sarah's. She squeezed it gently. ''And if I go, will you go with me?''

Sarah shook her head without even considering it. ''Even more than before, I've no choice. I cannot go, Mellie. *That* is Mary's child I would abandon, and I will not do so—not now when I am finally in a position to help him. I owe it to them.''

"But *are* you in a position to help him?'' Mel asked, forcing her to reconsider. "Are you truly?''

Sarah shrugged stubbornly. "I don't know, but I do know this . . . Last night I held that child in my arms and rocked him to sleep while he cried. I comforted him when he whimpered in fear, and promised him all would be well. I will not walk away from him now, Mel. I will not!''

"Then neither shall I,'' Mel declared. "We shall do this together. You need me, Sarah. And I'm staying!''

Sarah was hardly in a position to argue. Had it not been for Mel, she would be left now with no clothes, no spectacles, nothing at all. It was Mel who had thought far enough ahead to replace those items for her, and it was Mel who gave her the courage to continue. Sarah squeezed her friend's hand in return, and smiled up at her gratefully.

"I know you don't like me to say so . . . but I don't know what I'd do without you.''

"For better or worse, we're in this together,'' Mel said, and smiled down at her, her eyes twinkling. "In payment I shall only require your firstborn child.''

"Imagine that!'' Sarah said, and laughed softly. "And what if I shall never have a firstborn child?''

Mel's brows lifted. *"What if?''*

Sarah's cheeks heated.

"Hmmm,'' Mel said. "Only a week ago you would have sworn to me that I was out of luck entirely.'' She narrowed her gaze, studying Sarah. ''What has happened since then?''

Sarah glowered up at her. ''Not a blasted thing!'' she denied vehemently. And then glanced about the room, taking in her surroundings for the first time. ''God! I realize this may be a silly question, but . . . where the devil am I?''

Mel pursed her lips. ''Pulled out of the fire and cast into the frying pan,'' she answered cryptically, and then explained, ''In the master's suite, Sarah.''

Chapter 13

It was unfortunate that it had taken a fire to get her into this room, but Sarah decided every bruise and burn was worth it.

While the room adjoining the nursery had held very little of Mary, this one hoarded a wealth of memories. Sarah moved from piece to precious piece, recognizing some, exploring others. It was only when she came to a small portrait that stood upon a dressing table that she understood the depths of Mary's anger toward her. It had once been a sketch of the two of them together, their backs to each other, both looking at the artist. In the portrait, only Mary's half was visible; the other half that had been Sarah, was gone, cut away. Why had Mary displayed only half of the portrait? or had Peter? Sarah lifted up the picture and sat upon the bed, clutching it in her hands, contemplating once more the folly of their estrangement.

How was she to know, when she'd stood her ground in protest over Mary's marriage and had refused to return, that she would never again see her cousin alive? Such silliness it all seemed now. She'd been wrong to do so, had thought she might make a difference in Mary's decision. But when she looked back at it now, her motives were less noble and all the more clear.

She had thought she'd protested for Mary's good, but the truth was . . . Sarah had been afraid to be alone. She'd made up her *own* mind that she didn't wish to marry and had counted upon her cousin to be her life companion. Strange, even now, to think about it, but they'd had such a perfect friendship, and she just hadn't wished to give it up.

Selfish.

When Mary had chosen a life with Peter Holland over one with Sarah, Sarah had felt betrayed, and she'd reacted just like a spoiled brat. Mary had responded by cutting her completely out of her life, and the portrait in her hand was indisputable evidence of that fact.

When Sarah looked back on it now, she could scarce blame Mary at all.

And yet . . . how alone Mary must have felt . . .

Sarah certainly had.

Sarah lay upon the bed and rolled onto her belly, reaching over to set the little portrait on the nightstand beside the bed. She doubted anyone would notice she'd displaced it. And then she rose from the bed to look into Mary's wardrobes. Opening the doors, she discovered an extravagant selection of dresses, most of them designed with the long, slim lines that were popular in the early eighties. That was most definitely something she and Mary had not shared in common. Mary had always been the model of the latest fashion. Sarah had never cared a whit for the opinions of others. Perhaps that was a failing of hers as well. She thought it was, and yet she couldn't feel the least concern over it. She did, however, quite appreciate the style of these dresses and wished the bustle had never come back. She sighed. One could scarce find these styles any longer.

She closed the wardrobe doors and continued searching the room.

Where might Mary have hidden her last journal?

Did it even exist?

Had she become so depressed that she'd stopped writing at all?

God, Sarah hoped not, for in those journals Sarah hoped to find answers to her deepest questions.

A stack of books sat on a small table beside a blue silk tapestry chair. Mary had been an avid reader, and it didn't surprise Sarah in the least to find a place set aside for it within her own private sanctuary. She lifted the book on top of the stack: *The Return of the Native*, by Thomas Hardy. Beneath it was *Creole Days*, by George Washington Cable.

Setting the books down, she studied the room.

The bed, while it was big enough to sleep two, was entirely too small, it seemed, for Peter Holland's frame.

Had he ever spent a night here? She couldn't help but wonder, and the images that came to mind set her cheeks on fire.

She thrust them away, refusing to acknowledge them.

The paper on the wall was done in an ice blue with lavender sprays and cream-colored ribbons, and the heavy draperies in a deeper blue that hid the sun from view. She wondered how late it was. Through the crack in the curtain, fading sunlight crept into the room. Dust particles danced in its wake. As in the nursery, the carpet was a striking blue, covering brilliantly polished wood floors. Mary had loved the color blue, and her preferences were reflected throughout this room, as well as the nursery, and the house itself, though this room bore a decidedly feminine touch. Sarah surmised it must be part of an adjoining suite of rooms. The lack of men's clothing in the wardrobe suggested that fact as well. And there were indeed two sets of doors: one through which Mel had departed . . . and another that remained closed . . .

She stared at it, wondering if it led to Peter's room. She swallowed at the mere thought and ventured to the door.

Certainly she had no intention of opening it just now, though at some point she knew she would. That, however, she would leave for a time when everyone was out and she was left alone to explore. Pressing her ear to the door, she listened for sounds of movement. She could barely hear someone moving behind it in the distance, and she leaned a little closer to better hear.

The door wasn't completely shut. The latch had

not completely caught and when she leaned on it, it shifted, opening slightly.

Leaping away from the door, Sarah stared at it a moment in startle, and then realizing that if someone was inside, she would only have an instant to prepare herself, she turned and ran toward the bed. Her heart racing, she hurriedly crawled beneath the covers. And then seeing her spectacles, she reached out to snatch them from the bedside and put them on just as the door opened.

Sarah didn't look at the door. In fact, she closed her eyes and lifted her head to the sound. Her heart beat madly against her ribs, and she willed her breath to still. "Is someone there?"

"Me . . . Peter," he said, and Sarah's heart lurched a little as she heard his footsteps come nearer to the bed.

Cunning little vixen.

Peter hadn't intended to disturb her so soon. She'd been up practically all of the night, and her condition when he'd left her this morning was questionable. And yet, other than inhaling a lung full of smoke, she had seemed unharmed, and he hadn't seen the need to call a physician. Apparently neither had her *assistant*.

"I trust you slept well enough?" he asked her.

"Oh . . . yes, thank you." She pulled the blankets up just a bit.

Peter was feeling a bit ruthless perhaps, but he thought it long past his turn to enter the game. He sat upon the bed, taking immense pleasure in her little gasp of surprise. "Do you always wear your spectacles to bed?" he asked her.

Her brows lifted above the rim of her dark lenses. "Well! No, of course not," she said, and then rushed to explain, "But I am not in my own home, of course, and I know it makes some people uncomfortable—Mellie woke me some time ago. She brought them to me."

It was a perfectly reasonable explanation—the beautiful little liar.

She was quite a resourceful actress. Her eyes were closed, he thought, though he couldn't be certain. Her spectacles were so dark that it was difficult to see through them. "Not everything was lost in the fire," he told her, "but we'll not be able to go inside until they clean up the debris and make certain the structure is not damaged. Tomorrow perhaps, but for now they are still working on it."

"I see," she replied.

"The wardrobe is in one piece, though I cannot vouch for its contents. In the meantime, you are quite welcome to use whatever you find in this room. They were my wife's," he said matter-of-factly. "If I am not mistaken, the two of you are quite similar in build."

Her head lowered just a bit. "How generous, but I'm not certain I would feel very comfortable doing such a thing. They were your wife's after all."

"I can assure you, Sarah, she'll not mind."

She stiffened at his morbid attempt at humor. "Thank you, but it will hardly be necessary. My assistant brought me some of my own clothes."

He must be certain to be more aware of their comings and goings in the future. Somehow he'd missed a perfect opportunity to follow Mel. "How prudent of her," he said.

"She is quite foresight—"

He knew the very instant she opened her eyes, and he smiled softly at her reaction. She gasped at the sight of him.

"—ful . . ."

Sarah choked on her words.

Good God! It was all she could do not to shriek and glance away. He was dressed only in his trousers, no shirt at all, and she thought she would die with mortification. And yet what the blazes could she say to him? Not a blasted thing! Because she wasn't supposed to know he was seated before her— good Lord! on her bed! half naked! She couldn't even look away lest he wonder.

Her face heated to such a degree that she knew he must see her blush, but he didn't say a word, he merely sat there conversing with her much too pleasantly. Sarah didn't understand a word he was saying. His voice was a drone in her ears, overwhelmed as it was by the thundering of her heart.

She swallowed the knot in her throat and tried to focus on his words.

"I sincerely hope last night's fire will not frighten you away," he was saying to her. "I am committed to my son's education, Miss Hopkins, and am quite impressed with both your knowledge of the code and the way you have dealt with my son."

The words were recognizable, though they didn't seem to register. "What?" she asked.

His lips curved into a wicked little smile. "Will you stay?"

If Sarah didn't know better, she would think he was taunting her. She blinked behind her spectacles. "Where?"

"Here," he answered too patiently, and his eyes glittered with what Sarah thought was amusement at her expense. And yet it couldn't possibly be. "Will you stay and teach my son?"

"Of . . . course . . ."

"He's growing quite fond of you, I'm afraid."

"I . . . I should love to," Sarah maintained, trying not to gape at his lack of dress, "stay . . . and . . . and teach him."

"If you do not mind the move . . . this room is completely at your disposal," he told her. "It was my wife's, as I said."

"Oh," was all Sarah could think to say. "Well, no . . . I-I don't suppose . . ." She turned her head slightly. "But . . . does your room . . . a . . . a . . ."

"Adjoin it?" He was staring at her quite intently now, Sarah thought, and it was beginning to unnerve her. "Why, yes, it does," he said. Sarah didn't miss the strange note to his voice. Some odd sense of satisfaction? Was he toying with her? "I shall give you my word, however, to respect your privacy."

Suddenly she felt uncertain. That, she thought a little wryly, might just as well be attributed to the fact that she was alone in a room—in a bed at that—

with a half-naked man who was rumored to be her cousin's murderer!

Then of course, there was the simple fact that no matter how worldly she considered herself, and she was certainly no country cousin, she had never before seen a man unclothed, but she knew . . . she knew what happened between men and women . . . when they were attracted so.

And this man was most assuredly not just any man.

Mel was right, she suddenly knew for certain: She was not blind to the hunger in his gaze.

Sarah's heart beat wildly against her ribs.

She was conscious of each and every breath she took and of every gesture he made. God help her, he might be a murderer, but he was the most beautiful man she had ever laid eyes upon in her life. His chest was broad and smooth but for a sprinkle of hair about his pectorals and a thin line leading downward into his . . . trousers.

The images that tumbled through her brain heated her face and body until she was as warm as the blaze she had so narrowly escaped.

Her gaze lifted to his face . . . to his lips . . . and she couldn't help herself . . . she tried hard not to imagine what it might be like to kiss them. She had never kissed a man before, and hardly wondered about it, but this instant she found herself trying to imagine what it would feel like for him to press his lips against hers . . .

Peter could scarce keep a straight face as he sat before her, though somehow he managed.

He watched the flush creep from the collar of her nightgown to her cheeks and resisted the urge to reach out and touch his fingers to the heated skin.

His amusement faded abruptly when her expression changed from surprise and chagrin to something like desire, and his body responded with a vengeance.

Christ, she was lovely.

She was still wearing her soiled nightgown, and he wanted nothing more than to relieve her of it. Curiosity mingled with desire and drove him mad.

Were those breasts as supple as they appeared?

Her skin as soft?

Her cheeks as warm?

Her mouth as sweet?

He might not know who the hell she was, but his body didn't seem to give a damn. His blood heated merely at the sight of her. He felt his own flush begin to creep from his loins, up his belly, to his throat and face, and didn't bother to conceal his arousal. It was manifest now within his trousers . . . if she only dared to look.

He willed her to . . . for that wicked part of him that didn't seem to need a reason to want her, simply did.

His heart began a savage beat against his ribs as his body quickened.

Who was this lovely woman in his house?

And what did she want?

And Christ, did he want her!

There was no denying it. The evidence was pulsing hard between his legs.

He peered down at the outline of her limbs stretched long beneath the covers and reached down impulsively, laying a hand atop her. She stiffened at his touch.

"Sarah," he began, and halted abruptly, uncertain what to say.

If he didn't leave right now, this instant, he was going to frighten her away . . . that much was certain.

And then he would never discover the truth.

He willed himself to rise from the bed but somehow found himself seated still, unable to leave her, though he was well aware of the impropriety of his visit.

Then again, she had lost all rights, as he saw it, to worry about her honor, when she had come into his house like a thief in disguise.

Peter had once been an honorable enough man, but honor had gotten him nowhere: If you told your wife you cared for her deeply but didn't love her, she ended up a stranger in your house and suspected you of adultery. If you refused to open your personal life to the scrutiny of the press, they labeled you a sneak and a murderer, and somehow managed to plaster the most intimate details of your life upon the front pages of their yellow papers. You couldn't win.

No, *Sarah* had lost all claims to honor, and he didn't intend to play fair.

And yet he didn't want her scampering off with her tail between her legs either . . . not just yet, at any rate. He didn't even plan to tell Ruth what he'd discovered—not anyone, not until he knew what he was dealing with.

"I suppose I should leave you to rest," he said, though reluctantly. "You needn't worry about lessons tonight. It's much too late. You've suffered quite an ordeal."

"Yes, thank you," she replied, and her hand unconsciously fanned her throat. Peter wondered if she realized how telling the gesture was. He wondered, too, if she understood how hungry it made him . . . for the taste of her flesh upon his tongue.

He licked his lips gone dry and willed himself to stand. "I've taken the liberty of having a bath run for you," he told her, and watched, with satisfaction, as she forced a swallow. "Shall I call Miss Frank to help you or . . . can you manage on your own?" The very notion of having her naked within his bath hardened him fully.

"Please call Miss Frank," she answered, her voice more than a little trembly.

Not that he expected it to, but her gaze did not follow him as he rose from the bed. She was too smart for that.

"Sleep well, Sarah," he said, and left her before he could be tempted to stay.

Chapter 14

"**I** swear to you, Mellie, I think he must know!"

"Poppycock!" Mel replied. "If he did, I can assure you you'd not still be here in his home."

"I'm telling you, I think he does."

"Did he say anything to make you think so?"

Sarah winced as Mel began to scrub her back. Even as gently as she washed her, it stung. When she'd spilled the curtains from the window, flames had sprayed upon her, burning her. "Ouch! No, he said nothing," Sarah replied, "but I sensed it nevertheless. He was looking at me very strangely, as though he knew."

"Well . . ." Mel dipped the washcloth into the bathwater and then squeezed the warm water over Sarah's wounded back, rinsing off the suds. "That, of course, would have nothing to do with the fact that you were sitting half undressed before him," she suggested, her tone wry. "Maybe you should have a doctor look at this, Sarah."

"No doctor!" Sarah exclaimed. "That's all I need. For some physician to come in, examine me, and proclaim me quite healthy and capable of seeing!"

"You do have a point."

"And me? What about me? I am not the only one who sat there half clad. He was practically nude! Good Lord, Mellie, you should have seen him!"

Mel giggled. "I rather wish I had."

"Gawd! You are wicked!" Sarah exclaimed. "It was unbearable."

"Wicked?" Mel replied. "No, wicked is what I would call the person who started that fire last night. And *you* cannot tell me that not a single untoward thought crossed your mind, murderer or not, Sarah Woodard."

"It was all I could do not to die of mortification," Sarah swore, raising a hand. "Ouch!" she said again, as Mel washed a particularly sensitive spot.

Mel poked her head about to peer into Sarah's face.

"I swear it!" Sarah exclaimed. "I was absolutely horrified."

"If you say so," Mel relented. "You know . . . he certainly does have somewhat of a ruthless look about him, but I am having a devil of a time imagining him a murderer, I must tell you."

Sarah knit her brows. "How can you make such a supposition after so short a time, Mellie? The measure of a man's depravity is not written upon his face; even beautiful men are corrupt."

"So you think him beautiful?"

"I will not answer that. It has no bearing here."

"I beg to differ," Mel said at once. "And a man's soul is most certainly reflected within his eyes, Sarah. I have seen that man with his son . . ."

"Well, he can certainly love his son, yet still be a murderer," Sarah persisted.

"Perhaps," Mel agreed, "but I don't believe for one minute that he set that fire last night. Someone else did. The question is *who*."

"I'm not entirely convinced he didn't either," Sarah countered stubbornly.

"Of course not," Mel suggested. "Because he's a man, and you're quite determined to think the worst of him—and not just any man. He's the man who took Mary from you."

Sarah froze in startle at Mel's declaration and then reminded her, "You read the diary entries that were posted in the tabloids, Mellie. I sent them all to you. How can you forget them so easily? You certainly have a point about the fire, and his lack of motive there, and yet I cannot so easily forget what he has done."

"What has he done?"

Sarah's temper rose. "How can you ask that? He made Mary miserable and quite possibly killed her!"

"But what do you know for *certain* that man has done? Should a man not be held 'innocent until proven guilty'?"

"Not when we are searching for my cousin's murderer!"

"Well, but you'll certainly not find your *murderer* until you open your mind to the possibility that perhaps someone else is responsible,'' Mel reasoned. ''And then there is always the possibility that Mary's murder was simply the misfortune of a robbery gone bad. Just because the press was so quick to condemn Peter Holland does not make him guilty, Sarah.''

''Shhh!'' Sarah demanded, frustrated by Mel's logic. ''What if they hear us!''

Mel lowered her voice to an angry whisper. ''What if he is telling the truth? What if he is innocent, Sarah? Have you considered why it is you seem to *need* to blame him?''

''I don't *need* to blame him,'' Sarah denied vehemently.

''Don't you?'' Mel asked, and then changed the subject abruptly. ''Tell me . . . does he look as delicious unclothed as he does dressed?''

Sarah's face heated at the bold question.

He did, but good Lord, she wasn't about to confess such a thing!

It bedeviled her enough that she had been so flustered by him. ''How can you ask me that?'' It provoked her that Mellie was defending him, and even more so that she was making sense.

''How can I not?'' Mel replied evenly. ''It is not I who swore off men, remember. I am hardly alone by choice, you realize.''

''So you say . . . and yet I know it is not because you've had none courting you in the years since Andrew's death. What about that professor you were telling me about?''

''Which?'' Mel asked, much too conveniently forgetting his name.

"The one at the Institute. John . . . John . . ."

"Oh," she said, as though she hadn't given it another thought, "him . . ."

"What was his name?" Sarah persisted, trying not to smile.

"Cock. John Cock," Mel relented. "Good God, can you imagine bearing a name like that? Mrs. Cock? I hardly think so."

Sarah couldn't restrain her laughter. "I rather see your point."

"Lord, I can see it now . . . if they should happen to announce us at some gala . . . the Professor and Mrs. John Cock!"

The two of them giggled over the thought.

"I think I would die!" Mel declared. Then she confessed, "Actually, I have been thinking quite a lot about him. And I have thought that perhaps . . . well . . . I am not getting any younger, Sarah."

"What are you saying?"

"Only that I don't think I wish to spend all of my years alone. John is actually a very good man. I could do worse than to be Mrs. Cock."

They laughed together once more at the prospect.

Sarah grew quiet, listening, uncertain what to say. She had taken a stance once before against marriage, and it hadn't ended very well. The last thing she wished was to be a part of someone else's unhappiness.

Mel sensed her disapproval nonetheless. "You might have resigned yourself to a life without love, Sarah Woodard. And perhaps you don't need anyone at all, but I do. It isn't any fun to go to bed alone every night, when you know how gentle a man's touch can be.''

"Ack!" Sarah exclaimed. "Not you too!"

Mel shoved her down into the water unexpectedly, wetting her hair. Sarah came up sputtering.

"Why not me?" Mel demanded to know, sounding quite offended.

"Because you are sooo . . . well, it surprises me enough that you, as bloody independent as you are, with a successful career, despite that you have not had the financial backing that I have been privileged to have, would feel you *needed* a man. And furthermore, I just cannot imagine you relenting to such—such—"

"Desires?" Mel began to soap Sarah's hair with a vengeance. "Good Lord, Sarah! Are you made of stone? Have you never stared at a man's lips and imagined how they might feel upon your own?"

Sarah gasped, her cheeks heating with mortification.

"Have you never wished for him simply to take your hand? Have you never looked into his eyes and spied his hunger and felt your body respond to it?"

Sarah's hands went to her ears. Blast, had there been a spy in her room? She couldn't bear the thought of Mel knowing her guilty fantasies. "No!" she lied. "I have never allowed it!"

"Hold your breath," Mel commanded her, and when Sarah did, she dunked her under the water once more. "Then you are, indeed, made of stone," she said as Sarah came sputtering up out of the water. She came about to the front of the bath then and wrapped the soap within the washcloth, then dropped them both into the water. "There," she said, "that's as far as I go."

Sarah peered up at her, her brows knitting.

"But let me say only this to you, Sarah. Forgive me for speaking freely, but I think we know each other well enough by now that I shall take this liberty, no matter that you may be angry with me after."

"I shall not be angry with you," Sarah swore.

"Yes, well, we shall see."

"And anyway," Sarah interjected, "when have you ever *not* spoken your mind?"

Mel's hands went to her hips. "You were young, Sarah. So you made a mistake. You stood your ground against your cousin's decision to marry, and so you feel guilty about it. Well, get over it, confound it all! You cannot punish yourself for the rest of your life by clinging to some prideful stance you took in your youth. It is not a weakness to yearn for a mate. It is not a crime to love a man. Mary is dead and that is not your fault. She would scarce blame you if you changed your bloody mind now!"

Mel didn't seem to understand. It was not just *any* man she was drawn to, but Mary's husband, the very man who might be responsible for Mary's death, and the notion was unthinkable!

"*Let yourself feel, for God's sake, Sarah!* And stop! Stop being such an angry young woman—stop before you end up an angry old woman as well!"

Sarah stared at her friend with growing horror over her words.

"And," Mel declared, "stop judging others so harshly for not abiding by your own infernal rules!"

Sarah simply stared at Mel, unable to speak in her own defense. "Is that all?" she asked, torn between anger, sadness, and fear.

"Quite!" Mel assured. "I shall be back when you are through," she announced, and turned and stalked out of the bathroom, slamming the door in her wake, leaving Sarah without a towel, or clothes, or even a self-defense against the ugly truths Mel had flung at her so ruthlessly.

Chapter 15

Was that really what she was doing?

Punishing herself for taking a stance against Mary's marriage?

Did she truly need to blame Peter?

As much as Mel's accusations galled Sarah, she hadn't been able to stop thinking of them since Mel had left her. Mel had been her dearest friend for as long as Sarah had known her. She was only the third person, after her uncle and Mary, in Sarah's entire life whom Sarah had ever opened up to. Sarah doubted Mel would say such things if she didn't truly believe them.

Mel hadn't returned as she'd said she would, and Sarah supposed she was still perturbed over their discussion. Left to fend for herself, Sarah had found her way out of that monstrous tub that belonged to Peter Holland, and had rushed through his room and into her own, cursing Mel beneath her breath the entire way. Her cheeks burned now when she thought of herself tiptoeing through Peter's private bedroom—naked as the day she was born!

It wasn't until she'd shut the door behind her that she'd breathed a sight of relief.

In the back of her mind she wondered if Mel had left her there to prune in that bath so that Peter might discover her there. God only knew, after their *discussion,* Sarah wouldn't put it past Mel, because Mellie did indeed have a wicked streak as long as the bloody Nile—no matter that she denied it.

Even after Sarah was safely ensconced in her room, her heart continued to hammer. Peter had certainly barged in upon her once; she didn't think he would hesitate to do so again. She didn't bother to dress, however, as it was late already. Instead she drew on a fresh nightgown and crawled into the bed, despite the fact that the last thing she was, was sleepy.

She lay in her cousin's bed, and thought of her cousin's husband.

How wicked was that?

God forgive her, but for the first time in her life she allowed her thoughts to drift in that forbidden direction . . .

The memory of that look upon his face as he'd gazed at her made her heart beat just a little faster. A vision of him sitting here before her accosted her once more, and her breath quickened at the thought of his beautiful bare male flesh.

She hadn't been able to keep herself from peeking . . .

What *would* it be like to kiss him?

Did she dare even dream of it?

Something fluttered within her belly at the merest thought of him touching her, and her hand swept down, brushing herself gently over her gown. Her breath caught and she grew dizzy over the sensations that swept through her.

Was she truly such a prude?

Was she so afraid of letting down her guard that she could not even allow herself a private moment of appreciation for a man's beauty?

Her heart beat a little faster.

Why had Mel's observations angered her so?

And why couldn't she admit without so much guilt that she did indeed find Peter Holland appealing?

He *was* a beautiful man . . .

Her breath quickened at the mere image of him, and her body responded with a flush of heat that flooded through her, leaving her breathless in its wake. There was a slight dampness between her legs. Wide-eyed, Sarah reached down in shock to clasp a hand over it, denying it even as she felt the moistness seep through her gown.

Dear God . . .

She took a shuddering breath and swallowed a bit nervously as she arched upon the bed, stretching her legs, bracing herself against the sensations that threatened to overwhelm her.

Outside, the sun had completely faded to dusk. The curtains were almost completely drawn but for a sliver, and the room was darkening moment by moment . . .

With every breath she took, the next came more rapidly.

She turned to look at her cousin's portrait at her bedside and stared ... not thinking, only staring, only *feeling* ...

Her heart hammering fiercely now, she reached out and turned the picture down against the night-stand and stared at the ceiling.

What, dear God, was she thinking?

What was she doing?

Closing her eyes, she dared to picture his face once more ... that look in his eyes as he had so wickedly gazed at her breasts beneath her gown. If she imagined it, if she only dared ... she could swear she felt the weight of his hand upon her breast, pressing her down into the bed.

Daring to slide her hand down to the hem of her gown, she clutched it as though she would strangle temptation.

Let yourself feel, for God's sake, Sarah!

She heard Mel's words as though it were a challenge.

His face materialized before her once more ... so real she imagined reaching out and touching his cheek ... his jaw ... the feel of his skin beneath her touch ...

Dare she?

Warmth enveloped her at the very thought, and her skin prickled with gooseflesh as she lifted up her gown to her belly.

Oh, God ... dare she?

She swept her hand down to brush her dark curls,

and the sensation left her wanting. Something deep within her ached to be touched. Something she could not deny. Something she didn't *want* to deny.

Strange as it seemed, she could *smell* him in this room, though he'd been here only a short time.

Stranger yet was the notion that she should know his scent, but she did. She could swear that she did . . .

Squeezing her eyes shut, Sarah slid her hands back down . . . and dared to feel.

The last thing Sarah expected to see upon entering the nursery was Peter Holland seated on the floor with his son.

Despite that he hadn't spied her as yet, her face heated at the sight of him.

Don't think of it, she told herself.

She shook her head, watching them from the doorway.

This room had suffered minimal damage but for the right wall, which separated the nursery from the adjoining room. It was partially destroyed, and the unicorn's face was no longer entirely visible. One eye peered through the soot-damaged wall, and the shelves that had once held the toy soldiers and blocks so neatly had collapsed on one side, spilling little wooden men into a common grave upon the carpet. The smell of smoke permeated the room. Other than that, the structure seemed sound enough, and the room relatively unscathed.

Father and son sat on the carpeted floor, surrounded by little piles of damaged and dirty toys, while the sounds of reconstruction echoed from the other room. Peter's jacket was off. It lay on one of the small chairs that had been dragged away from the little table. His shirt was untucked and half unbuttoned as well.

Sarah tried not to notice.

They still hadn't acknowledged her as yet, so she watched them unheeded, taking these few moments to study them without the encumbrance of their scrutiny.

As she watched, Peter lifted up a little toy soldier and with the tail of his shirt began to buff it clean. It was only then that she realized how filthy his shirt was already, and the pile of cleaner toys that sat between him and Christopher.

Something like shock pummeled through her.

He was repairing his son's toys.

Those were not the actions of a man who had no heart.

Not at all.

She blinked, mesmerized by the sight of them.

It was becoming apparent to Sarah that he did indeed love his son. She didn't know many fathers who would take a day from their work to sit and polish little toy soldiers with such painstaking care. The two of them spoke in low tones, and Christopher giggled easily at something his father said.

Peter smiled, and Sarah's heart tripped a bit at the sight of it.

He had a brilliant smile, one that was filled with as much wicked masculinity as it was with little-boy charm.

She watched as he pressed a newly polished toy soldier into his son's hand, and tried to remain as inconspicuous as possible as she strained to listen to their discourse . . .

"This one is blue, Daddy?" Christopher asked of the toy soldier in his hand.

"It *was* blue," Peter corrected him. "Now it is more black. We'll have to paint him a new face, I think."

"All right," Christopher replied. And then asked, "Daddy?"

"Yes, son?"

"What is blue, Daddy?"

The question took Peter slightly by surprise.

He had to think about his reply an instant, because he didn't think he'd ever quite considered blue a *what*.

"Blue is . . ." He closed his eyes and thought hard about blue.

To answer simply that it was the color of the sky and sea seemed inappropriate. He wanted to express it so his son could comprehend. Christopher's world was one of scents and sounds and tastes and touch. "Blue is . . . tranquillity," he replied, opening his eyes and peering down at his son, and was satisfied with that definition. "Like the feeling you get," he elaborated, "when you are lying in a meadow in the sun on a warm day . . . and the sun is striking you upon the face . . . and the birds are chirping in the treetops."

Christopher seemed to accept that answer. He nodded. "What about black?" his son asked, still examining the toy soldier with his pudgy little fingers.

"Hmmm," Peter said. "Let's see . . . black is a tricky one, I think, because black can be empty . . . like a clean slate . . ."

Christopher's face screwed with confusion. "Clean slate?"

"No, arggh . . . that's not a good way to say it . . . Black is like . . ." He tried to think of something that had very definite boundaries . . . something his son had experienced . . . something that wasn't scary. "It's like the feeling you have when you are sitting in a big empty bathtub and the water is not yet running . . . understand?"

"Think so," Christopher answered, but his little face didn't express any measure of certainty.

"And then black can be frightening, too, at times, I think. Like—"

"Oh, yeah," Christopher interjected, though he was somewhat preoccupied with the toy soldier in his hand. "Sometimes I feel black," he said, and continued to inspect the toy soldier.

Peter looked down at his son, frowning. "You do?" he asked. "Explain, son."

"Well . . ." Christopher paused at his task a moment. "I think maybe it is the feeling like when I am standing someplace I don't know—like when Aunt Ruth takes me to the park—and I don't know where she is and I'm afraid to move." He went back to his toy soldier. "I think that might be black." He thought about his interpretation and then wrinkled his nose. "Is that black, Daddy?"

Peter considered his son's description an instant, thinking it was much better than his own, and then he scowled as he peered down at Christopher. "Yes, like that, I think."

Christopher sat silently beside him, and Peter suddenly had a strange feeling about his son's revelation. "Christopher," he asked, "do you always feel black at the park?"

"No, sir, I don't," Christopher answered, and shook his head. "Only when Aunt Ruth takes me, I do."

"Only when Aunt Ruth takes you?"

"Yes, sir."

"Why do you think that's so?"

Christopher shrugged. "Dunno, Daddy."

He couldn't shake the feeling that came over him suddenly. Christopher had never given him the first clue that he had ever been uncomfortable in Ruth's presence, but suddenly he found himself concerned. "Does she leave you alone, Christopher?"

"I dunno, Daddy . . . Sometimes she's quiet and tells me to stay and I get afraid she will go away."

Did Ruth walk away and leave him at times? Or did she simply lapse into silence? In either case, it obviously bothered Christopher, and he would have to take measures to remedy that.

"Well, I think I'll have a talk with Aunt Ruth and see how we can make it so you don't feel black when she takes you to the park anymore. I'm certain she doesn't realize."

Did she?

Christopher nodded, his attention returned to his toy soldier. "Daddy?" he said again.

"Yes, son?"

"What color am I?"

Peter had plucked up another toy soldier and had begun to clean it with the tail of his shirt, but he paused at the question. "What color are you?" he repeated, and tried not to laugh.

"Yes, sir," Christopher replied.

"Well, yellow," Peter said without hesitation.

Christopher's brows lifted. "Yellow?"

"Yep," Peter replied, a smile in his voice. "Bright, like the sunshine," he said.

Christopher's little brows drew together in confusion. "I thought you said that was blue Daddy."

Peter chuckled once more. This wasn't working quite as he'd hoped.

"I did, now, didn't I? But it's not quite the same as blue, son. Yellow is like ... well ... a room fully lit, every nook and cranny brightened by the light."

His little face twisted once more in confusion, and his tone reflected it as well. "I am yellow, Daddy?"

"Yep," Peter maintained.

"But I cannot see the light," he protested, and still the avowal was totally devoid of self-pity. His son was simply stating a fact. A multitude of emotions overwhelmed Peter.

Guilt, for one ...

Had he not been so bloody drunk that night ... drowning his anger and loneliness in a bottle, feeling sorry for himself . . . well . . . maybe his son would not be blind today.

"That," Peter told him, his voice softening, "is because you *are* the light!"

Christopher digested that particular bit of information, and didn't seem quite able to grasp the concept. "Daddy?" he prompted once more. "What color is Miss Hopkins?" he asked. "Is she blue, Daddy? She makes me feel like blue sometimes."

Peter considered his son's revelation. "Does she?" The truth was, she made him feel like blue too, Peter acknowledged, but not the sort of blue he'd described to his son, rather like the blue of an intense flame.

She made him burn.

"Yes, sir."

"Let's see . . . Miss Hopkins is . . ." He had to think about it a long moment, and still no answer seemed apparent. She was peachy cream, when he thought of the color of her skin . . . and deep rose, when he thought about the shade of her lovely lips . . . and cerulean blue, when he thought about her eyes. "I think she's red," he answered, finally.

The color of passion.

If there was one thing he sensed about Sarah, it was that she was passionate. He had heard her passion in her speech to him that first day, heard it in her snappy tone, not to mention he had witnessed the flush of her skin as she'd stared at him while he'd sat half naked upon her bed.

"Red, Daddy?"

Peter changed his mind suddenly as he considered her bloody lies. "No . . . she's black," he said.

"Black? Daddy!" Christopher protested. "I don't think she is black!"

"Black!" Sarah chimed in, and came forward into the room to offer her own protest. "You think I am black?"

Peter lifted a brow at her timely appearance. "Yes. Black . . . like an empty bathtub . . . or a clean slate," he told her, and watched her expression.

"Miss Sarah!" his son exclaimed, and Peter couldn't help but note the genuine enthusiasm in his son's tone.

Nor did he miss her smile as she acknowledged it.

She tapped her cane before her upon the carpeted floor as she entered. Peter watched her with dark amusement.

"I'm not certain I like that. Or even comprehend it!" she said.

"It doesn't matter," he told her. "It is merely my perception."

She stopped before him and he caught a glimpse of her delicate ankles as she lifted her skirt just a little. Christ, but he wanted nothing more than to slide his hand beneath her dress, up those lovely legs . . .

He willed himself not to think of it, though his breath quickened slightly. "How long have you been standing there listening, Sarah?"

She gave him a wry smile, and admitted, "Long

enough to feel quite ashamed for my eavesdropping.''

At least she had the decency not to lie about *that*.

''What color do you think my daddy is, Miss Sarah?''

Chapter 16

S arah blinked at the question.

"Well . . . I-I'm not certain . . ."

"Is he black, too?"

Strangely enough, Sarah thought as she peered at him out of the corner of her eye . . . he wasn't any longer.

Like the toy soldier in Christopher's hand, Peter Holland's layer of soot was beginning to fade. She refused to play, however, refused to say so. "I am certain I don't know your daddy well enough to say," she told him. "Neither does he know me well enough to call me black!" she objected, pretending affront.

He was smiling up at her, Peter was, with that strange smile he had given her earlier, and Sarah's breath caught at the sight of it.

Unbidden, the memory of what she had done the night before came back to taunt her.

Resisting the urge to flee his presence, she shoved

it at once out of her mind, lest she be too mortified to stand in his presence ever again.

"May I join you?" she asked them.

"Certainly," Peter answered, watching her still.

Sarah ignored him as best she could and lifted her skirt a little to sit with them. "So . . . what are we doing?"

"Cleaning my toys," Christopher replied matter-of-factly. "My daddy says he'll have to paint this one's face again." His own face fell then, and his expression saddened a bit. "I wish I could see it." The surface was flat, Sarah realized, the features lost within the polished wood, but Christopher's little hands continued to explore it determinedly.

Her heart wrenched for him.

And yet . . . this was the first time she had ever heard him utter a single lamentation. His father was right. Christopher was *yellow*. The little boy sitting before her had as much to teach them about dealing with life as any adult could. Sarah had earned herself a lifetime of woe by not accepting so much, and here this child had been dealt a terrible hand, and he accepted it without complaint.

"Would you like to know what I look like, Christopher?" she asked him suddenly, feeling a bit bold.

"But I can't see, Miss Sarah . . ."

"Why, of course you can!" Sarah assured him. "And you already know how!"

She reached out, groping for him, still very aware of his father's scrutiny, and then pretending to find him, scooted closer. Peter watched her now without a word, as though he were studying her every action with undivided interest. Sarah reached out her hand to touch Christopher on the shoulder and then slid her fingers down to his tiny hand, lifting it to her face. "Go on," she urged him. "See me with your hands."

Christopher hesitated, confused, and Sarah was certain her touch was as alien to him as the concept of light itself. She had watched father and son together, and the lack of physical intimacy between them was more than apparent. Neither did she think, judging by Christopher's comments about his aunt, that Ruth was overly affectionate either. She couldn't help but wonder why Christopher had implied to his father that he felt abandoned when he was with her. Could it be that she just walked away and left him alone? Feeling lost? Or did she simply not speak with him and thus he felt the lack of her presence? She wasn't the warmest person Sarah had ever met. She might love and protect Christopher fiercely, but she didn't seem to know how to show her affection.

"Go on," she urged him once more, when still he hesitated.

He did as she bade him this time, and Sarah closed her eyes, feeling his sweet little hand move against her cheek, her lips, her forehead . . . seeing her. He accidentally stuck a finger up her nose and she gasped softly and then giggled. He didn't apologize, but neither did he seem to realize what he'd done, and then he drew away suddenly. He was quite obviously not entirely comfortable with the exercise, but she could scarce blame him. He didn't know her so well.

"Now, what did you see?" Sarah asked him.

"A mouth and a nose," he declared matter-of-factly.

"Yes, indeed," Sarah agreed, and laughed softly. "One of each!"

Christopher responded with an infectious little giggle.

"Have you never done that before, Christopher?"

"No, ma'am."

"Well, whyever not?" she asked him. "Now it's your father's turn. Go look at his face, Christopher," she directed him. Christopher got on his hands and knees almost at once. His father gave her a somewhat protesting glance, but Sarah forced herself to ignore it.

She could scarce respond to what she was not supposed to see, after all.

This time Christopher didn't need a second prompting. He fell against his father's face, quite literally, drawing laughter from Peter's lips. He explored his father's face with careful precision, noting everything from his lips to the lobes of his ears. He even went so far as to pull at the hair of his father's brow.

"Ouch!" Peter exclaimed, but Sarah could hear the smile in his voice.

Her heart warmed at the sight of them together. She laughed softly.

"Shame on you, Peter Holland!" she declared suddenly. It was obvious that, indeed, this was the first time Christopher had ever *looked* at his father's face. "Men!" she exclaimed. "I shall never understand the lot of you. Afraid of a little touch!"

"Oh?" Peter replied, holding still for the onslaught of his son's tiny hands. "And you are not?"

"Hardly!" Sarah assured him, feeling quite superior at the instant. "Women are not nearly so afraid of intimacy, you see."

"Then perhaps you should like a turn, as well?" he challenged her.

Sarah's heart tripped at the challenge.

The thought of touching him left her breathless.

"No, I think not." Sarah refused him outright. "I hardly think that would be appropriate, Mr. Holland."

"So we are back to calling me Mr. Holland?" His brows lifted.

"Miss Sarah's nose is smaller than yours," Christopher announced, moving away from his father and returning to his toy soldier. "He has no nose . . ."

Sarah's heart began to pound against her breast.

"Tell me . . . why is it that you seem to need to retain a measure of distance, *Miss Hopkins*? Does it make you so uncomfortable to address me as Peter?"

Sarah swallowed.

Was she so obvious?

She wasn't very good at this pretense, it seemed.

Whatever had made her feel she could manage this scheme?

Did he know?

Something about the look in his eyes gave her a

sense of unease. And then she calmed herself, forcing herself to reason. He was hardly confronting her
about anything at all. He was merely offering her
the opportunity to *see* his face . . . as his son had
done to him . . . as *she* had suggested. And her de-
rogatory comment about men had been challenge
enough in itself. He was not the sort of man, she
reminded herself, to leave a gauntlet lying at his feet.

"What are you afraid of?" he taunted.

Sarah frowned. "I am hardly afraid of anything,"
she assured him, with more certainty than she felt at
the moment.

"Go on, then," he urged her. "I give you my
word I'll not bite."

His eyes held a mischievous twinkle that provoked her ire. The cad! He was enjoying this a little
too much, she thought.

"Very well," she relented, and hated that it
sounded so much like a pout. Peter might not be a
murderer, but he was certainly a rake, and he had
stolen Mary's heart entirely too easily.

She didn't wish to do this.

God help her, the last thing she wanted this moment was to touch him. After last night . . . after
what she had done . . . she could scarce bear the
thought of looking at him, much less touching . . .
those lips . . . that jaw . . .

He was waiting expectantly. He even went so far
as to lean toward her, and his smug and much too
patient expression made her hands itch to slap his
face.

And, well, why shouldn't she?

He would never know if she meant to, she thought as she recalled the way Christopher had fallen upon his face. Reaching out, groping, she gave the air before him a swipe and then one more, catching him squarely in the face.

"Aye!"

"My goodness!" Sarah exclaimed. "I didn't realize you were so near," she added too sweetly.

He was frowning at her now, and she smiled. "I'm beginning to think you are quite a dangerous woman to be around."

"I am soooo sorry!" she exclaimed.

"Are you?" Peter asked her, and was studying her once more. "You don't respect men very much, do you, Sarah?"

The observation surprised her, coming as it did in the wake of Mel's tirade. "Of course I do! Whatever makes you think such a thing?"

She began to *see* his face, giving it as little attention as possible.

"The things you say . . ." He peered up at her, and Sarah closed her eyes. "Unless it is simply me you do not like . . ."

Sarah ignored his speculation. "I respected my uncle enormously," she told him honestly. "But there are, in truth, not so many like him."

She tried not to think of the way his skin felt beneath her fingers . . . the warmth of it . . .

As she knelt above him, the scent of his warm masculine skin pervaded her senses. And dear Lord, but she became quite dizzy suddenly.

"Were the two of you very close?" he asked her.

Much too close!

God, they were too close.

She couldn't think. "What?" she asked him, a little breathlessly, her thoughts in danger of scattering.

"Your uncle. Were you very close?"

"Oh! Yes! Yes, we were! But he passed away . . . some years ago."

"I'm sorry," he said.

Sarah's hands shook. She tried to concentrate.

Unable to bear it any longer, she began to draw away, but before she could leave him, he placed his hand over hers and restrained her fingers upon his cheek, trapping it there.

"Afraid of a little touch?" he asked her, throwing her own words back at her.

Sarah jerked her hand from beneath his.

"It is only a face, Sarah," he taunted her.

"Scratchy face," Christopher interjected, reminding them suddenly of his presence. "Miss Sarah's is softer."

Sarah had completely forgotten Christopher though he didn't seem the least aware of that, as he was still busy playing with his faceless soldier.

Peter's hand reached out, touched her chin then, and Sarah gasped in surprise. His fingers slid to her cheek, cupping it softly. "Much softer," he affirmed, and closed his eyes. Sarah's heartbeat quickened at the look of relish upon his face . . . the gentleness of his touch. She swallowed convulsively as his touch grew firmer and his thumb caressed her face.

Dear God, she couldn't bear it!

Her eyes closed, and she leaned into his embrace.

"Much softer," he whispered, and Sarah let out a breath she'd not realized she'd held. Her hand covered his upon her face.

She forced her eyes open, her heart beating much too fiercely. She needed to be away suddenly, and desperately.

She drew his hand away quickly, as though it burned her.

"Yes, well . . ." She couldn't recall a time she had been more flustered. Her hands were trembling still.

"I think . . . I think I've forgotten something!" she stammered, and reached for her cane. She had enough wits about her to make it appear she was groping for it.

And then she rose and left the nursery as quickly as she was able.

Chapter 17

Sarah sat within her room—Mary's room—in her chair by the window, staring at the portrait of Mary she held in her hand.

She had panicked.

There was no other word for it.

She couldn't explain what had come over her, except that she had lost her wits and nerve and who knew what else.

There was something tangible between them, something that seemed wholly impossible and yet . . . and yet . . . it was there.

She could feel it.

And it wasn't her imagination because she saw it in the glitter of his eyes. It was a hungry glance she wasn't supposed to have spied, and yet she had . . .

Afraid of a little touch . . .

More than she could possibly have imagined.

Cad.

Without mercy, he had thrown her own words back at her.

Even now, with the memory of his touch, her heartbeat had yet to slow.

She studied the portrait she held in her hand. Had Mary felt this for him too? Had she been drawn to Peter in the same way? Had her skin prickled at his slightest glance? And had she dreamt of his lips?

Something fluttered in her belly at the thought of his mouth.

Had Mary dared to live these wicked thoughts?

Sarah could scarce bear that she had condemned her cousin for what she was feeling this moment—and for the very man she'd felt it for! God knew Sarah had come into his home ready to loathe him. With a start, she realized she no longer could. How could she despise a man who cared so very much for his son, who sat on the floor and polished little toy soldiers with him, who bought him taffy in the park and gazed down upon his child with such undisguised affection?

The only thing Sarah could not condone was the fact that he pushed his son so blessed hard. It was as though he drove Christopher out of some sense of . . .

What?

In truth, it was as though he could not accept Christopher's disability. And yet he accepted his son completely . . . It was obvious that Peter embraced his child. So did he push Christopher so hard out of some sense of personal culpability? Did he need his son to overcome his blindness in order to assuage his own guilt feelings?

Sarah wondered . . .

The truth was, however, that Christopher was an overly intelligent child. He did not appear to be overburdened by his father's expectations as Ruth had suggested. In fact, judging by all he'd said to his father, he had grasped everything she had taught him with a minimum of explanation and a maximum of comprehension. Even his speech patterns were hardly those of a six-year-old.

Whatever the case . . . it was growing more and more difficult to believe Peter was Mary's murderer.

She had to consider whether it was because she suddenly didn't *want* him to be . . .

A soft rap on the door startled her from her reveries. She placed Mary's portrait down upon the table. "Who is it?"

"It's Mel, Sarah."

Sarah rose up from the chair and hurried to the door. "Come in!" she exclaimed.

Mel didn't need a second invitation; she threw open the door and entered, shutting it quickly behind her.

"Where the devil have you been?" Sarah demanded of her at once.

"I am so sorry!" Mel replied. "Forgive me, Sarah, for not returning last night. But I think you'll be quite intrigued by what I've discovered."

"You left me all alone in that tub!" Sarah railed.

Mel's eyes twinkled with devilment. "Come, now, Sarah. You hardly need me to hold your hand," she chided. She lifted a brow. "Anyway, he didn't walk in on you, did he?"

"No," Sarah said, hardly appeased by the fact.

"Thank God! But he very well could have."

"Well," Mel reasoned, not the least bit moved by Sarah's complaint, "all is well that ends well, so they say."

Sarah gave her longtime friend a beleaguered glance. "Spare me," she pleaded with her. "So *what* did you discover?"

Mel took her by the hand and dragged her back to the chair. She seized her by the shoulders and sat her down upon the chair, looking rather pleased with herself. "You remember I told you about Peter's alibi?"

"Caitlin?"

"Yes! I spoke to her!"

Sarah's brows lifted. "You did?"

"She was with him!"

"Well, of course," Sarah replied, not quite following. Something suddenly twisted in the pit of her stomach at the thought. "How else could she be his alibi?" she reasoned.

"No," Mel returned, giving her a meaningful nod. "She was *with* him."

Sarah's gaze fell. Her heart sank. "I see." So he wasn't a murderer, but he *was* an adulterer. One was definitely worse than the other, but Sarah didn't particularly feel relieved. "So he keeps his lover in the house?" she surmised. "Mary was right, after all. He *was* betraying her."

"No," Mel said. "Not according to Caitlin. It seems he was quite inebriated that night, and did nothing more than pass out upon the floor—though that apparently was not his intention. Caitlin stayed to watch over him, because she was afraid he was in much too bad a state . . . if you know what I mean?'' She lifted a brow, then turned and went to the bed, sitting on the edge of it, facing Sarah. ''At least she stayed until she was certain he was all right, and then she went to bed—alone—in the servants' quarters. However . . . he *does* have a lover, and Caitlin seems to think her quite manipulative . . .''

Naturally Sarah was curious, though she tried to seem as unconcerned as she was able, considering the turn of the day's events. ''Who is she?''

''Her name is Cecile Morgan.''

Sarah's brows lifted. ''The woman who was here the night of the fire?''

Mel nodded meaningfully. ''Precisely.''

Sarah considered that, and said, ''I had the distinct impression she was a business partner of sorts.''

''It seems she's that, as well.''

Sarah frowned, still unable to connect the facts. ''But it has been six years since Mary's death,'' she reminded Mel. ''What has Cecile to do with anything at all?''

''That is the most intriguing part . . .''

Sarah wasn't certain she could agree.

''According to Caitlin, Peter's sister, Ruth, introduced the two of them seven-odd years ago. At the time Cile was married to J. W. Morgan, quite a wealthy older fellow. He was fifty-two to Cile's twenty-five—caused a bit of a scandal, the two of them did. At any rate, she and Peter met, and months later Cile's husband was found dead in his bedroom.''

"Do I truly wish to hear his cause of death, Mellie? Don't tell me she sent him to the grave with a smile upon his face," she remarked caustically, "because I think I will be sick if you do!"

"Hush, now, Sarah," Mel exclaimed, "and allow me to finish!"

Sarah glowered at her.

Mel ignored her. "Also . . . according to Caitlin, J. W.'s aged mother claimed to everyone who would listen that Cile had poisoned her son, but no one would ever believe her and Cile sent the old woman away to some hospital."

Sarah's interest was piqued. "Quite an interesting tale," she admitted.

"Isn't it, though?" Mel agreed, and lifted a brow suggestively. "Particularly when you consider the fact that merely three months later, Mary ends up murdered . . . here . . ."

"Are you trying to tell me that you suspect Peter once again?"

"If it is true that they are lovers . . . I'm afraid to say it, but yes. It is an age-old tale, I'm afraid; money and love and greed."

Sarah sighed. "So now he is both a murderer and an adulterer," Sarah said bitterly, and lifted up the portrait of her cousin once more. She stared at it, trying to imagine what Mary must have felt . . . all alone here in this house . . .

Mel watched her. "Sarah?" she began.

Sarah placed the portrait facedown within her lap. "Yes?"

"Be careful, dear. I am quite afraid that I might

have led you wrong where Peter Holland is concerned.''

''I am quite certain that I don't know what you are speaking of,'' Sarah said, refusing even to acknowledge her own feelings.

''I think you do,'' Mel returned, giving her a pointed glance. ''I saw him and his son together and perhaps gave him more favor than he deserved . . .''

Sarah sighed and confessed, ''Perhaps we both did.'' She absently toyed with the frayed back of the portrait, pulling it slightly.

Mel gave her a sympathetic glance. ''That is not to say he is guilty, Sarah. This is only to say that perhaps, just perhaps, he might be guilty after all. Somehow, the parts do not equal the sum. I cannot see that he would hire you in all good faith, and then try to kill you such as that.''

Sarah nodded, contemplating the truth of that observation.

''Perhaps someone doesn't want you here,'' Mel continued, ''but I cannot think it is he. Promise me,'' she demanded. ''Promise me you will remain on your guard.''

''I must,'' Sarah agreed, and vowed to redouble her efforts.

It certainly wouldn't do them any good at all for her to lose her heart to a murderer—not that she was losing her heart, mind you! But she was certainly a fool to have given him the benefit of the doubt.

She wouldn't do so again.

In her frustration, she tore at the frayed edge, pulling it away from the frame. ''Blast!'' she exclaimed.

"I broke it!" But curiosity led her to peer inside. She pulled the backing off a little further to find that the picture displayed was folded within. Her heart beat a little faster as she ripped the backing and pried out the picture, trying not to tear it. Her hands were trembling as she unfolded it.

"What is it?" Mel asked her.

Sarah swallowed the lump that appeared in her throat as she stretched out the portrait and turned it to face her. She tried not to weep as she stared at the full portrait of herself and Mary together. It had been folded so that only Mary was visible, but Sarah had been tucked neatly beneath.

Mary had not cut her so completely out of her life.

The knowledge flooded her heart with joy. She flipped the portrait over, only to find something scribbled upon the back in Mary's neat penmanship.

Out of sight . . . not out of mind. I love and miss you, dearest Sarah.

Chapter 18

〜◦✑◦〜

"**A**nd you never saw her before she answered your ad for employment?"

Peter considered the detective's question. He couldn't help but feel he knew her somehow, but it was less her face he recognized, and more her manner. "Never," he replied with certainty.

But it was about damned time he discovered who his houseguest was.

He had hesitated to hire a detective until he'd learned of Miss Frank's inquiries last eve. Caitlin had come to him quite concerned over what had begun as a casual conversation. It had, shortly thereafter, turned into an interrogation of sorts, and she'd been heartily afraid that she'd spoken out of turn.

He'd called an agency at once—though *not* the same he'd hired after Mary's death. Still, he wasn't certain how he felt about doing this once again. The last time he'd hired an agency, they hadn't discovered a bloody thing pertinent to Mary's murder. In the detective's estimation, Mary had simply been the hapless victim of a robbery gone bad, and yet the man had turned around and sold her journals to the tabloids—all but one, because Peter had never been able to find the key to open it, and by the time he'd decided to destroy the little lock, the detective had already leaked her journals to the yellow press. Peter had locked away the last of her journals afterward, without ever having read them. He hadn't been brave enough to hear Mary's final words.

"You say she was asking questions?" the detective asked Caitlin.

"Yes, sir," she replied.

"What sort of questions?"

"Well . . ." Caitlin seemed afraid to meet his gaze while she spoke, and Peter thought she was feeling guilty for disclosing so much. "No' much tae begin with," she said. "She was just wantin' tae know was it me there that night, and I did tell her that yes, it was." She turned to Peter then, and swore, "But I didna tell her anythin' really, Mr. Holland. I swear tae God, I didna!"

"It's all right, Caitlin. You did nothing wrong," he assured her. "It's not like my affairs aren't already public knowledge."

She knew what he was referring to and her face flushed with color. If it hadn't been for her disclosure of his condition that night so long ago, he might well be behind prison walls this instant.

"I'm sae sorry if I spoke out of turn," she told him, "but I didna think I was tellin' her anythin' she couldna find out from anybody else."

"It's all right, Caitlin," Peter repeated. "I'm glad you came to me."

"Between this and her résumé," the detective interjected, "we've a pretty good start."

"If you look at her résumé . . . she has a reference at the Institute, as well," Peter suggested. "Perhaps Mr. John Cock might shed some light for us."

"Did you ever speak with him?"

Peter's face heated a bit. He hadn't. He hadn't even considered it.

"I'll speak to him first," the detective suggested.

"Thank you Dave," Peter said, rising from his seat to see him off. "I have every faith you will get to the bottom of this."

"I shall certainly try."

Peter came around from his desk and shook his hand.

"Good day, Miss O'Connell," the detective said, and then left with Sarah Hopkins's portfolio in hand.

Peter had little doubt they would have their answers soon. The man was supposed to be good.

If Sarah had left them a trail to follow, then he would sniff it down.

Peter hadn't precisely objected to her taking Christopher to the park, but Sarah had the distinct impression he hadn't truly relished the idea.

He'd been behaving rather strangely the last week and a half, watching her a little too intently, as though he were waiting . . . for what?

She was beginning to be afraid that he'd discovered the truth and was merely watching for her to trip herself up. And yet he hadn't given her the first clue that he had.

She and Christopher, along with Mellie, had spent the afternoon enjoying a concert in the park. The three of them had sat upon blankets, enjoying the unusually warm March weather, and wishing the day would never end—at least, Sarah had wished it.

Christopher had fallen asleep in her lap, his little head resting sweetly upon her breast. And she had adored every moment of the embrace. He was such an insightful little boy, full of energy and ambition, and in every word he spoke of his father, his love and admiration were apparent.

Sarah had found herself viewing Peter through very different eyes—through the eyes of his blind son.

Christopher didn't seem particularly concerned about making his father proud. In fact, he seemed to hold little doubt of his father's esteem.

How could a man who could make a child feel so special be a murderer, too?

Peter Holland was a mystery, to be certain.

With Mel leading the way now, and lamenting the distance they had yet to go, she and Christopher held hands as they left the park and crossed Fifth Avenue. She listened to Christopher's exuberant renditions of the afternoon's concertos and smiled at his natural aptitude for music. Sarah wondered if it had to do with the fact that he seemed to remember entire passages so easily . . . He seemed to have incredible hearing and memory capacity. And his sense of smell was uncanny!

While Christopher had begun the day quite reticently, he was beginning to spiral out of his natural reserve into a rather boisterous little boy. She was so caught up in his enthusiasm, it wasn't until they reached the Twin Vanderbilt Mansions that she began to feel a sense of unease . . . as though they were being watched . . .

It wasn't difficult to remain inconspicuous on New York City's streets.

With the bustle of activity from Central Park at the end of the concert, Fifth Avenue was a melee. Peter followed his son and two female companions, remaining at a safe distance as they made their way home.

He hadn't trusted her alone with his son.

She might be beautiful as hell, but she was a conniving little witch, and he was bound and determined to discover what it was she was after. Her interest in Christopher had been quite clear from the first—she couldn't fake that kind of sincerity—but *what* did she want with him?

Peter had stood apart from them, watching while they'd enjoyed the concert. With no one about to scrutinize her every move, she hadn't even attempted to carry on with her pretense, other than that she had retained the use of her dark spectacles. Her attention, however, had been wholly upon Christopher, and her gaze clearly drawn to his son's every gesture. The way that she watched him, in fact, gave Peter a strange sense of familiarity about her.

He knew three things for certain after this morning: One, Sarah Hopkins was most definitely not blind. Two, for whatever reason, she cared about his son. And three, he couldn't stop thinking of her.

God, just watching her walk made him stiff as a cleric's collar.

And the thought of her lying within his bath last night had made him as hard as steel. Christ, he'd sat within his office, considering an investment proposal for a new restaurant akin to Delmonico's, and unable to concentrate on anything but the workings of his vivid imagination.

In his mind he had been able to see her lying within his enormous tub. He saw her, as in a dream, rise up from the frothy suds, her hair wet and rivulets of water and soap streaming down her face. He saw those moist lashes open and her blue eyes rivet upon him, and his blood simmered.

Even here, amid the masses, and though he could but see her at a distance, he found himself aroused by the thought of her.

But it was more than that.

The sight of her sitting there in the park with his son, holding him so intimately . . . had begun to give him insane thoughts. Somehow that gentle image made him yearn for something he'd not dared to yearn for in far too long.

Only this time he understood the perils of believing in a myth: *There were no happily-ever-afters.*

And yet, until now, he hadn't even considered the possibility of trying again. He had been perfectly content to simply be *Christopher's father.*

He was still content to be Christopher's father, but

suddenly he went to bed at night . . . and his hand reached into the cold space beside him . . . and his thoughts drifted to the room next door . . . and his loins hardened against the bed.

He never thought of Cile there anymore . . . in his bed. Nor was it any longer simply a means to satisfy his needs.

There were new needs he yearned to fill . . . needs he had never known he possessed . . . needs he had not even known with Mary.

Somehow this woman, this stranger in his home, had managed to awaken something within him that he'd never known existed. He'd heard of love but had never given it any credence. He hadn't believed in love—not with Mary—at least not love such as that lauded by the poets. No, but he had loved Mary . . . he just hadn't been *in love with her*. He had adored so much about her, but she hadn't invaded his every waking thought.

Sarah had.

Damn her to hell.

He was following too close, he realized suddenly.

Sarah turned to glance over her shoulder and stared. For an instant he couldn't tell whether she had caught him, or was simply curious about something occurring behind him. When she turned around once more, dismissing him, he decided it was the latter and waited until they crossed the street before he continued after them.

They were definitely being followed.

And Sarah was furious, though she knew she hadn't the right to be.

He didn't trust her—not that she particularly deserved that trust, but she was angered nonetheless, which didn't make the least bit of sense.

Was she hurt that he had somehow judged her and found her guilty?

Or was she angry with herself for failing?

What did he know? And why was he following?

She suddenly couldn't think. "Take Christopher's hand, Mel, please."

Mel turned and gave her a quizzical look. "Is something the matter, Sarah?"

Sarah didn't wish to make a scene. She certainly didn't wish Christopher to become aware of his father's presence, and less did she wish Peter to know that *she* had spied him. "Nothing," she assured, "I just have a bit of fatigue is all."

"Oh, dear . . . well, it has been quite a long day," Mel agreed, and took Christopher's hand in her own. She hesitated before crossing the street and led Christopher along to the next corner.

Sarah had to force herself not to peer nervously over her shoulder.

Calm yourself.

Think, Sarah, you need to think.

Perhaps he hadn't intended to follow them at all. Perhaps he had merely spied them together and was curious to see how they fared. He had no reason to suspect her after all. She'd been particularly careful in and out of his presence. There was nothing Sarah could point to that would say, *This is the instant he would doubt her.*

Had he spied her just a minute ago peering over her shoulder? Had she given herself away with her actions this afternoon? Had he watched them even at the park? Blast him!

Blast herself for not considering the risks!

Ahead of her, Christopher rambled on in an excited fashion, eager to tell his father about the afternoon's diversions. If Sarah hadn't been so distracted by the rat pursuing them, she would have felt overjoyed by his boyish enthusiasm. It was the first time he'd ever displayed such unbounded energy.

This was the little boy she had expected to find, not the quiet little sage she'd encountered.

She stepped into the street behind Mel and Christopher and couldn't help herself. She turned around to see if he was still following. She didn't see him. Not anywhere. Perhaps he hadn't been following them after all. Perhaps he'd simply spied them and out of curiosity had watched them together a moment before carrying on with his affairs. He wasn't there . . . not anywhere at all. She searched the passing crowds, hoping that he wasn't ensconced in some doorway, watching from some hidden perch.

Sarah was so preoccupied with studying the crowd that she didn't hear the thunder of approaching hooves . . . or the deadly clatter of carriage wheels . . .

Peter saw it too late.

He'd crossed back over Fifth Avenue to watch from a safer distance, and was helpless now to do any more than watch with terror as Sarah stood in tne middle of the street. He told himself the driver would spy her—impossible not to—but his speed increased.

And still she stood there, wholly unaware of the death rattle at her back.

Christ! Was she deaf?

"Sarah!" he shouted, and took a panicked step forward.

He couldn't reach her in time.

Impossible!

God help him, but she didn't move.

"Sarah!" She stood oblivious still, and he bolted into a run. "Sarah!" he shouted.

Chapter 19

❧

The impact took the breath from Sarah's lungs. Her head smacked the street with a thud that echoed in her brain. Daylight faded from light to black as Sarah was thrown.

When next she opened her eyes, a fuzzy pair of blue eyes stared down at her. Her head throbbed painfully. She closed her eyes once more. Focusing seemed impossible.

"You are bound and determined to get yourself killed, aren't you?" a male voice asked.

Disoriented still, Sarah tried to open her eyes again. Pain flared, and she closed them, moaning.

"Did you see that man?" she heard Mel ask furiously. "He didn't bother to stop! Did you see him?"

"I did," Peter answered, and his tone was deadly calm.

"What," Sarah stammered, "what happened?"

"That rotter tried to kill you!" Mel shrieked in outrage.

"My head hurts."

"It isn't any wonder," Peter said softly, his tone angry but subdued.

"He didn't bother even to slow down!" Mel added angrily. "Rotten dastard!" Peter must have looked at Mel then, because Mel said, "He most certainly is a rotten dastard and I'll not mince words. He could have killed her!"

"So I saw," Peter said.

"Is she all right, Daddy?" Christopher asked very near her. Sarah tried to open her eyes, and then reminded herself it was best not to.

She squeezed them shut. "Yes, I'm quite all right, Christopher," she replied, and with her eyes closed, tried to rise. "Ouch!" she exclaimed.

"Have you any notion," Peter asked her, "why someone might wish you harm, Sarah?"

Whatever was he implying? "No one did," she replied caustically, "until I met you!"

He reached out, hooking her beneath her arms. Sarah could smell his musky male scent, and she couldn't help herself—she let him drag her into his arms as he helped her to her feet, and she buried her nose against his sun-warmed shirt.

"Are you telling me this is my fault?" His tone told her he was hardly convinced. His hand at her back soothed her.

"Perhaps *you* could better tell *me*," she countered.

"What happened, Daddy?" Christopher asked. The poor child was still confused. No one had yet to enlighten him. Not that anyone seemed to have a clue as to what had happened. Sarah had not even spied the approaching carriage until it had been too late.

"I'm not sure, son," Peter said, and Sarah could hear the speculation in his voice. "But it seems to me that someone doesn't like Miss Sarah quite as well as you and I do."

He'd steadied her upon her feet only to dizzy her with his words.

"You like me?" she asked him with some surprise, and hated herself for the silly question. She'd spoken without thought.

Why did his silly declaration make her belly flutter?

And why should she care what he thought of her?

His breath was warm upon her cheek and his hand firm at her back. "Does that surprise you, Sarah?" he murmured.

Sarah dared not look at him. "I . . . I suppose that it does a bit." She hated that her voice sounded suddenly so breathless.

"Well, I do," he told her without hesitation. "I like you very, *very* much."

He just didn't bloody well trust her.

Sarah Hopkins was after something; Peter just couldn't figure out what that something was.

They sat together in the parlor, all of them—he and Ruth and Sarah and Christopher—in an easy atmosphere that reminded Peter of days with his own family, long ago. Before his father had begun to drink so much. Even then Ruth had been a serious young girl, removed from the family despite her presence, and full of her own thoughts. She sat in her chair, quietly assessing the pair sitting on, of all places, the floor of the parlor—Christopher and Sarah—with a general air of disapproval.

Peter could see that Ruth had not even begun to warm to Sarah's presence. He thought perhaps it had to do with Sarah's appearance. She was quite a lovely woman, and Ruth had never been able to accept that as a virtue in others. Peter thought it had to do with their mothers, but he couldn't be certain. Ruth had often begrudged his mother her beauty, and belittled her for it. Yet she hadn't particularly embraced her own mother's lack of it, either. Ruth seemed a woman lost somehow, and while he often regretted the power struggles between them, he also was pleased to give her a home where she felt needed and welcomed. He felt sorry for his half sister. Though she wasn't precisely unattractive, something about her made a man shrivel to his bones.

His gaze returned to the woman who had managed to hold his attention from the instant he'd laid eyes upon her. There was something luminous about her— something that drew him—something more alluring than mere beauty.

"Do you feel the difference, Christopher?" she asked. "Feel them more closely." She had a book of embossed metal sheets between them, and Christopher was feeling the raised dots with extreme care.

"Yes, ma'am."

"Which letter is that?"

"*F*," he said.

Sarah found his hand and placed her own over it, finding the letter Christopher was examining. She was taking great pains to play the part of a blind woman. "No, darling," she said. "That is the letter *D*. They are quite similar except one faces one way, and the other faces another."

"I'm sleepy," Christopher protested suddenly.

"Try, Christopher," Peter commanded him.

Despite his suspicions of Sarah, she was doing Christopher so much good, he could see. And she did seem to know her codes. Which led him to wonder . . . why would she have bothered to learn it so profoundly . . . if she weren't blind?

Who the hell was she?

The question plagued him.

Who was this woman who had taken so much time with his son? Who would sit on the floor with him and teach him the alphabet with such patience?

Sarah stilled and straightened. "Peter?" she said without looking at him. Damn, she was good, but not good enough. He knew better. He lived with a blind son, knew his every mannerism. He was not fooled.

"Yes?"

"If Christopher is tired, I hardly wish to push him."

Peter stared at her. Though she didn't look his way, she clearly knew his gaze was upon her and she straightened her spine, ready to do battle for his son. Why did that make him smile? Why did he not feel more wariness toward her than he did? Why did her pretense intrigue rather than anger him?

And why the hell couldn't he quit thinking of those damned beautiful lips of hers?

From the moment he'd first spied her, with her dark spectacles, his gaze had focused upon that mouth, and he couldn't seem to dismiss it from his thoughts.

He gazed down at his son, suddenly ready for Christopher to be abed—suddenly eager to be alone with Sarah. "Are you tired, Christopher?"

"Yes, Daddy." He tilted his head sleepily.

Peter turned to Ruth. "Take him to bed, please."

"Peter," Ruth replied. He knew it would be a protest; and he knew why. He also knew Ruth understood the look in his eyes. She didn't wish to leave them alone.

"Take him to bed, please," he repeated, and his tone brooked no argument.

"I can take him," Sarah suggested.

"No," Peter said quietly but insistently.

Giving him a disapproving glance, Ruth rose from her chair and took Christopher by the hand. "Good night, son," Peter said softly.

"Night, Daddy," Christopher replied, as Ruth led him away.

An uneasy silence fell between them once they were alone in the parlor.

"I don't think she likes me very well," Sarah said at last.

Peter saw no reason to deny the truth. "I think you are quite a perceptive woman."

"I have tried to speak with her," Sarah said, "but she doesn't seem to appreciate my efforts. I am sorry if I have offended her in some manner. I did not mean to . . ."

"You have not," Peter assured. "My sister is quite protective of her family. Overly so, I'm afraid. Since the death of my wife, Cile is the one person she seems to favor."

Sarah's heart began to race at the turn of their topic. "She must have loved your wife very deeply, then."

His voice was low, entirely too silky, as he said, "Mary?"

"Yes, your wife," Sarah reiterated.

"I honestly would not know how Ruth felt about her. My sister was never very vocal with her opinions of the women in my life until *after* Mary."

Sarah lifted her brows.

"Ruth knows, however . . . how distraught I was after my wife's death. It nearly ruined me . . ." He lapsed into thought. "Nearly ruined us all," he added sadly.

As difficult as Sarah found the subject, it was the first time he'd spoken so directly about Mary, and she didn't dare dissuade him from it. Her heart hammered against her breast as she listened. "I'm certain," she murmured when he didn't continue. "You must have loved her deeply." She sucked in a breath and held it, then released it.

"I'm not certain I knew what love was," he confessed, surprising her with the declaration.

She had to resist the urge to look up into his face, to peer into his eyes. "You didn't love her?"

He shrugged. "I did as much as I was capable,"

he told her. ''Mary was a delightful, bright, charming woman. I thought I could make her happy.''

But you made her miserable, Sarah wanted to remind him. *And everyone knew it.* Her eyes filled with tears she could not afford to shed. Not for the first time since arriving in his house, she was grateful for the spectacles to shield her grief. ''But you couldn't?''

''No,'' he answered. ''I tried, though perhaps not hard enough. Mary deserved more.''

His candidness confused her. She didn't know what to make of it. Why should he lie about his feelings for his dead wife at this late hour?

''She was an excellent mother,'' he added, and smiled a little wistfully. His gaze focused upon her once more.

Sarah knew it was true. She was a wonderful mother. Evidence of that fact was everywhere . . . from the charred little blanket she had begun to embroider for him . . . to the words she had spilled upon the pages of her journal—words that the public had been witness to, thanks to the press. She wanted to ask so many questions, but didn't dare. ''Perhaps . . . She forced her gaze to remain on the intricate design of the blue wallpaper. ''Perhaps I should be off to bed as well,'' she suggested. ''It has been a very, very long day.''

''It has, at that,'' he agreed, watching her. She could feel him.

Silence once more.

''I don't suppose you have any inkling who might

have wished you harm today?'' he asked her. ''That carriage intended you damage, Sarah.''

He needn't have reminded her. ''I said I did not, and I do not.''

''You are a very fortunate woman,'' he told her. ''That driver might have killed you.''

''Yes, well, I'm quite grateful he did not,'' she said, and started to rise.

''Me too,'' he answered.

Sarah blinked, and shivered at his words. She froze upon her knees. Blast, but how could such a simple statement like that affect her so? Her skin prickled. ''I think I should retire for the night,'' she suggested once more, and began again to rise, before he could manage to unsettle her again.

''What are you afraid of, Sarah?'' he asked her.

''Whatever do you mean?'' she asked, gaining her feet. She stood there, daring to face him, watching the casual way in which he reclined within his chair. He was slumped within it . . . his legs splayed out before him, slightly parted. He rested his elbow on the arm of the chair and leaned into his hand, studying her.

''I don't bite,'' he said.

''No?''

''No,'' he replied.

''Well, I do,'' Sarah snapped. This was not going very well, and she felt the need to leave at once. He was playing some game with her, she realized suddenly.

He stood abruptly, and Sarah turned to go before he could stop her.

He was faster than she was. He caught her and turned her about.

"What do you think you are doing?" she asked him, infuriated that he would dare to touch her. But she didn't chance looking him straight in the face.

"What's the matter?" he taunted her. "Afraid of a little touch?"

Sarah gasped as he reached out and removed her spectacles from her face. Instinctively she reached out to take them back, but once again he was too quick and Sarah swallowed as she forced her hands to her sides and closed her eyes.

"You have the most beautiful face," he told her, whispering. "Beautiful blue eyes . . ."

Sarah's heart tripped. "You take too much liberty, Mr. Holland," She informed him. "I should like you to return my spectacles at once!"

"Open your eyes for me, Sarah," he urged her.

She squeezed them tighter. "No! I will not. I am uncomfortable doing such a thing, and I would appreciate it very much if you would return my spectacles to me, Mr. Holland."

"I live with a blind son," he reminded her. "It is nothing I have not seen before."

"I am *not* your son, I should remind you, and neither am I your wife to be ordered about!"

"So you are not," he agreed, and slid his hand beneath her chin, raising her face for his inspection.

Sarah was at once too confused to respond. His thumb caressed her cheek, and she held her breath at the sensations that jolted through her.

Dear God, what would she do if he bent to kiss her now?

What would she say if he tried?

Her hand came up at once to grasp at his arm. She dug her fingers into his sleeve, desperate to be away.

"Good night, Miss Hopkins," he said, and there was a smile in his voice.

Sarah didn't know whether to be relieved by his dismissal or dismayed.

He wasn't going to kiss her?

She hadn't truly wanted him to, had she?

Lord, she was becoming so confused.

She knit her brows. "G-g'night, Mr. Holland," she stammered. He released her and she turned to go, dazed.

"Aren't you forgetting something?" he asked her.

Sarah stopped but didn't turn to him. "Forgetting something?" she repeated dumbly.

"Your spectacles," he said, coming up behind her and reaching around her to press her spectacles into her hand.

Sarah held her breath at the feel of him behind her. Her heartbeat quickened painfully.

"Sweet dreams," he whispered against her nape, his breath hot against her neck. Her knees went weak at the hand he placed on her shoulder.

"And to you," Sarah replied. Straightening, she inhaled a breath and walked quickly away before she could disgrace herself and melt at his feet.

Chapter 20

From the journals of Mary Holland:
January 5, 1880

I don't know what to believe.

Peter and I don't even talk anymore—he spends all his time with Cile. And Cile can no longer even look at me. She comes into the house and runs back to Peter's office to see him, hardly sparing me a word or a glance. Guilt? Anger? Does she loathe me? I cannot even tell what sentiments she harbors toward me, but it seems to me that the two of them would love nothing more than to have me out of the way. I want to confront her, but am afraid to. What if she should tell Peter?

What if they are innocent?

What if they are not?

Should I stand idly by and watch my family torn apart?

That is hardly the daughter my father raised.
I should talk to her . . .

Someone was watching outside the window.

Sarah was beginning to feel her time was running short. If she didn't uncover Mary's journal soon, she was going to lose everything.

She had a terrible feeling she was going to lose everything anyway.

It had occurred to her earlier that if Peter was not guilty, and he discovered her ruse—and even if he didn't—she was never going to see Christopher again. Having come into Peter's home as she had, so deceptively, especially if he was innocent, she was going to end with no recourse but to leave. Surely he would never allow her to see Christopher again.

Dear God, she *did* need him to be guilty.

But she didn't want him to be.

What a terrible mess she had woven for herself!

She went to the window once more, shoving the curtains aside and peering out. No one there, and yet there had certainly been someone watching earlier from across the street.

If Peter was *not* guilty, *who* was trying so hard to remove her from this house?

Someone was guilty.

Who?

Cile Morgan had yet to return to visit. Sarah had seen not a hair of her, and yet she was very aware of the anger she had borne Peter the night she'd stormed into his office. Her angry shouts had reverberated throughout the house. Why? Were they truly lovers? What had he done to make her so angry?

Impatient now, Sarah drew away from the window and began to pace the room. She'd called for Mel to come and awaited her now. Sarah only hoped no one spied her, because there was something she wished to do—something she needed to do before she ran out of time.

She put out the lights as she waited, hoping her silhouette was all the watcher could see from outside her window.

When the knock came upon the door at last, her nerves were on edge. She snatched the curtain closed and hurried to the door, opening it, dragging Mel quickly within.

"Hurry!" she said.

"What the devil are you doing?" Mel asked her. "I think that accident has left your brain quite addled!"

"That is entirely possible," Sarah admitted. "You should know the things I have been thinking. If they are not mad, I don't know what is." That she must prove Peter guilty if she ever wished to see Christopher again—and yet, dear God . . . she just didn't want it to be true.

"Why are the lights out?"

"Don't turn them on!"

"Sarah," Mel began, tilting her head as she peered through the darkness. "You are beginning to frighten me. Why are you sitting in the dark? This is hardly good for you. Something is going on here,

surely, but I think our time in this house is done.
I'm quite concerned about you."

"Not yet," Sarah begged her. "Someone has
been watching my room, Mel. I have spied them
from my window. Someone is watching now!"

"I am beginning to get a terrible feeling about this
place, Sarah. I don't think we are going to gain anything by remaining. I have found absolutely no evidence of Peter's guilt. In fact, everyone I have
spoken to here is convinced of his innocence. And
yet something is very, very strange in this house."

"I agree," Sarah said.

"So let us simply pack our bags and go," Mel
begged her. "There is no reason to remain in this
house another night."

Sarah's shoulders slumped with regret. "Mel,"
she began, "I cannot yet. One more night," she beseeched her. "Let me try just once more to find that
journal and then I promise we will go in the morning."

"Once more? What are you going to do?" Mel
asked, wary now. "Sarah?"

"I need your help," Sarah began. "Someone is
watching this room. I need to leave, but I need you
to make my presence known here . . . in case they
are still watching."

Mel shook her head. "You are making absolutely
no sense at all."

"Listen to me," Sarah begged her. "I only need
you to stay here and to keep the lights out; pretend
you are me."

"Whatever for?"

"Because I'm going to search his office and library, that's what for."

"Sarah!" Mel protested. "That is entirely too dangerous! What if he discovers you? What if he is guilty? How can you be certain?"

"I can't be, of course, but I need to search that office, Mel. I must! What if he is *not* guilty?" Sarah dared to ask.

"You are getting quite mad, I think. Whatever does that mean? If he is guilty, then you are a dead woman tonight!"

"No," Sarah persisted, "not that. It occurred to me to worry about something else entirely, Mellie."

"Good Lord!" Mel exclaimed. "I'm getting so confused. What the devil are you talking about?"

"Mel," Sarah began, "if Peter is innocent . . . what happens after tonight? How do I go to him tomorrow and say . . . 'Oops! I am not who I said I was and guess what. I'm Mary's cousin and I wish to be a part of Christopher's life.' How do you think he will react to that?"

Mel's shadow moved across the darkness to the bed. She sat down. "I see what you mean," she sighed. "I imagine he would not react very well."

"No," Sarah agreed. "Not very well at all."

"What a mess we have made for ourselves," Mel told her, reaching out and grasping her arm.

"Mellie," Sarah appealed, "I truly thought he was guilty of murdering my cousin. When I made this plan, I didn't consider the possibility that he might actually be innocent. It honestly never occurred to me. And now I stand to lose Christopher entirely.''

Mel nodded in the darkness. "Yes, I see."

"What am I going to do, Mellie?"

"God, Sarah, I don't know. Find that missing journal!"

There was an uneasy silence between them.

Then Sarah admitted, stomping her foot, "But I don't want him to be guilty!"

"Sarah," Mel began.

"No, don't ask it." She shrugged free of Mel's grip. "I don't know what I feel. I just don't know, but I do have to know for certain if he is guilty or not. I'll deal with the rest of my life tomorrow. Tonight I need to search for Mary's journal, and I hoped you would sleep here in my bed just in case someone is watching to see if I leave this room."

"Of course," Mel said without hesitation. "That's a simple enough thing to do, but I'm concerned about you. What if he catches you in his office?"

"He won't!" Sarah swore. "I'll make certain of it. I shall be careful. Are all the lights out yet? Is the house sleeping?"

"I . . . I think so," Mel replied.

"Good Lord, you took long enough to come," Sarah complained.

"I . . . I'm sorry, I was bathing when you called for me."

"It's all right," Sarah said, feeling at once contrite for her outburst. "It may have worked for the best, at any rate. It's late enough now that perhaps I can go straight to it.''

"Wait just a bit," Mel suggested. "Just in case. The night is young.''

"Very well. But when I go," she said, "whatever you do, do *not* use a light in this room.''

"I won't." Silence fell between them. "Sarah?" Mel prompted.

"Yes?''

"What is going on between you and Peter?''

"I don't know," Sarah confessed, and then added, "but something is, Mel. Dear God . . . I cannot breathe when he walks into the room, and I cannot think!''

"Fear?" Mel asked her, mistaking her meaning. "Are you afraid of him?''

"Only of myself," Sarah admitted, turning her back to Mel. "Mellie . . . oh, my God . . . I have these wicked, wicked thoughts . . .''

Across the street, the watcher watched from the darkened corner of a building, dressed in men's trousers and coat, and with her hair pulled into a hat. No one could tell her gender; she looked just like a scrawny boy.

Sarah Hopkins wasn't alone in that room, and the possibility that it might be Peter with her made the watcher sick to her stomach. She was too late. If he married the witch . . . if he brought her into his home . . . where would that leave *her*?

She couldn't let it happen.

She mustn't be afraid to take a stand.

It was time for her to take matters into her own hands, and not delegate to idiot men who failed at every task, lest their pricks or their pockets were at risk. Something needed to be done, and something needed to be done tonight before this went any further . . . before she lost everything . . .

Before someone suspected these accidents were not accidents at all.

Peter was beginning to: She'd spied the look on his face as he'd knelt over Sarah in the street. Once he'd been certain she was all right, his gaze had lingered in the direction the driver had vanished, and his expression had been much too thoughtful.

Tonight she had to do something . . .

Within the darkened window, two silhouettes moved toward the bed. The watcher waited, shuddering at the sight of them. She strained to see their faces, willing the shadows away.

She willed Peter out from the room—didn't dare blink her eyes, lest she miss his leaving. He couldn't stay. Damn! She had to be alone. She needed Peter to leave. What the devil were they doing with the lights out?

She held her breath until the door opened once more, and then she watched as one shadow slipped from the room and Sarah was alone once more.

The watcher loitered some time longer, with squinted eyes and unbroken concentration as the remaining shadow prepared for bed, and then she moved closer to peer into the window when all movement ceased.

Inside the room, Sarah Hopkins lay upon Mary Holland's bed. It gave the watcher a strange sense of déjà vu.

Tonight she would not take a passive role . . .

Chapter 21

The house was dark as Sarah made her way down the hall to the library. She would check that room first, before moving on to his office. She didn't dare chance going there first, just in case he'd remained late to work. It should take her some time to search the library, she thought, and by the time she was through, she hoped he would be gone.

Upon reaching the library, she found the door ajar and the room bathed deep in shadows. The drapes were open wide.

Brilliant moonlight fell across the rich wood floors and spilled at her feet. The scent of this room was predominantly one of old books, a familiar scent that brought back memories of her childhood . . .

She had been much too young when her mother and father had died, and so she remembered little of them. Only slivers of memories penetrated her consciousness. Her father's library . . . her mother's perfume . . . the sound of her mother's voice. Their deaths had been such tragic ones, two lovers alone on the cliffs of a beach, after enjoying too much wine. Her mother had lost her footing, and her father had tried to save her. Both had ended up on the rocks below, and Sarah, their only child, had gone to her uncle in Boston. The loss made her sad even to this day, and yet it was her uncle's death that had dealt her the hardest blow—and then Mary's . . . She'd always thought she and Mary would have the opportunity to make amends. And then suddenly her best friend, her cousin, her sister even, were gone.

And what did Sarah do? She came to Mary's home to atone for past mistakes and ended up losing her heart to the very man whom Sarah had belittled her cousin for loving.

The admission shocked her.

Was that what she was doing?

Losing her heart to him?

Somehow she was beginning to.

She could feel it. It was too easy to see him with his son, whom she thought of as her nephew, and love him for the love he gave. It was difficult to stop thinking of that face . . . that look . . . those eyes . . .

She needed to think . . . to concentrate . . .

She needed to search this library, and then his office, for that journal. It was her only hope of shedding any light on the last days of Mary's life. And it was becoming more than apparent that *something* was not right in this house. She just didn't know what that something was. It certainly didn't appear to be what she'd first believed—that its master was a murderer. And yet Mary had come here looking for happiness and had not left this house alive.

Something was amiss . . .

She began by searching the shelves closest to the door. She searched the titles on the lowest shelf, trying to determine some sort of order for her search. There were so many titles that it seemed an impossible task for one single night, let alone for one person: The first title she made out was *The History of England from the Fall of Wolsey to the Defeat of the Spanish Armada,* by J. A. Froude. Another title read, *Studies in the History of the Renaissance,* by Oxford classicist Walter Pater.

Her gaze traveled upward, searching for some clue as to the order of his library. A shining brass plaque, when she read closer, said *Nonfiction: Histories.*

Sarah decided to skip the section entirely, moving on to the next section, knowing that Mary had had very little interest in histories. Her cousin's interests had lain in the mystic's interpretations of life, in theology and in fictional classics.

She scanned the shelves, examining them through Mary's eyes . . .

Peter Holland's library was extensive, she realized. Her eyes caught titles of all sorts . . . from Thomas Hardy's *Far from the Madding Crowd* to Mark Twain's *A Tramp Abroad* and Bernard de Fontenelle's *De l'Origine des Fables.* His collection of contemporary works was commendable.

She reached to pull out the spine of *The Origin of Myths,* and froze at the sound of footsteps. Close, but too faint to be of any—

"Late night reader?"

Sarah started at the sound of Peter's voice behind

her, throwing her hands up in fright. Her heart leapt into her throat.

She hadn't realized he was so near! She cursed him for his lithe footfalls. She didn't know what to do, or how to reply. She was caught and what could she say?

"I seem to have lost my way," she said lamely. Her voice trembled nearly as badly as her hands.

"I see that," he answered rather sarcastically.

"I called for Mel . . . earlier," she improvised. "She never came. I . . . I thought perhaps I might find her . . . myself."

His tone was dubious. "In my library?"

"I-I wandered in . . . by mistake," she persisted, and turned to face him.

"And you stayed because . . ."

"I . . . I . . . was trying to find my way back out," she replied and cursed herself for sounding not only like a liar but an incompetent fool.

"I see," he replied. "So you were groping for the door just now, I presume?" He was looking straight at her, and even through the shadows she knew his gaze was focused on her eyes. She wasn't wearing her spectacles.

She swallowed convulsively as he took a step toward her.

His magnificent shoulders were bare, and Sarah could scarce keep her eyes from wandering over them. His face was cast deep in shadow, but moonlight glazed his shoulders bronze.

God, but he was a beautiful specimen of man . . .

And as terrible a liar as she was, she was in trouble!

What could she say to him now?

What excuse could she possibly give him for snooping in his library?

"Good thing I came along . . . wouldn't you say?" His tone was silky smooth, unnerving her all the more for its deliberate calm.

"Y-yes," Sarah agreed. "I-I was q-quite lost."

"Well, then . . . I would be most pleased to show you the way," he told her, and took another step toward her.

Sarah swallowed once more.

He knew, she realized as he neared.

He knew.

"Th-That would be wonderful . . . I-I can't seem to gain my bearings."

"The bloody hell you can't," he snapped suddenly. "It rather seems to me you find your way about quite well . . . for a *blind woman*."

"I . . ." She didn't know what to say. "I do the best I am able."

"Do you now?" he taunted her; and his gaze raked her even through the shadows. He stood before her, and Sarah's heart began to cartwheel within her breast. She backed against the bookcase, stopping only when she could not retreat any farther.

"Yes," she answered breathlessly. "Yes, I do."

His face was entirely too close to hers now, his eyes too knowing, his mouth too near. Despite that her heart was beating madly and that she was frightened of the repercussions, she couldn't seem to stop staring at his lips . . .

"Who are you, *Sarah Hopkins*?" he whispered softly.

The scent of him filled her lungs, dizzied her.

He moved closer.

"Whatever do you mean?" she answered fearfully.

"I've been waiting," he said, his words slow and deliberate, "very, *very* patiently for you to come and tell me what it is you are after . . ."

Sarah couldn't respond.

Her throat constricted and her chest suddenly felt too tight to breathe.

Oh God! He knew!

But what precisely did he know?

She thought she might faint in fear. The expression on his face grew more ruthless as he stared at her, and her legs began to tremble. She hated herself for that weakness.

"*Who* are you?" he repeated. "*Why* are you here?"

Sarah sucked in a breath.

In panic she tried to push past him, refusing to answer his questions.

He seized her by the arm, dragging her back, forcing her once more against the bookcase. She smacked her head against a shelf and her knees buckled under her.

"Look into my eyes," he commanded her.

Sarah turned away, unable to bear his scrutiny,

unable to face him. At her sides, her hands clenched and unclenched nervously.

He placed his hand behind her head and forced her to face him. "Sarah?" he demanded.

Sarah couldn't bring herself to speak.

She just couldn't say it!

Suddenly she felt so ashamed of the lies—and afraid! Afraid of the truth.

He had let her into his home, trusted her, and she couldn't even find regret for her deceptions.

Someone was responsible for Mary's death, but somehow she knew in her heart in that instant that it wasn't him.

Peter was innocent.

She could see it in his eyes. He wasn't afraid of the truth or even angry, only determined to know.

And suddenly she was the villain here . . . suddenly she was the liar and the thief!

Suddenly she didn't know anything at all.

She wanted to run, to take Christopher away and shield him from harm.

But that wasn't all she wanted.

God help her, but there was something else she wanted more.

Chapter 22

She was like a frightened animal, caught in the hunter's snare. Terrified.

Frozen.

Peter could see it in her face.

Tears welled in her eyes and glistened by the light of the moon, reflecting the light like tiny diamonds. They were expressive eyes, eyes that revealed things her lips never would have spoken. Had he chanced to peer into them even once, he never would have believed her scheme.

Christ, but she was a beautiful little liar.

What the devil did she want?

"Who are you?" he demanded once more, moving closer . . . needing the scent of her. He couldn't help himself. The scent of her skin was more intoxicating than any drink ever had been. "Sarah," he whispered, and lowered his mouth to hers.

The first taste of her lips sent his pulse skittering.

God, but her mouth was soft . . . so soft . . . and beautiful . . . and sweet . . .

She didn't fight him and the blood surged through his veins. His heart hammered.

"Sarah," he whispered once more, and she trembled beneath him. She turned her face from his kiss and her body shuddered.

In fright?

He didn't give a bloody damn.

He pressed his body harder against her.

Somehow he didn't give a damn about anything at all at the moment . . . only the sweet taste of her mouth, and the heady perfume of her female skin.

He breathed in deeply, burying his face against the curve of her throat, filling his lungs with the alluring scent of her.

He lifted his gaze to look into her eyes, a man drowning in his own passions.

He was drowning and he didn't care.

Beautiful blue, even by the light of the moon.

Christ, but a man could lose his soul in those eyes . . .

Sarah's heart thundered with fear . . . and something more . . . something she didn't dare acknowledge.

He shifted, pressing himself against her, and she nearly went black with the sensation of his body so hard against hers.

It was as though he were melting into her, his body seeking to fill every curve.

"Look at me, Sarah!" he whispered fiercely, tilting his hips against her. Sarah's breath caught at the suggestion of his body. Her own body responded with a flush of heat that dizzied her.

She looked up at the ceiling, unable to meet his gaze. "I can't!" she cried softly, desperately. "I can't!"

"Goddamn you," he hissed, and slid his hand up the back of her head, forcing her to acknowledge him once and for all. His lips came down hard upon hers, insistent and feverish.

"Dear God," she whimpered into his mouth, and melted into his embrace. Her hands went about his neck, clinging to him, even as she loathed herself for her reaction to him.

"Sarah," he murmured, lifting his mouth from hers, and the single word was like a sigh.

He tilted his head to lock his mouth over hers once more, and she moaned softly in the back of her throat.

Nothing in her life had ever felt so heady as this.

Nothing she'd ever known had ever made her body quiver so deliciously.

His hand slid down her back. Sarah held her breath. Some part of her knew she should stop him . . . now . . . before it was too late . . . but she couldn't speak to say so, didn't dare utter a sound. Her body was no longer her own to command. Desire flooded her. His hand slid to cup her bottom and Sarah went weak in her knees. Something convulsed deep within her, an answer to his body's silent question . . . a question her body instinctively understood and answered without any will of her own.

God forgive her, but she wanted this—wanted her cousin's husband with a passion she had never known.

He shifted his weight into her, setting a knee between her thighs and prying her legs slightly apart, and her body convulsed once more. At the same time, he cupped her chin in his hand and lifted her face. He kissed her lips, plundering depths of her mouth with a sweet ferocity that took the air from her lungs and left her breathless.

"I want you," he whispered, cocking his hips fully against her. *"I want you, Sarah . . ."*

His fevered declaration left her completely defenseless.

Somehow her body understood what he'd meant with those heated words and the simple tilt of his hips, and she reacted with shameless abandon. Heat flowed through her, spilling into her most private places like a river of warmth. The tips of her breasts cried out for the pressure of his touch.

In that instant it didn't matter that he was her cousin's husband.

It didn't matter that he might be her murderer as well.

It just didn't matter.

Nothing mattered.

God forgive her, but all that seemed to matter was the way he was making her *feel*.

His hand squeezed her flesh just a little too hard, and Sarah sensed the hunger in the desperate gesture . . .

Heaven help her . . . she wanted this too . . .

Christ.

Peter couldn't think any longer. He tangled a hand

in her hair, reveling in the feel of it sliding through his fingers . . . like softest silk.

The sensation melted his brain.

It had been much too long since he'd felt this way . . . much too long . . .

It didn't matter who she was.

His body didn't give a damn.

He wanted to bury himself inside her . . . wanted to drag her down to the floor and feel her wrap her legs about his waist. He wanted to . . . God help him, but he wanted to take her with all his lustful energy. No gentle intimacy as between longtime lovers. No meaningless tumble. He wanted to give her everything his body had to offer, everything, but not gently.

His hand slid along her back and under the seam between her buttons. His fingers reveled in the feel of warm flesh, craving more. With one swift motion, he popped the buttons from her dress, scattering them over the shelves and floor. The sound of them spraying over the hard wood quickened the beat of his heart. She cried out softly, but didn't protest, and the blood in his veins melted into his groin, setting him on fire.

Had she ever known a man?

Mel had said she'd had a fiancé—was that a lie as well? He hoped.

Her body's response was passionate and instinctive, and he was afraid to ask. If she had given herself to *him* . . . The notion somehow turned his gut. If she hadn't . . . would he feel compelled to stop?

He bent to kiss her once more, sliding his tongue

across the seam of her lips . . . delicious . . . sweet
. . . warm . . . everything he had imagined they
would be and more. He craved the taste of her unlike
anything he'd ever craved before.

No whiskey, or port, or wine, had ever held such
allure.

If she didn't deny him . . . if she didn't protest . . .
now . . . this moment . . . while he had a thread of
sanity left in his fevered brain . . . he was going to
strip her bare and lay her right here on his library
floor.

His body quickened at the thought.

"I want to see you," he told her, his voice shuddering with desire, and it was the only chance he
intended to give her. It wasn't much of a chance to
stop him, but he was hardly a saint and he wasn't
in the bloody mood to earn points for Saint Peter.

To hell with honorable intentions.

To hell with the consequences.

To hell with anything and everything that stood
in his way.

He tilted his hips once more, pressing her back
into the shelves, and she clung to him.

He looked into her eyes, and they were as lust-
filled as his own. Her arms tightened about his neck.

Peter didn't need further encouragement.

Greedily covering her mouth with his own, he
thrust his tongue within, tasting the intoxicating
warmth of her mouth. His tongue slid deeper, meld-
ing with hers, and his heart leapt with satisfaction as
her sweet tongue began to spar with his own.

Christ, he wanted this.

His hands slid to her shoulders as he kissed her, and he couldn't help himself. He gripped her shoulders, pressing her back against the bookshelves, cocking his hips without mercy and lifting it against the heat of her.

No gentleman's courtship this, he wanted her to feel him.

He wanted her to know . . . wanted her to feel *all* that he wished to give her.

He wanted to possess her fully.

Sarah gasped for breath as he rocked against her, revealing the depths of his hunger in the hard lines of his body. Her brain went fuzzy and her mouth entirely too dry, and she couldn't even have protested had she tried.

But she didn't wish to.

She wanted this.

Her body cried out for all that he would give her and more.

Instinctively her hands slid down his back, to his buttocks, her breath coming in tiny pants as she dared to take that firm flesh into her hands. As in a dream, she tilted her head for his kiss, reveling in the heat of his lips upon her mouth.

He ended the kiss with a wicked but gentle lick upon her lips, then kissed her chin . . . then her neck. When his mouth opened upon her flesh and his teeth bit softly into her throat, she cried out in pleasure and instinctively dug her fingers into his buttocks, drawing him to her.

She didn't care how she might appear.

For the first time in her life, she only cared about what she was feeling.

His arousal hardened fully against her, pulsing, seeking . . . and Sarah thought she would swoon at the sensations that spiraled through her.

She couldn't think anymore . . . didn't wish to . . . only feel . . .

He lifted his lips to her lobe and growled softly, a rich animal sound that sent her pulse racing and scattered the last of her thoughts. She trembled with pleasure as his hands slid to her back once more, seizing her dress and drawing it open.

Slowly, deliberately, he moved his hands down her spine, popping the remaining buttons and peeling her dress to reveal her. He pushed the bodice to her waist and slid his hands down, taking her rear into them. Without warning, he lifted her up against him. Sarah cried out as his mouth covered her breast through the material of her corset. Her arms tightened around his neck, and her breath came in ragged gasps.

Oh, God . . . God . . . what was she doing?

Nothing had ever felt so right in all her life.

Never had she craved anything more than she did the feel of his lips upon her bare breast. She willed him to undress her . . . willed him to continue . . . willed him never to stop.

She didn't care just now what the blasted consequences were.

He dragged her down to the floor.

Sarah followed him without protest, accepting his

mouth as it covered hers once more and he pulled her beneath him.

Never would she have believed that two lips could feel so perfect.

He rose above her, kneeling, staring down into her eyes. Sarah stared back without fear. His face, lit with moonlight now, was beautiful, his lips glistening from their kisses, and his blue eyes glittering feverishly.

Sarah thought he might be trying to compose himself.

She didn't want him to.

"Don't stop," she urged him in a whisper, and slid her hand into her corset, unable to bear the ache at her breast.

"I had no intention of stopping," he promised her, his eyes piercing her through the shadows. "No bloody way!"

He watched her. Smiling slightly, he bent forward to take the tip of one breast into his mouth, biting her gently through the soft material. Sarah cried out in sheer pleasure, casting her head back and whimpering softly under the sweet assault of his mouth.

He fell upon her fully then, and she gasped in delight at the feel of his hard body pressing her into the carpeted floor.

In that instant they became a writhing tangle of limbs, and Sarah lost herself completely in the pleasures of her flesh. He lifted her skirt, sliding his hand between her legs, and she knew it had gone beyond the point of return.

The first feel of his hand between her thighs sent

a jolt of pleasure sweeping through her. When his fingers slid into the moistness of her body, she thought she would die. Her heart hammered fiercely and her body convulsed under his touch. Like a concert pianist, he played her.

She cried out, reaching to tug at his clothes. Panting softly, desperate to feel his naked flesh against her, she fumbled with the buttons of his trousers, knowing instinctively that only he could soothe the ache that was beginning to build to a crescendo within her.

His own breath ragged, he lifted himself slightly and reached down, ripping the trousers open. He shrugged out of his pants, never lifting himself from atop her, exposing himself completely, and Sarah sucked in a breath at the sight of him bared. She didn't protest as he lifted up her skirts and her knees along with them. Her heart leapt into her throat as he lowered himself and settled his head between her legs.

Oh, God . . .

Oh God . . .

He wasn't going to do that . . . not that . . .

And yet he did . . .

Sarah's breath left her entirely. Her heart somersaulted against her ribs.

His tongue darted out and slid into her body, tasting her, and Sarah thought she would die with the incredible sensations that rocked through her.

She was his to do with as he would . . . she didn't care anymore.

He was showing her pleasures she had never known existed . . . and she didn't care.

Peter was lost in the throes of his own pleasure.

Christ, but she tasted so damned good.

His body shuddered with satisfaction when she wrapped her legs around his neck, embracing him. Drunk with his own desires, he pressed his lips against her sweet flesh and moaned at the heady taste of her upon his mouth.

He couldn't wait to feel himself within her . . .

There was something wholly satisfying about the feel of her lying beneath him, her dress in tatters and her legs spread for his pleasure.

He had never dared take such liberties with Mary. Mary had been too sweet. Cile had tempted his most wicked desires, but Sarah was the first woman he had ever craved. She was the first woman he had ever wished to know completely. He wanted to taste every inch of her flesh, know every sweet curve of her body.

Sliding his hands beneath her rear, he lifted her to his mouth, and his body convulsed with pleasure at the tiny sounds she made in the back of her throat. Fierce satisfaction flooded him, and his body pulsed hard, craving to know the feel of her.

He couldn't wait any longer.

He slid up her body and looked down into her face, warning her with his gaze before his mouth fell upon her lips, tasting them with as fierce a hunger as he had below. He growled deep in the back of his throat when she didn't protest and slid a hand down to guide himself into her body.

Pure sensation rocked through him at the feel of her so warm and soft and wet, and he thrust within, growling with unadulterated pleasure when she arched backward to accept him fully. He felt her maidenhead give to accept him, and his body shuddered violently in response.

She was his.

Sarah cried out in pain.

He stilled, looking down into her face, his heart pounding, the significance of the moment not lost to him even through the haze of his desire.

And then he was lost completely and he couldn't stop.

Sarah bit into her lip until she tasted her own blood.

She thought she would faint over the pain until he began to move within her once more, easing the throbbing ache with every stroke. She gave herself fully to him then, daring to answer his every thrust with one of her own. Upon her lips, the taste of her own body lingered . . .

Something wicked took seed within her.

Reaching out, she wrapped her hands about his neck and boldly drew him down, urging him once more to kiss her. She craved the blend of their bodies unlike anything she'd ever craved before.

No taste had ever been so sweet or so heady.

No pleasure ever so wickedly delicious.

Deep within her, something began to coil and tighten . . . a thin veil of sensation she suddenly needed to explore more than she needed even to breathe. She closed her eyes and followed it to someplace she'd never dared to go before . . . some heady place where her body was no more than an illusion and the pleasure was the only thing physical.

She dared to seek it . . . with every roll of her hips . . . with every gasping breath.

And when at last her body convulsed in pleasure, tightening around him, she cried out with joy.

With a savage thrust he spilled himself within her, and his answering cries of release filled her heart with a joy and completion she had never understood until that very instant.

In that moment Sarah understood for the first time how Mary could throw away all she had striven for—for this.

Because in one final, desperate thought, she knew she never wanted to leave Peter's arms.

Forgive me, Mary, she pleaded silently.

But she couldn't help herself . . . she reached up to hold him, clinging to him desperately as tears flooded her eyes.

Chapter 23

⌒⌒⌒⌒⌒

*D*arkness flooded the room.

With the curtains drawn, only the minimal light found its way in. But that didn't dissuade the watcher. She knew her way around the house well enough that she wasn't intimidated by the lack of light to see by. Her heart thumping a nervous beat against her breast, she leaned back against the door, staring at the sleeping figure upon the bed . . . waiting . . . to be certain Sarah had not awakened at the click of the latch when she'd closed the door behind her.

The blood sang through her veins, a song of anticipation.

This time . . . she wasn't going to leave her fate in the hands of some incompetent man! All her life men had abandoned or ignored her, left her to fend for herself. And she had never any choice but to swallow her pride and go on.

No more!

That night . . . so long ago . . . she'd had to weasel

into his house with some petty excuse just to open the bloody window in the nursery . . .

Damn Peter.

He had never wanted for anything. Not ever!

Her gaze narrowed on the bed. Pride gave her the resolve she needed to carry this through, desperation drove her.

Women such as that—even blind, and it galled her—didn't have a care in this world.

And she resented Peter for being like every other man—for being swayed by a pretty face.

Sarah Hopkins was everything she despised in a woman, and damn Peter for wanting her anyway!

She was not going to be left once more with nothing!

Not if she could help it!

Pushing away from the door, she moved closer to the bed, desperate to keep some measure of control over her life. She didn't feel anything for Sarah at all. It was not like her life could ever amount to anything anyway. She was blind. What good was she, save to teach others of her kind? It was not as though her life would be wasted when she was dead.

She was a burden, as was Christopher, and no more.

She should be happy not to suffer anymore.

She approached the bed as quietly as she was able, smiling with satisfaction as the figure remained so still in her slumber. In the sheltering blackness of the room, she could barely make out the silhouette of a woman lying on the bed.

Sarah was on her back, her pillow over her head.

How perfect: She couldn't have asked for better.

Not long now, before Sarah Hopkins was out of her misery.

She reached out, her fingers touching the pillow, her heart thundering. She slid her fingers up the cool sham and tentatively pressed on the pillow, testing it.

And then she took a deep breath and shoved with all her might—until she could feel the outline of Sarah's face beneath her hands. And still she pressed harder, her own body trembling with the force of her grip upon the pillow.

Sarah jerked awake, her hands going at once to the pillow. She expended a startled scream into the down. Her shrieks muffled by the down, she struggled fiercely. She could feel Sarah's gasps for air, violent breaths that were never forthcoming. She felt the convulsions of her lungs as she struggled for her last breaths and smiled at the final shuddering of Sarah's body as it stilled beneath her weight.

And still she did not release the pillow—didn't dare, not for the longest time—afraid that if she did . . . that somehow Sarah would gulp a lifesaving breath and then scream for help.

It might have been seconds or it might have been hours before she dared to release the pillow at last. And when she did, her legs went weak with relief at the stillness of Sarah's body upon the bed. Her heart hammered fiercely as she reached out once more and plucked up the pillow between two fingers, as though it were suddenly soiled, and then pulled it to one side of Sarah's face, leaving it covered, but not completely.

She stood there only a moment longer, staring in awe at the stillness of the body lying before her on the bed.

Such power in the act of murder.

So easy . . .

Mere minutes ago there had been life flowing through those limbs and now they were stilled forever. Her own breath came in soft, exhilarated pants, but she was not enervated by the struggle at all. No, she was energized.

No time for regrets.

She peered up at the window then, and urged her feet to move toward it. Like that night so long ago, she hurriedly opened it, lifting it just far enough to appear that someone might have fled from it, and then turned and walked quickly away toward the door.

She paused only once to peer back at the bed.

Behind it, the curtains fluttered gently with the night breeze. It was an unusually warm March night of the sort that drove lovers out to coo at each other under the twinkling stars.

A peaceful scene if ever she'd spied one.

It was done. For better or worse, it was over.

If it was determined that she was murdered, Peter would face the consequences. This time, who would be his alibi?

Turning her back to the deed, she drew the door open, not so concerned this time with the click of the door as it latched once more behind her.

She made her way quickly down the hall, toward Christopher's room, and nearly shrieked in fright as she found him pulling the door shut as he came into the hall. His little white gown almost glowed in the darkness. He paused at the sound of her gasp and stilled, his little hand on the knob, but he said nothing.

He simply stood there, frozen.

A instant of fear shook through her as she realized he knew she was there . . .

Until she remembered . . . he was blind.

He wouldn't and couldn't know who she was, she reminded herself . . . unless she spoke to confirm it.

He remained frozen at his door . . . as though listening, and then when he determined it safe, he pulled his door all the way closed and ventured into the hall, turning instinctively in the direction of his father's room. Likely he'd had a nightmare and was off to sleep in his father's bed.

Well, let him, she thought, and smiled as she watched him hurry down the hall before she made her own escape.

Sarah couldn't stop weeping.

How could she tell him the truth?

And then again, how could she not?

He shifted his weight to one side of her and peered down into her face, holding her still. Her heart wrenching, Sarah turned away from him, unable to look him in the eyes. His hand tightened about her waist.

He drew her nearer. "Sarah?" he whispered. "What's wrong?"

Sarah's sobs grew a little desperate. She couldn't look at him, couldn't face him.

What had she done?

"Sarah," he appealed, his voice soft. "Don't you think it's about time you told me?" He surprised her with a gentle peck on the cheek.

Her heart squeezed a little at the sweetness of his gesture.

She was so confused—so afraid . . .

He reached out, taking her chin in his hand, and turned her face to his. "Look at me," he commanded her, though not unkindly.

Sarah refused. "I-I can't," she cried softly. "I c-can't!"

"You *can*," he countered, his voice low but insistent. "And you *will*. Look at me, Sarah."

Sarah forced herself to obey him. He had a right to know, she told herself. She couldn't keep the truth from him forever . . . nor did she wish to. She took a shuddering breath. "H-how long have you known?" she asked him.

He held her gaze without blinking. "Since the morning after the fire," he told her truthfully.

"Oh, God!" she said, and tried to turn away again. He wouldn't let her. He held a finger at her cheek, forcing her gaze to remain on him.

"Who are you, Sarah?" he demanded to know. "Who are you, and why have you lied to me? What the bloody hell do you want with my son?" His tone lacked the fury that would have made her tremble in fear of him. She couldn't imagine him a murderer—couldn't imagine him harming anyone or anything.

But was she simply hoping?

Did she only wish to believe him innocent?

How could she know for certain?

She squeezed her eyes closed.

"Let's begin with something simple, shall we? Sarah is your true name?"

"Yes," Sarah replied.

Had Mary ever spoken of her? Would he know her by name?

She opened her eyes to peer into his. "Sarah Woodard," she said, bracing herself for his reaction.

Even in the darkness of the room, she saw his brows rise, and knew that he knew her. "Mary's—" His voice caught.

"Yes," she replied once more, and began again to sob. She couldn't help herself. She couldn't believe she'd betrayed her cousin so bitterly tonight—couldn't believe she'd put herself in such a position—couldn't believe she was lying now within Mary's husband's arms.

He reached out at once, surprising her with his reaction to her disclosure, placing his fingers gently at her eyes, brushing the tears away. "Shhh," he said. "Hush, Sarah."

Sarah shook her head.

"Why?" he asked her, and there was confusion in his voice. "If you wished to see Christopher, why did you not simply knock on our door? I would have welcomed you with—"

Sarah shook her head, lifting her own hand to her

face, wiping her own tears. "You don't under-stand," she told him.

"Then help me," he pleaded.

"I didn't simply wish to *see* him," she confessed, and took the hem of her dress into her hand, squeez-ing it.

He stared at her in the darkness, and Sarah couldn't have spoken to save her life. An uneasy silence fell between them. She knew the instant he understood her silence, because his brows twitched and his lips formed a hard line.

"I see," he said finally, and she could see that her words had wounded him.

She cried softly. "I-I thought—"

"That I was guilty," he finished for her, and turned away.

Sarah nodded. Though he wasn't looking at her, she knew he felt it, because his hand was still resting on her face.

He let his hand drop away as he stared out the window, his face beautiful by the light of the moon. In that instant Sarah wanted so badly to reach up and touch the tiny cleft in his chin. She hadn't known he'd had one before now, hadn't dared to study his face so closely. She wanted to slide her fingers up and caress his cheek, to beg his kisses once more. To plead his forgiveness. His skin took on the blue-black tones of night, and his eyes ap-peared all the bluer for it.

"I'm sorry," she said, and took a deep breath to keep from bursting into tears. She thought he might be struggling with his anger, but she couldn't be certain.

He wouldn't look at her.

He peered down at her suddenly, and his expression took her breath away—so much pain there. "Why should you be?" he asked her coldly. "Everyone else thought so." His eyes glittered suspiciously.

God forgive her, but she had to ask, though she knew the truth in her heart. "Are you, Peter?" she dared ask, her heart hammering fiercely.

His features tightened, and she knew he was struggling with his emotions by the tick in his jaw. His eyes narrowed. "Guilty?" he said, staring angrily at her. "Is that what you are asking me? Am I guilty?"

Sarah didn't turn away. She held his gaze, her heart beating like thunder in her ears. She had to know! Though in her heart she knew the answer, she had to hear it from his own two lips.

Some little part of her still doubted his innocence.

Someone was guilty.

His expression shifted from anger to pain and then returned to anger. He lowered his face to hers, until his lips were just a breath away. "Do you make it a habit of making love with murderers?" he asked her coldly.

Sarah refused to answer. Tears pricked at her eyes.

He knew the answer to that question without a doubt: She had given him something tonight that she had never thought she'd give to any man. Not ever! How dare he say such a thing to her when he knew . . .

"That is a cruel thing to say," she told him, and tried not to betray the pain his words had struck into her heart.

"And *your* question was put forth from the kindness of your heart, no doubt?" he snapped in return. "And your lies to me and to my son were perpetrated for our own good?" he added scathingly. "You make love to me, Sarah, and have the nerve to ask that question?" He glared down at her.

Sarah tried to rise, but his arm about her waist prevented her; he jerked her nearer . . . so close she could feel the beat of his heart against her bare arm.

"I don't have to listen to this!" she shouted up at him suddenly, her nerves near to shattering under his anger. She couldn't bear it!

"You do," he said softly, calmly, though with no less determination. "You do have to listen to this and you *owe* me and my son an explanation, *Miss Hopkins*!"

She tried to rise once more, yet he jerked her down easily with a shift of his hand to her breast. "Please!" Sarah beseeched him. "Can't you see . . . I had to know!"

He continued to glare down at her.

"That is my cousin's child, Peter! And I loved her more than anything," she swore, trying to make him understand. "I loved her truly and I betrayed her once already . . . can't you see?"

He said nothing, and Sarah begged him with her eyes to understand. "I needed to be certain," she said again, trying not to cry. "I needed to know. Please . . ."

Still he said not a word, and Sarah had only once before felt such terrible shame . . . the day she'd learned of Mary's death—that day she'd realized she'd forever betrayed the one person in her life, besides her uncle, who had ever mattered to her.

"Peter," she pleaded.

He didn't answer.

This had been her one chance to absolve herself and she'd failed—failed because in trying to redeem herself, she'd betrayed once again . . .

How could she possibly have grown to care so deeply what this man thought of her?

Why did she suddenly feel as though she wished she could crawl into some hole in the ground and never come out? Why did her heart suddenly feel empty and cold? Why did he have to look at her so sadly? Why couldn't he simply be angry and ease her conscience?

Anger, she could deal with—she was angry with herself.

Why did she have to feel such an overwhelming urge to hold him?

Why did all of her reasons for all of her actions suddenly pale before the look of pain in his eyes?

Because she'd spied the love there when he'd watched his son, and heard the adoration in his voice as he spoke with him. Because somehow every gesture between the two had endeared them to her—father and son. Because her body didn't seem to know that her heart was reluctant. Because he hadn't held blindness against her, but had given her flowers in the park when he'd thought she couldn't see them.

Because she remembered the sound of his voice, reassuring her as he'd carried her from the flames and then after . . .

Because she was a bloody fool.

Because if he told her he wasn't guilty, she would believe him.

Because her heart cried out for his caresses.

Because . . . because . . .

She had for the first time in so long felt the warm embrace of a family, and she wanted it back—with him!

"Are you?" she dared to repeat. "Guilty?"

"No," he answered, and Sarah released a breath she'd not realized she held. He turned away from her then, and Sarah reached up with a shuddering breath to touch her hand to his cheek.

The look in his eyes as he'd made love to her had made her feel more of a woman than anything had before in her life.

She smiled softly, though he couldn't possibly see her, his gaze once more upon the window.

"I believe you," she told him. "I want to believe you," she confessed.

His gaze returned to her, and this time there was evidence of tears glistening in his eyes. "We both failed her, Sarah," he said out of the blue.

Sarah blinked at his confession and nodded, her lip trembling softly.

He bent to kiss her suddenly, a soft peck on the lips, and Sarah drew her arms around his neck, daring to embrace him. She pressed her quivering mouth to his, offering her tongue. He cried out a low, keening, tortured sound and took her offering into his mouth, kissing her back with a passion she had thought already spent.

"Sarah," he whispered against her mouth, and deepened the kiss. She could taste the tears that coursed from his eyes onto her face.

Or were they her own?

She didn't know anymore . . . didn't care.

She didn't have to ask him. He knew what she needed. He made love to her once more, this time with all the slow sweetness their first mating had lacked, and Sarah dared to accept his comfort and his tenderness . . .

She dared to accept his caresses and his kisses . . .

Dared to return them, as well.

For the first time in her life, she opened her heart. Though she might regret it come the morning light, tonight she dared.

This instant it didn't matter that he was her cousin's husband—nor did it matter that she had condemned Mary for loving this man!

All that mattered at the moment was that he filled a place in her heart that had long been empty. Selfish or not . . . Sarah was going to greedily take every piece of his heart he was willing to give.

Mary's lesson in death had been clear; life was entirely too short.

Chapter 24

It wasn't until the wee hours that either of them stirred.

Lying on the library floor, cuddled with Peter in a tangle of clothing and limbs, Sarah awoke to a brightening sky. Through the window lace, the glow of morning crept in like a lover returning for the night, swiftly but quietly bestowing his embrace.

In the gentle light of morning, the arms around her seemed less a dream. She waited for a sense of regret to assault her, but it never came. His arm about her waist merely left her content in a way that she had never known possible. He snuggled sleepily at her back, drawing her nearer to him, and she could only smile at that simple gesture he had done so often throughout the night. It was as though he couldn't seem to draw her near enough, and it left Sarah feeling connected in a way she had yearned for so desperately.

It left her smiling.

He nuzzled his face into her hair and Sarah sighed

contentedly, refusing to think of the consequences of last night's actions. Save one . . . as she remembered where they lay . . .

She peered up and over his shoulder at the door. It was open. Blast, they had not even given a single thought to who might walk in on them.

"Peter," Sarah whispered, stiffening in his arms.

He mumbled sleepily at her ear.

Sarah elbowed him. "Peter!" she said, and tried to wiggle free of his embrace.

That alone managed to wake him. "What's wrong?" he asked, allowing her to sit upright. She snatched up her bodice and replaced it as best she could, covering herself. The back of it gaped open, her buttons scattered about the room.

Well, it couldn't be helped, she told herself, though her face heated.

He looked so like a little boy in the morning light, she thought, with his rumpled hair and sleepy eyes. She loathed to think what she must look like to him. He was staring up at her, his lips turned slightly at the corners, as though he knew her thoughts.

"We should dress," Sarah said in a frantic whisper.

He grinned up at her, a lazy grin that was no less mesmerizing for its lack of intent. "Says who?"

Sarah narrowed her gaze at him and resisted the urge to smack his arm. "Says me! What if someone should find us here?"

He shrugged. "Then we tell them the truth . . ."

Sarah lifted a brow.

His grin widened. "We tell them you lost your

way and that I, being a good host, was helping you find it.''

Sarah frowned at him as she gathered the remains of her clothing, and made to rise.

He was up on his feet too swiftly for her even to realize his intent, until he had swept her into his arms and was carrying her out into the hall.

She shrieked in alarm. ''What are you doing? Put me down!''

His grin was infectious. ''Make me,'' he said, sounding so like a little boy that Sarah laughed despite her mortification.

He carried her all the way to his room, opening the door, and then straight to the bed.

''Not here!'' Sarah squealed as he went to place her down upon the bed.

He stopped abruptly and drew her back up, staring down at the bed. Sarah followed his gaze to the sweet little child who lay curled within his sheets.

''Damn,'' he said in a whisper.

''He's beautiful,'' Sarah said, clinging to his father's neck as she stared down at Christopher's angelic face.

Peter was frowning. ''He must have had a nightmare,'' he whispered back, and Sarah could hear the concern in his tone. ''He has them on occasion. He claims the boogeyman comes into his room at night.''

He turned from the bed suddenly and carried her into the adjoining room, shoving the door closed behind him. He leaned back on it, with Sarah still in his arms.

"Poor child," Sarah said with a sigh. She couldn't help the image that accosted her suddenly of herself and Peter asleep in bed . . . and little Christopher climbing in beside them. Wouldn't she love to put her arms around him and draw him into their embrace . . .

The image left her longing for something she hadn't ever dared to . . .

"Sarah," he murmured, drawing her closer. "Please don't regret last night. Tell me that you don't."

Her heart might not, but her conscience did. She couldn't help it. What would Mary say?

"I'm certain you're exhausted," he said suddenly, seeming to understand her hesitation. He pushed away from the door and carried her to the bed, his expression troubled.

He froze midway across the room.

"Sarah?" he whispered, his brows drawing together.

Sarah remembered at once—Mellie! Oh, God, what was she going to say to her? How would she explain? Her face flushed with heat. "Put me down!" she hissed.

He did, and Sarah took a deep breath and turned to push him out the door.

He didn't budge.

"It's best I tell her," Sarah said with growing panic, urging him to go. He seized her by the arm, holding her still. Something about the way he gripped her drew her gaze to his face. He was staring at the bed. Sarah tried to look, but he didn't let her.

Panic struck her.

She jerked away from him and turned to the bed. The sight that greeted her stole the blood from her face, and the words from her lips.

She blinked once, then twice, then passed out.

Peter had only left Sarah's side long enough to speak with the police. He'd hoped they wouldn't wish to disturb her. She'd suffered enough with her loss. Not surprisingly, she'd been perfectly stoic, only clinging to him while they'd come to remove the body, and he'd held her, feeling both helpless and responsible at once. Her grip on his arm had been the single clue to her state of distress, because to look upon her, one would have thought her perfectly composed.

She'd walked away the instant the body had been removed, closed his door, and burst into tears, and this time, when Peter heard her sobs, he hadn't walked away from that damned door. He'd pushed it open and gone to her. He'd held her and comforted her.

It hadn't been enough.

She'd wept on his shoulder until he was certain she hadn't any tears left at all, and still she'd sobbed. Ruth had sedated her, and she had been asleep ever since.

He was beginning to wonder if she'd ever wake up.

Damn these cops.

They were not going to leave until they spoke with her—as though they thought he might find a way to rid himself of her as well. God damn them to hell. Even after all this time, they were too willing to see him hang. It was as though they'd thought to set him as an example all those years ago, and when that had failed, they'd held their grudges and bided their time. The looks they gave him now told him clearly that they would like to see him nailed for this.

They might just get their wish, because Sarah was his only alibi and he didn't wish to ruin her reputation.

He sat on the bed beside her, wishing he could somehow lift her up into his arms, along with his son, and just leave . . .

But would she go with him?

He doubted she would.

And why should she?

He wanted to protect her. Something had snapped inside him when she'd fallen into his arms after seeing her friend lying so still upon the bed, her eyes open in death.

The image would haunt him for some time, he thought.

His conscience would prick him until the day he died.

How the hell could he have allowed two women to die in his home?

His wife . . . and he shuddered to think the second might have been Sarah.

Poor Mel.

He stared down at Sarah as she slept, reluctant to wake her, though he knew he must. The detective sergeant was still waiting.

God, but she was beautiful in slumber . . .

He'd made her sleep in his own bed—he hardly expected her to rest in the other after what had transpired there.

The last thing he wished to do was wake her . . . she slept so peacefully . . . like an angel, and he thought he could watch her this way forever . . .

Looking down at her now . . . he understood what it was about her that had seemed so familiar. She was like Mary in so many ways, though there wasn't the least family resemblance between them—except in the shape of their eyes. In temperament and wit, however—all of those things he had loved in his wife—she was much the same. And yet . . . the one way they were very different was that Peter could never see Mary perpetrating such a scheme as this for any reason whatsoever. Sarah had one thing his wife had not—pluck—and he chuckled inwardly at that observation.

Nor could he see Sarah hiding her feelings . . . couldn't see her moving her bed into the nursery . . . couldn't see her dwelling on her suspicions, rather than facing them. No, Sarah would march into his bloody office, box his ears, and ask him what the hell he was doing.

That was what he had needed all those years ago, when he'd buried himself so completely in his work that he'd neglected everything and everyone around him. He had needed someone to come in and tell him so—to assure him that even if his business failed, he would not fail them—that it didn't matter how much money he made, or where they lived, or who their friends were.

Instead, Mary had crawled away to her little sanctuary, and Peter had let her. He hadn't understood her turmoil at the time. And yet, staring down at the woman lying within his bed, it occurred to him for the first time ever . . . that perhaps he'd had reason to feel his own anger as well. No, it had not been the right thing to do . . . to let Mary slip away. And yet he was human, too, and he'd needed her to come to him as well.

And she never had.

He'd needed her to understand the incredible sense of responsibility he'd borne and had needed her to reassure him. He hadn't been fighting so bloody hard for the money. He'd struggled so hard to give his young wife the one thing that had always seemed out of his reach—a respectable name.

Mary had come from a wealthy and respectable family, and now that he thought about it, perhaps that in itself was part of the reason he had married her. He'd wanted the respect of his peers, something he had never received, though in all aspects he was their equal. His own father had worked himself into an early grave trying to gain it.

Instead, Peter had felt as though he'd dragged Mary down to his level.

Every time he'd looked at his wife, he'd thought about how lonely she must be. Her friends had drawn away. Invitations had dwindled to a minimum. And what had he gone and done? He'd drawn away from her as well, in guilt and in shame.

Damn it all to hell!

They'd been so bloody young.

They had hardly had a chance.

And yet . . . here in his bed was another . . .

Sarah was all the good things that Mary had been—but Sarah was more.

In the short time he had known her—God, but it was true—he was growing to love her. Sarah had somehow found a way into his closed heart. He'd watched her with his son, and his heart had swelled with undeniable emotion. She dealt with Christopher with genuine love—yes, love, he realized, now that he knew who she was. And now he understood her concern and her sincerity toward Christopher from the very first day.

God, and he'd watched her stand up to him and had admired the hell out of her even as she'd infuriated him. He shook his head. Even when she'd smacked him with her cane, he had chuckled to himself.

Crazy, but he smiled now just thinking of her in a fit of temper.

Damn, he wanted her.

But not just in his bed.

He wanted her for his wife.

"Sarah," he whispered, reaching out and placing a hand at her shoulder to wake her. "Sarah . . ."

She opened her eyes sleepily, still very sedated, and then closed them again. He had to wonder in that moment how much laudanum Ruth had given him to administer in her tea. He hoped Ruth knew her doses, but was certain she must, because she used the opium-laced serum for every ailment, it seemed. Peter suspected it was addictive, but what the hell did he know? It seemed to him that Ruth walked about in an endless anesthetic state. And God only knew, she didn't need the damned laudanum to draw her into that distant world of hers. The only time he knew his sister's thoughts, it seemed, was when she was railing at him.

"Sarah," he said, and shook her gently.

She tossed her head, as though trying to regain consciousness, and finally opened her eyes to stare up into his face. She said nothing, and Peter frowned at the dazed look in her eyes.

"The police are here," he warned her. "They've asked to speak with you."

Her lips parted to speak, but she couldn't seem to manage. She lapped at her lips with her pink tongue . . . and the sight of it filled his loins with instant heat, despite the gravity of their situation.

Damn, what the blazes did she do to him?

"Police?" she asked, almost drunkenly, and brushed the loose strands of hair from her face. She looked so like a little girl that he had the urge to bend forward and kiss her on the nose.

She filled him with such a myriad of emotions.

He reached out to touch her brow, his heart hammering at the flush of her skin beneath his fingertips.

"They wish to speak . . . with me?"

"Yes," he told her. "Shall I allow them in? Or can you manage to go to them?"

"I think I can go," she said, and tried to rise, but

stumbled forward onto her hands. "I . . . I'm a bit dizzy," she said, looking confused.

Peter hadn't warned her that he was going to sedate her, and suddenly he felt guilty for doing so.

"I think perhaps I should bring them here," he said, frowning as she righted herself once more.

She shook her head, trying to clear it, he thought. "I . . . I don't know why I feel . . . so strange."

And then her gaze met his. "Is it . . . is it about Mel?" she asked, and the question made her lips tremble. She squeezed her eyes shut, and Peter knew she was trying not to cry.

"Yes, Sarah."

She peered up at him once more, and her beautiful blue eyes were filled with pain and sorrow. "She . . . she never . . . she didn't deserve that!"

"No," Peter agreed, and reached out this time to brush the hair from her eyes. So soft. "She didn't."

But it wasn't Mel the culprit was after, if anyone, he reminded himself.

It was Sarah.

His gaze was drawn to the window. It had been left open last night . . . Had Mel opened it? Why would she have done so? This city was hardly the place to be leaving windows open late at night—not at street level.

Something cold went through him in that instant, something like a premonition . . .

Or a memory . . .

The window had been shattered in the nursery . . . but he recalled that it, too, had been left ajar. It had been shattered in the intruder's departure, not by his entrance.

"It's my fault," Sarah said, sobbing quietly. "If only I'd not asked her to sleep in my bed . . ."

"It's *not,* Sarah."

"That should have been me!" she cried.

Thank God it wasn't, he thought, though he refrained from saying it aloud. *"It's not your fault,"* he repeated with conviction.

She glared at him defiantly. "It should have been me!"

He understood her sentiments better than anyone could. How many times had he said the very same of himself over Mary? And still it wrenched his gut to hear the lament come from her lips.

She froze suddenly and peered into his eyes, her own filled with fear. "Oh, God, do they suspect me?" she asked, and shuddered.

He shook his head. He knew that of a certainty.

She took a breath of relief. "You?"

"Are you up to this?" he asked her, ignoring her question.

She looked down at the bed, shaking her head. "Yes . . . yes, I think so . . ." She sat up as best she could, wobbling a bit in her drugged state. Peter helped her to rise.

"Am I decent?" she asked him, inspecting herself.

"You are beautiful," he told her, and meant it from the bottom of his heart. She was wrapped in a simple woolen dress—*drab* was more the word for it. And her hair was mussed from sleep, her eyes swollen with tears. The tip of her nose was more red than pink, and her cheeks a bit too pale. To him she was the most beautiful creature he had ever laid eyes upon.

''Are you ready?'' he asked her.

Sarah nodded, and Peter rose from the bed, determined to protect her at all costs.

No matter what she decided to confess, he would support her.

Chapter 25

⟨⟨⟨◦⟩⟩⟩

66"Tell me again why you asked Miss Frank to sleep in your room, Miss . . . Miss . . . What did you say your name was?'' the detective asked her. He tilted a slightly narrow-eyed look at her. "It is Miss, isn't it?"

"Yes . . . yes, it is." Sarah's gaze went at once to Peter, who was leaning against the doorframe, as though ready to escort their inquisitors out at any instant. Sarah was still a bit groggy from her nap and wasn't certain how to respond to their swaggering attitudes.

Peter nodded, urging her to go on. By his expression, and his stance, it was obvious to Sarah that he didn't care for them in his home, that he only tolerated them because he must.

Judging by the looks on *their* faces, however, they were all too happy to be here once more.

Sarah felt an instant dislike for them and their prejudgment of Peter—never mind that it hadn't been so long ago that she had been guilty of judging him too.

Or perhaps it was just that very thing . . . that the accusations written all over their faces reminded her of her own sin against him, and it filled her with guilt and regret.

"Woodard," she replied, her hand going to her temple. God, but she was getting a headache. She felt hungover somehow, without having had the first drop of wine. It must be because she'd cried herself to sleep, because her nose was still stuffy and her head cloudy, as well.

The detective stood there, staring at her as though he thought her guilty, too. But then, Sarah supposed they always had that particular look in their eyes—she had just never been in a position to be its recipient.

Poor Peter to have to suffer it once more.

Her gaze returned to him standing at the door. He was an imposing figure of a man, with his height and his dark features.

It had been so easy to believe him guilty.

Though she now knew he had been falsely accused, she *had* thought him guilty as the devil. How did she tell these men, with Peter present . . . that she had thought the same of him as they did . . . enough to have lied to come into his home . . . enough to have endangered her best friend's life?

Tears pricked at her eyes as she thought of Mel.

She despised the smug look on the detectives' faces, and wanted to bolt from the bed where she sat to slap the smirks from their lips.

"Go on, Sarah," Peter urged her, his voice soft but encouraging.

Sarah's gaze met his once more. He knew exactly what she was contemplating, she felt.

"Tell them," he urged her.

Sarah averted her gaze and clasped her hands before her, praying silently that she would not harm him with her confession to these bigoted men.

She knew why they loathed him. It wasn't so difficult to see. He was one of them, and he had *dared* to make more of himself. He had dared to rise above his birth. She knew Peter's beginnings . . . remembered from Mary's letters. His father had been a man of moderate means, who had given all he had possessed to his son. He had sent him to college to study and had left him every penny after his death, in hopes that Peter might make him proud.

And yet . . . didn't these men see that Peter had suffered for his successes?

Didn't they see that he would never fit in with those whose money was old and respected?

She hardly envied Peter's position at all. All the things that she had taken for granted, he struggled with. Even as a woman with means, though she suffered some discrimination over the simple fact that she was not born a man, she knew it was not the same as dealing with those clannish ideals.

Sarah inhaled a breath, knowing she had no choice but to cooperate with these men, and said, "I . . . I asked her to sleep there because . . ." She dared to look Peter straight in the eyes, and continued, "Because I thought Mr. Holland was responsible for my cousin's death.''

They turned toward Peter, both of them, their smirks now becoming leers. Sarah wanted so badly to throw them out of her room, but this wasn't her house, and she hadn't the right. Nor had Peter, she realized more than a little resentfully.

They said nothing, and Sarah continued. ''I am ashamed to say I lied coming into his home,'' she revealed to them truthfully. ''And I asked Mel to take my place last night because . . . well, it was my intent to search his library and his office.''

''For what, Miss Woodard? What were you searching for?''

Sarah had yet to tell Peter. He hadn't asked. ''My cousin's journal,'' she told them.

The detective lifted a brow. ''The missing journal?''

''I thought it would shed some light on Mary's death.''

One of the detectives began to scribble notes, while the other continued to ask questions. ''And why did you feel the need to switch places with Miss Frank? Did you feel yourself in danger?''

''Not in danger, no,'' she replied at once, and frowned at them.

''You must have,'' the detective said, dismissing her denial. ''Did you feel you were being watched?'' he asked as well.

Sarah narrowed her eyes at him, hating that he was putting words in her mouth and quite ready to say so. She would have liked to tell them to go to the devil right now, and simply not answer any more questions, but she wanted Mel's murderer uncovered. "Someone *was* watching the window from across the street," she told them. "I noticed them first sometime before dusk, and they never left the alley, so I called for Mel to come."

The detective's brow lifted. "So you have no doubt this was not some simple rape or a robbery, then?"

Sarah gasped in horror at his question. Rape? She hadn't even thought that a possibility! "Oh, God, no, was she . . . ?"

He shook his head. "There is no evidence to verify that fact, no," he answered, and Sarah glowered at him for even bringing up the horrible possibility.

The detective who had been scribbling stopped now and went to the window, peering out. "You saw them from the window next door?" he asked her.

"Yes," Sarah replied.

"These rooms are seated at the corner of the house," Peter explained. "Her window faces Twelfth Street."

"So you left Miss Frank to sleep there in your room?" the other asked her.

"Yes," Sarah answered.

"And what time was this, do you recall?"

Sarah shook her head. "I'm . . . not certain. I . . . I didn't look at the clock. But it must have been late because Mel didn't come right away, and when she did . . . the house was already dark. Everyone seemed long abed."

"And where did you go from here?" the detective

asked her, while Peter silently looked on from the doorway. The other detective came away from the window and began to scribble his notes once more. Sarah took a deep breath. Not that she would consider lying about something so important, but she dreaded speaking the truth, and she had no doubt where his questions were leading.

She lifted her chin, swallowing. "The library."

"And how long did you remain there?"

Sarah suddenly couldn't meet the detective's gaze. Nor did she dare look at Peter.

Her heart hammered ruthlessly against her breast.

She wasn't stupid; she knew exactly what her confession would mean.

"Miss Woodard?" he prompted, his tone firm.

"Sarah," Peter called her.

Sarah looked up into his eyes, and he shook his head, telling her without words that she needn't speak a word, that he wouldn't tell if she chose not to say. His instinct to protect her moved her deeply, but she knew full well that he would be the one to answer for Mel's death if she didn't speak up now to absolve him. These men were only too willing to point the finger at him once again. She could see it in their expressions, tell by their arrogant stances. They were gathering their information against him . . .

And yet if she told them the truth . . . if she admitted where she had been all of the night . . . her reputation would be ruined forever.

Given the two choices—Peter's life or her honor—there were no decisions to be made at all.

She took a deep breath. "I was there all night," she disclosed, and held Peter's gaze. She could see in his expression that he was stunned by her confession.

The detective who had asked the question lifted a brow when she turned to look at him once more.

"All night?" the other asked her, lifting his head from his notes.

She lifted her chin a bit higher. "Yes, sir," she replied more firmly.

"Sarah," Peter cautioned her.

Sarah chose to ignore his warning.

"And did you perchance find what you were searching for . . . in this library?"

"No," she replied.

"What, then, were you doing in Mr. Holland's library all night?"

Sarah faced the detective squarely and said, "I was with Peter."

Both of them stared at her.

Sarah's gaze reverted to Peter. His eyes were closed suddenly and she couldn't read them.

" 'With'?" he asked her. "Define 'with,' Miss Woodard," he added with cold disdain.

"I think she has answered quite enough," Peter said suddenly, stepping in.

It was clear to Sarah that her disclosure had done more than surprise them. She knew anger when she spied it.

"Saved once again, eh, Holland?" said the detective who had been scribbling.

"Are you willing to testify to that fact, Miss Woodard?" the other snapped at her.

"Yes," Sarah answered without hesitation, looking him in the eyes. "I am."

"I think it's time you two ran along to gather your dirty money, don't you think?" Peter asked them coldly.

Sarah held her breath. It was a bold reference to the state of corruption of the New York police force, and she winced at the murderous expressions on both detectives' faces.

"I hope you realize what you are getting yourself into, Miss Woodard," the one who had been scribbling told her.

"The truth, I hope," Sarah answered.

"Gentlemen," Peter said, enunciating the word as though it were a farce. He stepped away from the door, essentially dismissing them, wordlessly ordering them out.

Sarah released her breath only as they turned to go.

"I trust you'll see your own way out," he told them both as they passed him.

"Lucky bastard, is what you are," the scribbler said low, no small amount of disgust evident in his tone. "Lucky bastard!"

And then they were gone, leaving Sarah and Peter alone.

"My head aches," Sarah said.

"Probably the laudanum," Peter told her. "I gave you a bit in your tea earlier to help you sleep."

She lifted her brow. "That explains it."

Peter couldn't believe what she had done.

"Those men are quite rude," she said.

"They don't particularly like me," Peter said in agreement. He couldn't believe the sacrifice she had made for him today. Essentially she had blackened her name with her confession. He had no doubt, given a few dollars, those corrupt little bastards would leak the story to the yellow press. And perhaps they'd even do it for free—they loathed him enough. But damn, he hadn't expected Sarah to give up so much for him. He'd been bracing himself for another investigation of which he would be the focus. He wouldn't have blamed Sarah in the least for protecting her honor; he was willing to do the same for her.

He was moved beyond words at what she had done—and without hesitation.

He didn't know what to say. He stood there feeling responsible once again.

"Sarah . . . you didn't have to do that," he told her after a moment, breaking the silence between them. He closed the door behind him as he entered the room. "But I thank you."

"Yes, I did have to," she replied, holding his gaze. He admired her for that, for never shying away. "It was the truth, Peter. I couldn't have lied."

He couldn't let her suffer over this. If she would let him, he would make it right. "You realize what you have done to your reputation?"

Sarah shrugged, and he wanted so much to take her once more into his arms, to kiss those beautiful lips and put the color back into those pale cheeks.

The memory of their lovemaking made him burn even now.

God, but how could she do that to him? Make him want her even at a time like this?

He came to the bedside and stared down at her. She turned her face away, and he went to his knees beside the bed.

"Sarah," he whispered.

She turned those beautiful eyes on him, and he held his breath as he gazed into them.

Those eyes were so filled with pain.

He wanted to make everything better for her, but he seemed to turn everyone's life inside out. He couldn't seem to make even himself happy, much less another human being—except for Christopher. But Christopher was so easy to please. His son accepted everything without fail. He never complained and his spirit was a joyful one. He had tried so hard to take Christopher's example in life.

He was willing to try to make Sarah happy.

He *wanted* to try.

He wanted the chance.

He *needed* to be the one to put the smile back on her lovely face.

He needed to make things right, once and for all.

"Sarah," he said with a bit more courage. His heart beat at a frantic pace as he tried to form the words.

Her gaze remained on him, beautiful blue and full of something other than pain . . . Dare he hope she might feel something for him, too?

God, he wanted that—with all his heart, he realized in that instant.

"Marry me," he asked her. "Let me make it right."

She sucked in a breath, as though she would cry out, but she didn't and tears filled her eyes.

She didn't answer for the longest moment, merely stared, and Peter held his breath for her answer.

He wanted this suddenly—more than he wanted to breathe.

He wanted Sarah Woodard as his wife.

He wanted one more chance.

And this time . . .

God . . . this time . . .

He thought he loved her.

No, he didn't think it! *He did,* he was certain.

The evidence was in the pit of his stomach as he waited for her to reply.

If she said no, he didn't know what he would do.

She tilted her head and reached out to touch her fingers to his chin, and Peter closed his eyes. His heart hammered violently against his ribs.

She blinked down at him. "No," she answered.

The single word was like a punch to his gut. He couldn't blame her and yet—goddamn it!

He opened his eyes to find a tear sliding down her cheek, and he swallowed, and caught his hand before he could reach out to wipe her sorrow from her face. His stomach turned, and his heart felt suddenly too weighted for his body.

"I understand," he said, his jaw tautening, but he suddenly couldn't stay in her presence any longer.

"I should let you rest," he said, and rose from his knees, releasing his hands at his sides.

He left her quickly.

Why had he thought she would agree to it?

With his past, what had he to offer any woman . . . except his heart . . . and his goddamned money . . . though why the hell should Sarah believe in him when he had failed Mary so miserably?

She didn't need his money.

He had nothing to give.

Chapter 26

I t was a beautiful day for a funeral.

The sun was shining through the budding trees—no shade because the oaks were not yet adorned in their verdant green coats, but Sarah was certain it would be a perfect place on a hot summer day to come and visit.

She listened to the drone of the pastor's voice as he gave his graveside service, hardly absorbing a word he spoke. She was aware only of the hands upon her shoulders, strong hands, Peter's hands. He stood behind her, as though bracing her . . . as though he thought she would crumple if he released her.

And she might.

She stared at the freshly laid soil, so rich and moist—dampened with a billion tears.

Mellie would have loved the flowers Peter had chosen for her grave site—a brilliant display of violet and white tulips that made her think of spring in all its splendor. How fitting that the collection should remind her of a time of renewal, because she chose to believe that Mellie's spirit had been reborn into a place where there would be no suffering and no unhappiness. No loneliness. It was in that place she thought of Mary too . . . and her uncle. And perhaps they were all together now, sending her love and goodwill.

That was the way Sarah chose to see it.

Mellie's parents had passed away years before, and she hadn't a man in her life, or children to grieve at her grave, but Sarah knew her presence would be greatly missed by all who had loved her so dearly. Melissa Frank had touched the lives of so many people. She had given of herself so freely and generously that she hadn't had time for a life of her own. How many lives had she touched at the Institute alone?

Sarah would never forget her.

Everyone Sarah had ever loved had left her— through no fault of their own, but they had—her parents when she'd been just a child, and then her uncle and Mary, too.

Now Mellie.

It had never been easy for Sarah to open up to anyone. She'd closed up almost completely after her parents' deaths. She remembered watching her uncle and cousin together from a safe distance, never feeling quite a part of their world. Her uncle had persisted with her for years, until at last he'd drawn her out. Sarah had been too young when her parents had died, and so she didn't remember a bond with them

at all, but she remembered vividly the day she had
first *felt* part of a family . . .

Her age, she was unsure of, but she thought perhaps she might have been eleven. She had refused
to sit for a family portrait, believing that her uncle
had asked her to join them only out of the kindness
of his heart. And so she had pretended illness every
day until the portrait was finished, and then she had
miraculously recovered. Her uncle had never forced
her to sit with them—and instead asked her to watch
from her safe little perch, telling her stories that had
kept her in the room. Sarah had stayed, wishing the
entire time that she were sitting at his side, along
with Mary—and feeling a little betrayed that he had
given up so easily when she had weaseled out of the
sittings.

And then had come the day he'd unveiled the finished portrait. To Sarah's shock and her joy, there
she had been, sitting beside him through the magic
of the artist's brush.

Seeing them together had made a difference,
somehow—though she realized much later that it
had been evident all the time. His love for both *his
girls* had been in his every gesture, and Mary had
never begrudged her a single smile or hug from her
dear father.

They had been her family.

How could she simply come forward now and
steal what was rightfully Mary's?

It didn't matter.

Even if she could do such a thing . . . Peter had
only asked her to marry him in order to salvage her

reputation. Why should they both suffer when she had made that decision as clearly as he? She could have saved herself.

But she hadn't.

So why should he marry her now when he didn't love her?

The last thing Sarah wished was to end like Mary, bitter and alone despite her vows.

No, she had made the right decision.

Her gaze scanned the cemetery. Only a fistful of people here, most she didn't know—friends of Mel's from the Institute. When they glanced her way, Sarah felt a stab of guilt, as though somehow it was her fault that Mel was no longer with them. So she couldn't face them. She avoided their gazes, scanning the street ahead of her.

Reporters.

Peter had guarded her from them when they'd first arrived, and they'd remained at a distance, heeding his warning glances in their direction. Sarah knew, however, that they did so only out of respect for the service being held. As soon as it was over and they attempted to leave, she was certain they would hound them once more.

And she wasn't wrong.

Peter had literally to shield her from their assault of questions as they departed—never mind that many of their inquiries were directed at him. He ignored them all and held her by both shoulders, guiding her out from the cemetery and into his waiting calash.

Once they were inside the carriage, he sat beside her, but turned to peer outside.

Sarah didn't know what to say to break the silence between them.

It was an uneasy silence that left her feeling empty and lonely in a way she had never known before.

She had insulated herself so well against everyone, except for a few . . . and now they were gone, and the one person she could turn to was the one person she had no right to.

He was Mary's husband.

He was Christopher's father.

And she had begrudged Mary both.

"I didn't realize you were searching for her journals," he said abruptly.

Sarah peered up into his face, swallowing her grief.

His blue eyes lacked any luster this morning; they reminded her of a dreary, foggy morning, one that promised eternal rain.

"Yes," she replied, and averted her gaze. "I had hoped they would reveal something of Mary's death." There was no point in lying any longer, or in keeping the truth from him.

He might as well know it all.

"I never cared to read it."

She turned again to look at him, and there was a new glitter in his eyes.

Tears?

"Why not?"

"I suppose I was afraid of what I might learn," he answered honestly.

Sarah hoped he would continue, but wasn't certain what to say to make him do so. He had said last night that he had failed Mary. Her gut told her that his statement harbored a wealth of information, but she didn't dare pry. It was one thing to hear it in Mary's words, but another entirely to hear it from his own two lips. After all she had put him through, she didn't dare pry.

"I promised her so much that I never delivered, Sarah," he said, and peered down at the floor of the carriage. He slumped down into the seat, cupping his chin in his hand.

Sarah wanted to reach out and take that hand into her own, to hold it in her lap while he spoke. She didn't dare, however. She clasped her own hands together, instead, and closed her eyes to listen, hoping he would continue.

"The truth is, I didn't kill my wife. I swear to God, Sarah."

"I believe you," Sarah assured him at once.

"I didn't kill her, but I took away her spirit and her joy. So in a sense, I might as well have." Sarah watched him, listening, her heart thumping mercilessly. His sincerity and heartfelt emotion were in his every word, and she wanted to reach out and take him into her arms.

"I'm just as guilty as that bastard with the bloody knife," he added, and turned to look into her eyes.

"We both failed her, Peter," Sarah murmured, and she did reach up to take his hand from his face. "She was like my sister, and I turned her away when she most needed me."

Their gazes held.

He squeezed her fingers just a little, and with it, the breath from her lungs.

His gaze fell to their clasped hands.

Sarah followed it, blinking at the sight of them together—his so much bigger and so much darker, hers smaller and pale.

She was aware that his hands shook . . . hers as well . . . but she didn't care.

She closed her eyes and put her heart in that gentle embrace. And suddenly every sensation in her body was centered in their joined hands.

Together they lifted their hands between them, entwining their fingers, feeling every nuance of every breath and every heartbeat in that gentle touch.

She opened her eyes to find that his were closed, and she swallowed convulsively at the raw emotion that registered on his face.

She turned away and jerked her hand free, her heart hammering fiercely.

She couldn't let herself feel this . . . couldn't let herself take the *one* thing she had denied Mary.

How *just* would that be?

Not at all, she decided, and turned to stare at the floor of the carriage.

What she needed, now more than ever . . . was to find out who was responsible for Mary's and Mellie's deaths. Because she knew in her heart the two were connected, and she needed to know Mary's son would be safe.

She needed those things more than anything, and she needed to go home . . .

Before she lost her heart and soul to a man she hadn't a right to.

Ruth's face was florid with anger. "She's a liar, Peter!"

"Yes, she lied, but not with malicious intent," he said, defending Sarah. "She was merely seeking the truth."

"And what else?" Ruth returned caustically. "She's here looking for something, I'll warrant."

Peter held his tongue. It was Sarah's place to say, he thought. Nor did it make him feel particularly good to say she had been searching for evidence against him. And yet he understood why she had done all that she'd done, and he couldn't blame her. He couldn't say that he would have handled the situation the same. It was his way to confront issues directly, and he might have come marching into the house demanding answers, rather than disguise himself as a blind teacher. And yet Sarah's motives had been honorable enough. She had been looking out for his son's best interest, even if not his.

"Why are you defending her?" Ruth accused him, narrowing her eyes in condemnation. "She doesn't deserve a defense!"

Peter's jaw tautened.

"You love her, don't you?"

He gave Ruth a pointed look. "If I love her, Ruth, it is no crime."

Ruth threw up her hands in defeat. "You never learn your lessons, do you?" she said to him, and turned away. She stood there an instant, facing the door, and Peter refused to defend himself for loving Sarah. She swung about to face him. "And Mary's cousin, no less! How can you?"

Peter responded to her questions with silence. There was no reasoning with Ruth when she became so irate and irrational. He would simply let her vent, and then if she wanted explanations later, and asked him reasonably, he would answer her as well as he was able.

"I tried to tell you she was trouble, Peter," Ruth reminded him bitterly, "and mark my words when I tell you this is not over. I have a terrible premonition about that woman. Send her away," Ruth begged. "Send her away now before it's too late!"

"Ruth," Peter began, and tilted her a concerned look. She was acting strangely, he thought, almost desperately. And why she should be so frightened of Sarah, he had no inkling. He wouldn't send Sarah away. "No," he told her firmly. "Sarah is welcome in this home as long as she wishes to stay, and you will help me to make her feel so," he demanded of her.

"No!" Ruth shouted. "For Christopher's sake, I will not!"

"For Christopher's sake?" She wasn't making sense. He wondered if the laudanum she took so often had clouded her thoughts. "Sarah would never harm Christopher," he assured her. "Everything she has done, she has done for my son."

Ruth shook her head, and there were tears in her eyes. "You don't understand. Her very presence here endangers him."

"Sarah would never harm him," Peter maintained.

"No, but someone else may!" she shouted at him. "Don't you think it rather coincidental that Mary is murdered, and then nothing for six years—all is quiet until Sarah arrives? And now Mel Frank is dead, and who is next?" she reasoned with him. "Send her away, Peter," she begged.

Peter shook his head, denying her request. Something was definitely not right, but he refused to believe Sarah responsible. And the last thing he was going to do was send her away when it was possible she was in danger.

"No," he said.

"Confound it!" Ruth cursed him, slamming her hands down upon his desk. "You are going to regret this, Peter! We are all going to regret this!" she swore, and pivoted on her heels, sobbing.

"Ruth," he said, surging up from his chair, trying to reason with her, but she bolted out the door. "Ruth!" he shouted, wanting to reassure her, but she didn't stop and he let her go.

He wanted to assure her that he would *not* fail them again, but he couldn't blame her for being afraid. His gaze fell to the glass of port sitting before him on the desk and he lifted it up and hurled it against the wall, contents and all, shattering glass and spraying sweet liquor with such force that a droplet landed on his lip. He didn't lick it off, but swiped it away angrily.

Damn, but he would not fail them again.

Chapter 27

Sarah had been sitting, staring blankly for the past half hour, trying to find an outlet for her anger, rather than allowing herself to feel the weight of defeat.

Two days after the funeral, they had received another visit from the police department, bearing news that they had closed the investigation into Mel's murder without bothering to try to find her murderer.

How could they possibly do such a thing?

Did it suddenly no longer matter who the murderer was now that Peter had an alibi?

Was it only a valid investigation if the defendant was someone of Peter's means?

Did Mellie's life simply not matter because her family name was not Belmont or Vanderbilt?

They had concluded that Mel was the victim of a break-in . . . just as they had with Mary . . . because the bloody window had been left unlocked and open for anyone to come in. Sarah wanted to know what thief came in and suffocated a woman, and then turned again to go, leaving everything of value still in its place!

What bloody sense was there in that?

How could they leave it at that so easily?

The injustice of it all staggered and angered her beyond words.

Peter was watching her, frowning. "I'm sorry," he offered. "I know she was dear to you."

Sarah nodded.

It was difficult to look him in the eyes just now, knowing she must go.

There wasn't anything left for her to do here. Peter was innocent, she had no doubt. He was aware of any danger to Christopher now, and he would guard his son well, she had no doubt.

It was the most difficult decision she had ever made.

Uncomfortable with his scrutiny, she stared down at the bed.

"I'm leaving, Peter."

"Leaving!"

"Yes," Sarah said, and her eyes stung. "I think, perhaps, I should go . . ."

Why did it hurt so badly even to think of leaving?

Why did she suddenly wish she'd never met him at all?

Why did it feel like her life was over?

It was certainly not!

What was wrong with her?

"Sarah," he said, and stepped forward, then froze. "Don't go . . ."

Sarah swallowed and looked up into his eyes. And

in that instant it was like peering into a looking glass, so familiar were the emotions evident there.

Their gazes held, locked.

He couldn't let her go.

He'd be damned if he'd simply stand here and watch her walk out of his life.

His gut wrenched at the mere possibility of losing her.

Never in his life had he needed someone more—*needed!* And that realization scared the holy hell out of him. Not even facing his inquisition years before had terrified him more. In the short time he had known her, Sarah had become a vital part of his home and more . . . his heart.

He'd be damned if he'd just let her go without a bloody fight.

He wasn't certain what came over him in that instant, but he shrugged out of his coat, all the while staring at her. He wanted her to know how much he loved her—how much he needed her. He unbuttoned his collar, then the rest of his shirt, and pulled it off with purpose. He threw it on the floor.

"What are you doing?"

"What does it appear?"

"It appears to me you have gone wholly mad!"

Probably.

But he didn't give a bloody damn.

"Peter!" she shrieked as he moved toward her. She sprang up from the bed.

"Mary is dead," he told her cruelly, "and I am not." He damned well wasn't going to allow her to use that as a barrier between them.

"Peter!" she cried out as he closed the distance between them.

She turned to scramble over the bed.

He caught her and took her into his arms. "And neither are you," he told her, catching her at the back of the neck and cradling her face in his hands, forcing her to look him in the eyes.

"We mustn't!" she sobbed.

"Why? Tell me *why* we mustn't. And it damned well better be for better reason than because of Mary, because Mary is dead!"

She stood silently, staring up at him, her eyes filling with tears.

Christ, he wanted to kiss them away, wanted to make love to her more than he'd ever wanted anything in his whole damned life.

"Tell me why!" he demanded, and bent to kiss her beautiful mouth, just a gentle peck, but he couldn't seem to help himself. He craved the taste of her fiercely.

"Sarah," he beseeched her.

Tears stung Sarah's eyes.

His grip on her hair was just a little too tight and his embrace a little too rough, but she couldn't voice an objection to save her life. With the mere memory of his kisses, she melted into his arms and silently begged for him to take them once more. She couldn't give them, didn't dare, but she yearned for the touch of his mouth on her own, gentle but insistent.

"Don't go," he begged her, and Sarah closed her eyes, ignoring the pull of her heart.

She didn't *want* to go.

She never wanted to go.

Craving his kiss, she dared to turn her lips up to his, silently begging him to taste her mouth.

He didn't disappoint her.

Sarah cried at the feel of his mouth. The touch of his lips was like manna to her soul. Tilting her head, she parted her lips and dared to slide her hands up and about his neck, clinging to him.

"Peter," she said, and whimpered softly as he deepened the kiss.

His response was a low moan deep in the back of his throat, and Sarah's heart leapt at the raw sound of it. That he wanted her was unmistakable; she could feel his desire clearly in the hardness of his body.

She didn't protest—couldn't—when his hand went about her waist and he laid her back on the bed, following her down.

She couldn't stop it.

Didn't want to.

She hadn't the will.

Her body convulsed, begging for a lover's embrace as he laid his body down upon her, pressing her into the bed. And Sarah moaned with delight at the feel of him covering her so possessively.

"I need you, Sarah . . ."

He pressed his arousal against her, making his meaning clear, and the words spewed from Sarah's lips. "I need you, too," she whispered, and cried out softly as he increased the pressure of his hips. "I do . . ."

That was all Peter needed to hear.

He hadn't gotten to this point in life by letting opportunities pass him by—and this was one such opportunity for which he'd rather die trying than lose.

He wanted to make her his, wholly his.

Sarah was everything he had ever wanted in a woman and more. He wasn't going to give her up, not unless she chose to go, and he didn't intend to let her choose without a battle.

And he wasn't going to fight fairly.

His hands stroked the curve of her thighs, her hips, encircled her waist, reveling in every beautiful inch of her lovely body, while his mouth ravaged her lips with a hunger he could not contain.

Sweet, beautiful lips . . .

The taste of her dizzied him.

The scent of her intoxicated him . . . drove him to the brink of madness.

Like a man possessed, he traced every curve and every hollow of her body, wanting to know her. He made promises with every touch, and hoped she read them with her heart.

If she left him, he was going to make damned certain she never forgot him.

And if she stayed . . . he would be sure she never regretted it for an instant she breathed.

He pressed his lips against her brow, and whispered, "I think I love you, Sarah . . ."

Sarah's heart jolted.

The beat of her heart thundered in her ears. Her hands trembled as she reached out to cup his face and hold it in her hands. He had spoken it so low, barely a whisper . . . so she couldn't know for sure.

Had she only imagined it?

Dare she believe it was true?

He took both her wrists in one hand and drew them away from his face, smiling down at her. Releasing her hands, he moved to one side of her and urged her over onto her stomach, then pinned her hands to the bed above her head. Sarah thought she would die when he bent to nibble on the back of her neck, tiny kisses interspersed with bites and a caress of his tongue to soothe it. Her hair was still in pins, but she didn't care that he mussed it . . .

Didn't care about anything at all . . .

All she cared about this instant was his breath so hot against her flesh. When he released her hands to unfasten the buttons at her back, Sarah didn't move . . . didn't dare . . . She lay frozen upon the bed, her breath coming in soft pants, her heart hammering so fiercely she thought it might burst.

I think I love you, Sarah . . .

The echo of his words made her heart leap yet again.

Unlike the first time in the library, his hands were gentle as they worked the buttons of her dress, and he bent to kiss her bare skin after he loosened each one, peeling back her dress slowly, sending shivers down her spine with every touch of his hot lips against her skin.

When he had her fully unbuttoned, he slid the bodice from her shoulders and drew it from beneath her. Sarah gasped at the feel of it as it slid off her arms, and beneath her. Her breasts spilled free from her corset, and then he started to work on the lower buttons at her back. One by one he unfastened them, and Sarah swallowed convulsively as he bared her.

The first time he had undressed her it had been under a cloak of shadows, but just now, he revealed her flesh to the light. Sarah held her breath at the wicked pleasure it gave her to give herself to him so fully.

"So beautiful," he murmured at her back, and it sent quivers down Sarah's spine. She gasped as he pulled off her dress at last, sliding it from her, and then her undergarments—so skillfully and efficiently, as though he'd removed a thousand before.

The thought gave her a twinge of jealousy.

She didn't wish to think of him with anyone else.

And then suddenly she was wholly bared beneath his scrutiny, and was keenly aware that he was not. Without warning, he slid down to nibble at her bottom, and Sarah bit her lip as he moved lower still to taste her so wickedly.

She clawed desperately at the bedclothes.

God, but he was a wicked man!

And Lord help her, she loved all that he was doing to her.

She reveled in every touch of his hands . . . every caress of his mouth upon her body . . .

"Turn around," he whispered, and Sarah's heart lurched a little at the command.

The notion of lying there fully exposed to him both terrified and thrilled her at once. She did as she was told, couldn't seem to help herself. With merely the sound of his voice, he did things to her . . . to her mind, body, and soul.

Her heart beat fiercely as she turned around and her breath caught at the hunger evident in his eyes. Cool air caressed her breasts, while his eyes, like smoldering blue flames, bore down on her, inspecting her, warming her as no fire ever could.

A slow smile turned his lips as he reached down and began to undo the buttons of his trousers.

Her heart jolted a little harder, and she held her breath as she watched him bare himself to her, not daring even to blink.

Peeling open his trousers, he pulled them down, shrugged out of them as she watched, and then his drawers followed, until he stood before her as naked as Adam.

God, but he was a beautiful man—his body perfectly formed, from his wide shoulders to his chest and narrow waist.

He fell to his knees, and Sarah thought she would die with anticipation of his touch. She knew, from the things he had done to her the first time, what he intended, and her body quivered at the mere thought.

Heat began to coil deep within her, a delicious thread that ignited at the promise of his kisses.

It was wicked, what he craved . . . wicked, what she wanted.

Peering down between her bared breasts, she watched him open his mouth, felt his lips upon her, and her head fell backward in surrender as he made love to her with his mouth.

Sarah had never dreamed she could crave his

touch so deeply . . . Somewhere at her core, she ached for him to fill her, touch her deep into her very womb!

She loved him—God, but she loved him!

Forgive me, Mary, she thought, and if she spoke the plea aloud, Peter ruthlessly ignored it.

Thank God! Because if he dared to stop now . . . if he walked away this instant, Sarah thought she would weep.

She needed him to fill her . . . needed him to make love to her . . . needed him to need her . . .

She needed him to love her.

Chapter 28

H e hadn't meant to say it.

The words had slipped from his tongue, but entirely too easily, and damn it all, he didn't wish to recall them!

He did love her.

And he wanted more than life to please her.

More than anything, he wanted that.

For the first time in his life, this wasn't about his own pleasure. It was about hers.

He wanted to sink into her, feel her wrapped about him, hold her face in his hands and kiss her lips until she moaned sweetly into his mouth. He wanted to taste the sweet elixir of her passion . . . wanted to feel her body tremble beneath him.

He wanted to pleasure her until she cried out his name.

More than anything, he wanted to hear her whisper *I love you*, though he knew it was more than he could ask.

He would be content just to hear her cry out in pleasure.

He reveled in the taste of her, lost himself in the throes of her passion, and tore himself away only when the throb of his own body grew insistent and painful. He drew himself up then, looking down at her as she lay on the bed.

Her eyes had been closed, but she opened them now and peered up at him. They were glazed with desire. Her skin was flushed deep rose, her lips bruised from his kisses. And he had the sudden primeval thought that he would kill any man who dared touch her this way.

He bent forward, pinned her between his arms, and took her mouth with a ferocity he hadn't realized he could possess.

Sarah closed her eyes, reveling in the taste of him. He pressed her once more into the bed, and her body cried out in impatience. She shuddered at the feel of him so hard against her softness and shifted her hips to seek him. She didn't wait for him to enter her, didn't care that it seemed bold. Reaching with total abandon, she gripped his buttocks in her hands and thrust forward, drawing him so deeply into her that she felt him surge to the hilt. He cried out and the sound of it set Sarah's body on fire.

He began to move, and it was the most delicious sensation she had ever imagined.

"Peter," she cried out softly, but she couldn't think any longer.

His arms encircled her, embracing her, while his

lips and tongue caressed her face, her lips, her eyes, her nose . . .

She wanted to be with him always . . .

Wanted him never to stop.

She dared to open her heart.

"I love you, Sarah," he whispered once more, and her body exploded with pleasure. Sarah had never known such bliss existed. He cried out as she shuddered beneath him, and he lunged forward just once more. "I love you," he whispered, and found his own release, filling her, trembling as he held her.

Sarah clung to him, and never wanted to let go.

She clutched his head to her and dared to whisper against his ear.

"I love you, too."

And she smiled as he sighed against her throat.

Sarah hardly slept all night.

Impossible to sleep with all that she had yet to contemplate.

She and Peter had not left his room even for the evening meal. They'd made love yet again, and then had crawled under the covers to sleep. But lying next to him, Sarah could scarce even close her eyes.

He made her feel alive in a way she hadn't ever known—every breath, every heartbeat magnified, every pore of her skin yearning for his touch.

It was impossible to deny this feeling that overwhelmed her.

Sarah thought she would die if she couldn't wake in his arms every morning for the rest of her life.

And yet . . . Mary had once felt the very same . . . and for this very man.

How could Sarah awake each morn and look into his eyes, and know that she had disapproved of him for her cousin—and in the strongest manner possible?

It was because of him that she and Mary had not spoken ever again.

No, she amended to herself . . . it was because of her.

It had been *her* own insecurities that had driven them apart. She had been terrified of losing her best friend—so terrified that she had pushed her away.

What sense did that make?

And now was she doing it again?

Was she so afraid of losing someone else in her life that she wasn't even willing to let him in?

Was she simply using her guilt as a shield to keep him at bay?

She had so much to think about.

Peering over at Peter, she saw he was still asleep, his expression peaceful in slumber, and she wanted to touch her hand to his cheek, but didn't dare.

Carefully extricating herself from his embrace, she slipped out of bed and quickly dressed, pondering the man she had grown to love.

He never seemed to bat a lash at her fits of fury. He faced her with calm resolve, and knowing him now, she wondered that anyone could ever think him capable of harming another human being. It only took a single look at him and Christopher together to know for certain that deep down he was a gentle man, even if at first glance he seemed intimidating. She had never once heard him raise his voice to his son.

Needing time alone to think, she stole away from the room as quietly as she was able, closing the door gently behind her.

Chapter 29

Peter awoke with a smile on his face.

Reaching out groggily, he clasped Sarah about the waist, vaguely aware that the shape didn't quite fit, but too sleepy to open his eyes. He dragged her closer and kissed her on the nose.

"Yuck!" Christopher cried out, and Peter's eyes flew wide to find his son struggling to be free of his embrace. He swiped his face with his little hands. Peter released him and he sat on the bed. "Yucky!" he exclaimed once more.

Peter chuckled, though his gaze at once scanned the room, searching for Sarah. He frowned when he didn't find her there.

"Morning, sport," he said.

"Mornin', Daddy."

He wondered how long she'd been away, and where she'd gone.

"What are you doing here, Christopher?" he asked his son.

"The boogeyman was in my room again last night!"

His son's imagination was quite vivid and quite normal, but that was all it was, his imagination, and Peter had yet to be able to convince him of that fact.

"Not him again?"

"Yup!" Christopher said, nodding.

"Christopher," Peter began.

"I swear it was, Daddy!"

Peter glowered at his son's emphatic tone. He certainly wasn't about to call Christopher a liar, but neither did he think it was entirely healthy for the child to continue to believe such things. Ever since he'd been able to talk and relate his fears, he'd been claiming visits from *the boogeyman*. Peter had wondered at first whether it was some memory from infancy, because Christopher had always had the most remarkable aptitude for remembering things—more than anyone he knew. Sometime later, however, he'd discovered that Christopher had overheard the servants talking about his mother's death. He hadn't been happy to learn that his son knew every gruesome detail of his mother's tragic end. It only stood to reason, then, that his subconscious would create this *boogeyman* for him to fear.

Christopher was getting better, however. In the beginning he would wet his bed rather than rise and go to the bathroom, because he'd been too terrified to let the boogeyman know he was awake. Peter probably hadn't handled it the best way possible, but he hadn't been certain how else to do it. He certainly hadn't wished his son to be afraid of every shadow, so he'd forced Christopher to go to bed each night in his own bed, telling him that if he should chance to waken, that he could run to Peter in the night, or call for help and Peter would come. Christopher's room was in shouting distance, and there was nothing wrong with his son's lungs.

In the beginning Christopher had come running to his bed every night. Lately, however, he slept more soundly, and it was only on occasion now that Peter awoke to find him curled up beside him.

Not that it was a disappointment this morn, but he certainly had expected to awaken to a far different embrace.

Where had she gone?

And did he dare ask his son?

He decided it was best not to.

"I was so scared, Daddy! But I din't even cry!" Christopher continued excitedly. "He came to my bed even and I din't cry!"

It was at times like this that it wasn't so difficult to believe his son a child. His little old man was just a little boy, after all, and despite his disappointment over Christopher's continued nightly visitor, he smiled at that thought.

"What happened? Did you scare him away?" Peter asked jovially, reaching out to pat his son's head.

"Yup!" he replied excitedly. "I think I did, Daddy!"

"Thatta boy," Peter cheered him on, dropping his hand to his son's shoulder. "And did he run away?"

"Nope," Christopher replied, shaking his head. "He just started to cry."

Peter laughed at the sober expression on his son's face. "You made him cry, did you?"

"Yes, sir," Christopher told him.

"And how did you manage to do that?" Peter asked him.

Christopher's little face screwed. "Well, I dunno, but I think it was 'cause I told him he smelled like Aunt Ruth."

Peter tried hard not to chuckle. His shoulders shook, but he restrained his laughter. "You did?"

"Yes, sir."

"And then he started to cry?"

"Uh-huh!"

"Maybe he won't come back now," Peter suggested. "I'm certain he doesn't like that you think he smells like Aunt Ruth."

"Maybe," Christopher agreed, nodding. "But maybe if he does," he added excitedly, "then I will just beat him up this time!"

Peter couldn't contain his smile at his son's bravado. "I'm certain you will," he told him. "I've never had any doubt you could."

Christopher beamed with pride. He smiled so widely Peter thought his face would split. "So now I'm not scared anymore, Daddy."

"Good for you!" Peter exclaimed, and resisted the urge to tackle him and steal another hug. Christopher seemed to be getting too big for them of late, and though it was what Peter had hoped—that he would feel independent enough—it gave him a little twinge of regret to see his only son growing up so swiftly.

"How would you feel about a little brother or sister, Christopher?" he asked suddenly, surprising even himself with the question.

Christopher's expression became animated. "Really, Daddy?"

"Really, son."

"A brother! Oh, yes!" he exclaimed.

Peter smiled, picturing a house full of children . . . In addition to the brother for Christopher, he saw little girls with dark hair and blue eyes as deep as the sea and temperaments as fiery as their mother's.

"Is Miss Sarah going to be my new mommy?" he asked, and Peter had to catch himself from answering yes. He damned well hoped so, but he was well aware that he couldn't force her.

"I hope so," he answered.

Christopher nodded fervently. "Me too, Daddy!"

"I'm glad we both agree," Peter said, laughing, and reached out to pat Christopher's leg.

"Can we go ask her now?" Christopher pleaded at once. "Please, please, Daddy!"

"It's not so simple as that, son," Peter said, and then a wicked idea entered his head.

Perhaps it was.

Who could refuse that little face?

Who could look at his son and not feel a tug in their heart?

It wasn't quite the fair thing to do, but then, as

he'd already determined, he wasn't going to play fairly.

He wasn't going to lose her—not if he could help it.

"Why don't you do that, Christopher!" he suggested, his eyes narrowing mischievously.

Christopher had fallen back on the bed, bouncing up and down. "Do what, Daddy?"

"Ask her," Peter proposed.

Christopher stopped bouncing and went still. "To be my mommy?"

"Yes, sir!" Peter exclaimed, suddenly excited by the prospect. "Listen . . . you go and find her and ask her, and then come back and tell me what she says to you."

"All right, Daddy," Christopher agreed, and crawled off the bed. "I'll go ask her."

Peter grinned, wishing he could somehow eavesdrop on their conversation. "Just don't tell her I sent you," Peter told his son. "And ask her as nicely as you can."

"Yes, sir!" Christopher exclaimed, disappearing an instant as he knelt to retrieve his little cane from where he'd obviously left it on the floor. He rose and hurried to the door.

"And if she says yes, son, you can have all the taffy you want!"

"Oh, yippeee!" Christopher exclaimed, and did a slightly awkward leap of joy. "I'll be right back!" he swore, throwing his hand into the air, and Peter grinned as he watched his son go.

He lay within the bed long after the tap-tap of

Christopher's little cane vanished down the hall. Crossing his arms behind his head, he considered dressing and following behind him to hear what was said, but decided against it, because he knew his son would fare better without him.

Still, he'd like to see the look on Sarah's face when Christopher asked.

What would she say?

The image made him smile.

"Sarah Woodard," he whispered, "you're not going to walk away from us so easily."

Chapter 30

What a mess Sarah had created for herself.

Try as she might, she couldn't seem to find the clarity of mind she needed to unravel her way out of her tangled life. She'd sat alone in the library since leaving Peter's bed, trying to make sense of the myriad feelings she was experiencing.

She fumbled with a forgotten button she'd found on the floor, tossing it from one hand to another, trying to determine her best course of action.

Should she go?

Or should she stay?

Could she walk away?

She sat there contemplating those things until the soft tap-tap of a cane alerted her to Christopher's presence in the corridor.

"Christopher," she called out as he passed, dropping the button on the floor. It landed with a faint clatter on the hard wood.

He paused in the doorway.

What time is it? Sarah wondered. Was Peter still abed?

"Miss Sarah?" he called out a little uncertainly.

"Good morning, Christopher," she said, smiling at the silly grin that appeared on his face. She took a deep breath and invited him in, determined to begin setting things right at once.

Christopher was foremost on her mind, after Peter.

He turned to enter excitedly, swinging his little cane before him. He was dressed still in his nightgown, had obviously come straight from his bed. Sarah had never seen him look quite so adorable.

Her arms ached to hold him.

"Christopher," she said, "would you mind very much sitting in my lap . . . just this once?"

"No, ma'am!"

"C'mere then," Sarah urged him, and he did. She lifted him onto her lap, but he didn't release his cane at once. Sarah let him keep it, though it smacked her on the forehead as he settled himself.

Rubbing her head, she tried not to laugh at his oblivious expression. He was just too excited this morning, and she was flattered to think it might be because he was happy to see her.

"I'm glad you came to me this morning," she said, "because I have something I wish to tell you."

"Me too!" he replied at once. "I have something to tell you too!"

Sarah laughed softly at his unbridled enthusiasm.

"You want to go first?" she asked him. "Or would you like me to?"

"Ladies first! My daddy always says that," he

told her, nodding. "You can if you wanna, Miss Sarah."

"Very well, then . . . in that case . . ." Sarah inhaled a breath, uncertain how to proceed. "Well, I have a few confessions to make . . ."

"Confession?"

"Yes," Sarah explained, leaning forward and putting her arms around him. "You see, a confession is when . . . well, in this case it is when you have not quite spoken the truth about something . . . and you wish to set it right."

Christopher thought about that a moment, and commented, "Like when you say you like rice but you really don't, 'cause you think they feel like too many bugs in your mouth?"

Sarah wrinkled her nose at the image. "Well . . . yes," she said, "somewhat like that, Christopher. You don't like rice?"

He shook his head and made a disgusted face. Sarah nipped her bottom lip to keep from laughing.

"Well, then! Why don't you speak up and say something?" she suggested. "I'm certain your father and Aunt Ruth wouldn't force you to eat bugs! Yuck!"

His little brows drew together. "Well, I did tell my aunt Ruth," he said, and pouted. "But she said I shouldn't waste my food."

Sarah lifted her brows. Ruth was, indeed, somewhat of a battle-ax, she decided. Old biddy. "Well!" she exclaimed. "Next time, if I am with you, I promise to stand up to Aunt Ruth for you."

He smiled.

"That is . . . if you think you'd still like to have me around after I tell you my confession."

"Oh, I will!" he assured.

Sarah inhaled a breath. "Well, we shall see . . ."

"In fact," he added, sounding entirely too much like a little old man again, "me and my daddy would like you to marry us!"

Sarah drew back in surprise. "Marry you?"

"Uh-huh!"

He nodded, looking so earnest that Sarah's heart skipped a beat. "He said that? Christopher," she urged him, "tell me . . . what exactly did he say?"

"Ummmmm." Christopher made a face that seemed suddenly uncertain. He stuck a finger in his mouth. "Well, I think I'm not supposed to tell you that," he explained.

Sarah lifted her brows in surprise. "You are not supposed to tell me?"

Could he be speaking the truth?

Could Peter truly wish to marry her?

He shook his head, and seemed reluctant even to speak now.

"I see," Sarah replied, and then added, regaining her composure, "Well, if your father would like to know what I think about *that,* Christopher, then he will have to ask me himself. Don't you think?"

He nodded, and Sarah decided not to pursue that particular topic, because she suddenly couldn't bear to discover they were nothing more than the fancies of a little boy. "Christopher," she prompted, "about my confession . . ."

He waited patiently, but Sarah had a difficult time

putting the confession into words he might understand. She decided the best course was simply to say it.

"Remember I told you I was a teacher?" she began.

He nodded.

"Well, I'm really not a teacher, Christopher."

His little brows drew together into a bewildered frown. "You're not really my teacher?"

"Well, I have been teaching you, yes," she amended, trying her best not to confuse him.

"Then you are my teacher!" he replied, with irrefutable logic.

Sarah sucked in a breath. "Well, yes, in this instance, but it's not what I do for a living . . . teach, that is."

"You don't?"

"No," Sarah replied. "I don't."

"All right," he said, and Sarah waited for him to say something more.

When he didn't, she continued. "And remember when I said my last name was Hopkins?"

He nodded.

"Well, that is not the truth either."

He was frowning now, his little brow furrowing. "What is it, then?"

"Woodard."

"All right," he said, and shrugged.

"Does that name seem familiar to you at all?"

He shook his head.

"Well," Sarah continued, disappointed though she had no reason to be, "I suppose it wouldn't be.

At any rate, I knew your mother well."

His little face lit up. "You did?"

Sarah nodded, smiling. "Yes, I did," she affirmed. "In fact," she continued, "I knew her *very* well."

"Was she very nice?" he asked, nodding still.

Sarah smiled fondly at the memory of her cousin. "Oh, yes! Very nice!" she exclaimed. "And I loved her very much. She was my cousin, you see."

"Cousin?"

"Yes," Sarah said. "Somewhat like brothers and sisters, except not so closely related. My mother and her mother were cousins. Understand?"

He nodded. "I wish I had a baby brother," he lamented, changing the subject. "But maybe when you marry my daddy you can bring one home?"

Sarah blinked at the innocent request.

She grinned, but didn't dare reply. She didn't wish to encourage him needlessly.

"Your mother was my best friend, too," she said, returning to the discussion.

"Really?"

"Yes," Sarah answered, and sighed. "She was."

"Well, I don't really have a best friend," he said. " 'Cept maybe my daddy."

"He's a very good best friend to have," Sarah assured him.

"And somebody killed my mommy when I was just a baby," he added matter-of-factly. Hearing it so frankly from his lips gave Sarah a start.

"You know about that, Christopher?"

"Yes, ma'am," he answered, his expression saddened now. ''And I think that was a mean thing to do!''

Sarah hugged him a little tighter. ''Yes, me too,'' she agreed, and leaned her cheek against his head. ''You know . . . we had a big fight before she died, your mother and I . . .''

''You did?'' he asked her, leaning into her embrace.

''Yes, I'm afraid so.''

''Why were you mad?''

''That story will have to wait until you are grown, I think, but it really wasn't your mommy's fault,'' she assured him. ''It was mine.''

''It was?''

That he seemed surprised by that made Sarah smile a bit. ''Yes, it was, I'm ashamed to say. And the worst part is that I never, ever got to tell her I was sorry.''

He nodded. ''I bet she was really sad about that.''

''Yes, I think so,'' Sarah agreed. ''But I hope and pray she knew I loved her, anyway.''

He nodded. ''I think maybe she did, Miss Sarah.''

Sarah kissed his head and closed her eyes, praying it was the truth. ''You think so?''

''Yes, ma'am—but I know what you can do, if you wanna.''

''And what is that?'' she asked him, opening her eyes, realizing the hardest part of her confession was yet to come.

''Well,'' he began, ''my daddy says she went to live in Heaven, and that Heaven is a place where you talk with your hearts. And I think if you talk to her like that, she will hear you, Miss Sarah. Have you said I'm sorry really hard?''

Sarah smiled at his description of Heaven. ''Yes, I have. I have said it with all of my heart, Christopher.''

''Then she knows,'' he said with certainty. ''My daddy says she hears everything now—sorta like God, 'cept she's not God, you know?''

Sarah laughed softly. ''Yes, I think I do. You know what else I think?'' she told him, squeezing him gently.

''What?''

''I think your mother would be very, very proud of you, Christopher.''

He beamed.

''But, Christopher,'' she continued, taking in a fortifying breath, ''there is something else too.''

''All right.''

''You know when I said I couldn't see . . . that I was blind?''

''Yes, ma'am.''

''Well . . . I really can see.''

He cocked his head a little in confusion. ''You mean the doctor fixed you?''

''No,'' Sarah said. ''You see, I was never blind.''

His little brows drew together in confusion, but he said nothing.

''I'm sorry for the lie,'' she offered him, hoping it was enough, and feeling it was inadequate. ''Do you hate me now?''

He shook his head. ''No . . . but I don't really

know why you would wanna say you were blind if you wasn't.''

"Well, I had a very good reason," she said, "but it was still a lie, and for that I apologize, Christopher."

"All right," he said, and then added, "but I don't really care about that, 'cause I'm glad you're not. I don't like it much," he disclosed.

Sarah's heart went out to him. "I'm certain you don't, darling, but you know what?" She lifted her hand to his cheek and hugged him to her.

"What?"

"I think you are the bravest person I know," she told him with certainty.

He pulled away. "You do?" he asked in surprise.

Sarah smiled. "Yes, I do!"

"Well," he told her, nodding once more, "I *am* pretty brave."

Sarah laughed. "Are you now?"

"Uh-huh, wanna know why?"

"Why?"

"'Cause I scared away the boogeyman last night!"

Sarah blinked, not quite understanding. "You did what?"

"Scared him away from my room! My daddy says he is just a nightmare, but I can really smell him, and he smells just like a smelly girl," he added with a scrunch of his nose.

Sarah's heartbeat increased its rhythm. "You mean to tell me someone comes into your room at night?"

He nodded soberly. ''Uh-huh, the boogeyman.''

Her brain tried to focus on what he was telling her, but confusion muddied her thoughts. Her heart pounded. ''Why do you think it's the boogeyman, Christopher?''

'' 'Cause I thought it was my aunt Ruth, but I asked her and she said no, it was the boogeyman, and if I didn't stay asleep, he might take me away.''

Terror swept through Sarah. Why would anyone tell a child such a thing?

''Your aunt Ruth told you that?'' she asked, wanting to be certain she hadn't misunderstood.

''Yes, ma'am.''

''And why did you think it was her?''

''Because it smells like her. Yuck!''

''Christopher?'' Sarah began, shuddering at the thoughts that passed through her head suddenly. ''Does this . . . boogeyman . . . ever harm you?''

He shook his head. ''No, 'cept he used to scare me, but not anymore.''

Sarah swallowed the knot that rose in her throat.

''You are such a big little boy,'' she told him, but her mind was racing with the possibilities.

Could Ruth possibly be Mary's and Mel's murderer?

But why?

It didn't make sense, but then, murder was not a sensible crime.

''Has this boogeyman ever spoken to you, Christopher?''

''No, ma'am . . . but he cried last night.''

''Cried?''

"Yes, ma'am."

Sarah tried to imagine what possible reason Ruth might have to wish Mary dead. And then Sarah, too—not Mel because it hadn't been Mel who'd been the intended victim. It had been Sarah all along . . . the fire . . . the carriage . . . and Mel had been in her bed, too.

"Christopher?"

"Yes, ma'am?"

"What does this boogeyman do when he's in your room?"

"I dunno," he said, "but I think he lives in my closet."

Sarah inhaled a breath. Her heart began to pound a little harder. "Your closet?"

"Yes, ma'am."

Chills bolted down Sarah's spine. "Why . . . why do you think this, Christopher?"

"Because I found a book there one time," he said. "It's smelly just like him."

Dear God! Could this be the missing journal? Had Ruth hidden the incriminating evidence in his room, knowing that he would never understand its contents?

Sarah's heart leapt into her throat. She gasped and stood at once, sliding Christopher from her lap. She took him by the hand. "Show me, Christopher!" she demanded.

"I din't know what it was!" he swore, sounding terrified all at once. "Did I do somethin' wrong? I din't touch it again, Miss Sarah!"

"No, no, darling," she assured him. "But I need

to see it. Can you show me, Christopher?''

He nodded.

''Show me,'' she demanded once more. ''Show me that book!''

Chapter 31

Peter climbed the stairs at Fifth Avenue and Thirteenth Street, taking the steps two at a time in his haste. Ruth had delivered to him a letter from a very irate Cile, claiming he had missed yet another meeting with August Belmont, and that he could "go straight to proverbial hell."

Damn, but if he had, he didn't know it. He didn't remember scheduling one, nor agreeing to a meeting at all. He was certainly preoccupied of late, but he damned sure would have remembered that. Mr. Belmont's was not a name he'd easily forget, not even with Sarah as a distraction.

He rapped on the door at the Morgan estate and waited impatiently for Cile's doorman to answer. It took him longer to respond than Peter had patience to wait.

"Mr. Holland, sir." He opened the door wide and stepped aside. "Shall I tell Mrs. Morgan you wish to see her?"

Peter stepped into the foyer and glanced into the parlor. "Please."

"She has been indisposed most of the day, sir, but I know she will wish to speak with you. Please make yourself at home and I shall tell her you are here."

"Thank you, Simon."

"Of course, sir," he replied. He bowed and stepped away, and Peter moved into the parlor to wait. He was far too tense to sit and so he wandered the room, pausing at the piano to clink a few keys. He wondered idly if Christopher would enjoy learning to play. His ear for language was certainly remarkable enough. Peter thought perhaps the same skills were required for music as well. And Christopher didn't have any sort of hobby to amuse him.

He plucked a few more discordant notes and decided his own ear was quite lacking.

Did Sarah play? He wondered.

And what had she said to Christopher?

He hoped his son had softened her a little because he damned well intended to ask her again himself. Peter could scarce think of anything that would please him more than to crawl into his bed each night and wrap his arms around his sleeping wife— Sarah.

He didn't want anyone else—couldn't imagine ever wanting anyone else. The sweet taste of her lingered on his lips, and the scent of her in his lungs . . . the sound of her voice upon his heart.

Even now, she was all he could think of.

He glanced out into the foyer.

Damn . . . he wished Cile would hurry because he wanted to go home. He'd left without even telling

Sarah good-bye, or where he was going. Though he'd looked for her and Christopher both, he hadn't found either one and he'd had to hie out the door. Judging by Cile's mood the last time he had seen her, Peter hadn't wished to anger her further by making her wait. Nor did he wish to hurt her, and in truth, he owed it to her to tell her about Sarah before someone else chanced to.

"Well, well," Cile said.

Peter turned to find her standing in the doorway. "Hello, Cile."

She tilted her head coyly. "If it isn't our *front page headliner* himself."

"Christ!" Peter sucked in a breath. "The *Times*?"

She lifted her brows. "You mean to say you've not seen the papers yet?"

"No, I've not."

"I see," she said. And then lifted one brow higher. "Preoccupied?"

"A bit," Peter admitted.

"You don't seem to like things quiet, do you? I leave you alone for ten minutes, and you embroil yourself in another murder." She made a clucking sound with her tongue.

"Cile . . . I know you're angry with me . . ."

"Not at all," she denied. "I am quite well, Peter." She sauntered into the room and went directly to her bar to pour herself a glass of sherry. "In case you haven't noticed through our years together, I am quite resilient."

"Dispense with the sarcasm, Cile."

She turned around and leaned against the bar, sipping at her glass and eyeing him over the rim. ''I suppose I am pouting a bit,'' she said honestly.

Peter lifted a brow.

''You have completely ignored me,'' she protested.

Peter nodded, and sighed. ''I'm sorry.''

She averted her gaze. ''I know.''

''There were never any promises between us, Cile.''

She turned to look at him again, and her eyes were glazed a bit with unshed tears. ''I know that too.''

Silence fell between them.

''I never told you,'' she began, ''all those years ago . . . because of Mary . . . and then, well, because I sensed you didn't wish to hear it, but I loved you, Peter. I love you still. I want you to be happy.''

He didn't know what to say. ''Cile . . .''

She lifted her fingers to her lips. ''Shhh.''

He hated hurting her.

''Do you love her, Peter?''

He met her gaze directly. ''Yes, I do.''

''You know what, then?'' she said, moving away from the bar and walking toward him. She smiled softly. ''That's all that matters.'' She was obviously trying not to cry.

She stopped when she stood before him and lifted her fingers to his face, giving him a fond look. It was the first time he had spied anything at all in her eyes, the first bit of warmth she had ever allowed him to see. ''I have watched you withdraw more and more, Peter darling. And I was never able to draw you back. Please believe me when I say I am happy for you if only you are happy.''

He smiled at her. ''You've always been a good friend to me, Cile.''

''And I shall continue to be so,'' she promised without hesitation, dropping her hand at her side. She winked then and said, ''If only you would stay out of the papers, darling. You are quite terrible for my reputation, you know!''

He chuckled. ''Cile, *you* are quite terrible for your reputation.''

She giggled. ''True.'' She tilted him a glance. ''But gad, you are a cad even to say so!''

Peter laughed, and then winced and shook his head. ''I suppose the papers were brutal?''

''Oh, God!'' she exclaimed. ''Quite! I cannot believe you haven't seen them yet.''

He sighed. ''So I am a murderer again?''

She shook her head. ''Uh, not quite.'' She laughed. ''But speculation abounds, my dear. You are involved, I think, in an array of questionable activities, none of which are quite respectable, and yet neither are they illegal, thank God!'' She laughed again. ''And you are a despoiler of innocent young girls as well.'' She winked at him. ''Just the sort of slightly dangerous man women seem to adore.'' She sipped at her sherry. ''Oh! And Belmont sent a messenger this morning, you might as well know. He isn't withdrawing his investments, but he did wish to know my feelings on the reports.''

''Belmont!'' Peter shook his head. ''Cile, I don't

remember receiving any requests for a meeting. I'm sorry that I missed another with him.''

Cile's brows lifted. "You haven't really missed any at all. I'm sorry to say that I lied the last time.'' She tilted her head a bit and gave him a coy little glance. "Forgive me?''

Peter narrowed his eyes at her. "You mean to tell me that we didn't have a meeting this morning?''

Cile made a bewildered face. "No. Whyever did you think so?''

"Because . . .'' Peter blinked. The note. Who had sent him the note if not Cile? "You didn't send a messenger this morning?''

She shook her head, denying it. He knew she wouldn't lie to him again. Why should she?

"Peter?''

Peter's brows drew together. He glanced down at the floor, and then into her eyes once more. "No meeting this morning with August Belmont?''

She shook her head.

"And you didn't send a messenger telling me to come posthaste?''

She shook her head once more. "I've been abed all morning, darling. Why do you think it took me so long to receive you? I had to dress, you know.''

Peter wasn't listening. Who the hell would have sent him the note? A very uneasy feeling slithered through him. Ruth had handed him a note . . . from Cile . . . penned in what looked to be Cile's elegant scrawl. His brows collided as he studied Cile's face. She wasn't lying . . . he knew her too damned well.

Something wasn't right here.

Someone had wanted him out of the house.

"I have to go," he told her.

"Now? So soon!"

"Emergency," he said, and turned and rushed toward the door.

Chapter 32

Christopher led Sarah to the wardrobe in his room. He opened the doors and fell to his knees at her feet and crawled at once into the curtain of clothing. Two tiers of his clothing hung in perfect array, and the closet seemed unremarkable until he began to toss out the collection of mementoes and toys he had hidden within the wardrobe.

He tossed out an old shoe—one of his own, she thought, judging by the size, but its mate never appeared. He tossed out a handkerchief—what appeared to be his mother's—and a wooden horse, and a soldier, too. After that came an assortment of items, some of them recognizable, some of them not, though it was clear each item had been well used and cherished. He paused, and backed out of the closet, dragging with him a small leather-bound book. He brought it to his nostrils, making a disgusted face, and then thrust it toward Sarah.

Sarah took it from his hands, examining it. "How did you discover it there, Christopher?"

"Just found it," he said. "These are my toys," he explained. "I save 'em there so Caitlin won't throw 'em away when she cleans my room."

"I see."

"They feel good," he told her, groping for an item—the handkerchief—and exploring it with his hands. "This one is soft," he explained, pulling it through his hands. "I think it was my gramma's, my daddy said it was." Sarah could see that it had an initial embroidered on one corner and she made a mental note to check it later. This instant, however, all she could think of was the journal in her hands.

Ruth's journal? There wasn't any identification, except for the distinctive odor even she recognized as Ruth's—a strong, sickeningly sweet floral scent. It was a blend of scents, actually, none of them the least harmonious, and it was only in that instant she recalled the scent in her room the night of the fire.

Taking the journal with her, Sarah sat on Christopher's bed.

"I think the boogeyman musta lost it, do you think?"

"Perhaps," Sarah agreed, shuddering.

"I think that was why he was crying," Christopher proposed.

With trembling hands, Sarah opened the journal to its very first page.

The date was December 5, 1878 . . .

Damn Peter.
   He's never wanted for anything. Not ever! From Father he received his due respect. From

his whore of a mother he received love! What have I ever had but silence and time to dream—time to plan!

Bloody man's world, this is—I've no choices available to me at all, have I, but to depend upon a man! It isn't fair! Isn't right! Simply because I've not been blessed with a face that draws men to my side, I have nothing at all, nothing! Not even the assurance of a place to rest my head at night! I hate men! Hate them all!

Sarah blinked at the vehemence of the entry, stunned by the anger apparent in every word written.

"I wanted to show him where it was," Christopher said, distracting her, "but I was afraid."

Patting the bed beside her, Sarah called him to join her. "Everything will be all right, sweetheart. I promise," she told him, and swore to herself he would never have to lie there another night listening to the boogeyman in his room.

She skipped a few pages . . . scanning the entries. They were mostly short ones, hardly a sentence, and judging by the dates, they were not kept every day. The very next entry, for instance, was dated January 19, 1879. Sarah skipped that one and turned a few pages, stopping at a particularly long entry marked

January 16, 1879 . . .

Peter met a woman today—Mary Cavanaugh. Ridiculous the way he follows her about. One

might think him a dog the way he drools after
her!

What fickle pigs men are!

Well, Mary will not win with her silly little
doll face and her childish giggles. Her face will
droop one day, and then what will she have?

Father abandoned Mother, left her to wither
and die once her looks no longer appealed to
him! He'd found himself some young harlot to
replace her within a month of her burial. I
wondered even that he might have hurried her
to the grave—morbid as that thought might be,
I have always suspected it to be so. So he'd
gone and married his younger woman—and
then had expected me to raise their son! How
just was that? To expect me to devote myself
to a little boy who would simply grow to leave
me someday—just as my father did to my
mother—just as he then did to me!

Mother gave him the best years of her life—
cooked and cleaned for him, doted upon him—
and for what thanks?

Women such as Mary Cavanaugh don't have
a care in this world. For me, nothing comes
easily—nothing is ever certain! I must rely
upon myself and no other, because there is no
one I can count on—not even Peter!

Sarah took a deep breath and turned another page.
Such anger in Ruth's words. How terrible to feel so
alone and bitter.

The next entry she stopped at was dated June 10, 1879 . . .

He's going to marry the bitch!

Sarah sucked in a breath at the malevolence of those words. This had been Mary Ruth had been speaking of, *her cousin!* Anger suffused her. Why couldn't she have been there at Mary's side to stand beside her? She swallowed the knot of emotions that rose to choke her breath away, and turned to look at Christopher, who was standing silently before her now.

"Will you read it to me?" he asked her innocently, as though sensing her gaze upon him.

Sarah shook her head, though he couldn't see her, unable to speak for an instant. She reached out to touch his cheek, patting it gently. "I don't think you would like this," she assured him, her voice trembling just a little. She patted the bed once more. "Come here and sit by me, Christopher."

He climbed on the bed and sat beside her.

Sarah put her arm about him, drawing him nearer. She took a breath when he leaned against her, and she dared to turn another page.

September 25, 1879

How dare Peter come to me and say to my face that Mary's beauty has been a terrible burden all her life! So the rich little brat isn't certain

*she wishes to marry him because it frightens
her. Poor thing . . . she cannot be certain
whether it is her face or her heart he loves her
for! How dare Peter in the same breath console
me by telling me I should never have to wonder
that a man might love me for my heart instead
of my face!*

How dare he!

*I hate him, and I hate his little society
darling!*

"Miss Sarah," Christopher whispered at her side,
but she didn't hear his words, only the drone of his
voice as she forced herself to read another entry, not
quite ready to believe what her instinct was whispering to her.

January 28, 1880

I am not feeling very welcome.

*I've given Peter everything, and what do I
get in return? A battle at every turn! I live
every day of my life in fear that he will push
me out of his life and his house! Simply discard
me . . . as our father did so easily.*

*My head aches at the mere thought.
Laudanum does not dim the pain.*

*Peter's marriage is laughable. He has gone
so far as to admit to me that he doesn't even
love her! How can he be so willing to give a
stranger so much—everything? His wife does*

not bear his blood as I do—and me, he discards without a thought! I live on what little he gives me when it pleases him—when he remembers! And to her he gives everything!

Why should it surprise me? My own father never cared enough to leave me a measly portion of his assets, meager though they were. He left everything to his namesake, his pride, his joy, his son! He left everything to his one child who hadn't needed anything at all—his one child who could easily make his way in this fool world without any help—and nothing at all to the child who had no means to survive, unless she had a man in her life—shallow, vain creatures!

The unfairness of it all makes me long to spit in the face of every man!

And what has Peter done with Father's inheritance? He's driving his business into the ground, that's what he's doing. If it weren't for me—that I'd introduced him to Cile—Peter would be a bloody pauper today.

He owes everything to me!

Everything!

His house is my house, his money my money. Everything is mine! I loathe having to go to him and beg for every scrap of clothing I place upon my back. Loathe him for making me come to him crawling—for not thinking enough to come to me instead! He takes my sacrifices in vain, and never thinks how humiliating it might

be for me to come to him every time I need
something . . . anything.

He's no different from any other man—
swayed by a pretty face. Mary Cavanaugh is
all that is loathsome in women, and damn
Peter for wanting her anyway!

Well, I'm not going to be left once more with
nothing!

Not if I can help it!

My head hurts! I am not going to be run out
of my own home because suddenly I am no
longer needed here.

Mary will go before I do!

Sarah blinked in horror at what she was reading.
She flipped pages in shock, stopping at the date of
her cousin's murder . . .

April 15, 1880

By now it is done!

Wish I could be there—anxious to know how
all fared. But tomorrow will be soon enough. I
do not wish to draw suspicion.

I cannot see this as death—no, I refuse! It
is rather a birth! My own! I think I shall not
even sleep tonight, waiting for the morning to
discover the news! So long I have waited! Only
a few short hours more . . .

"My dear God!" Sarah exclaimed in horror.
"What, Miss Sarah?" Christopher asked low.

Sarah peered down at the child at her side. She had been so drawn up in the journal she hadn't heard a word he'd spoken to her. "What's wrong, Miss Sarah?"

Sarah sucked in a breath and brought her hand to her cheek, realizing for the first time that tears had been streaming from her eyes. She swiped them away and set the journal down on the bed, unable to read more at the instant.

She needed to find Peter, needed to show him the journal.

Lifting her hand to her mouth, she tried to compose herself, tried to think of what next to do. She didn't wish to leave Christopher alone, but neither did she wish him to be present when she spoke to his father.

She knelt before the bed, taking Christopher by the shoulders. "Christopher, darling . . . I am going to ask you to do something for me," she told him.

He nodded, and Sarah reached out and took the journal into her hand, then pressed it into his.

"I want you to take this to your father's room, and I want you to hide with it under the bed. Can you do that for me?"

His expression reflected his confusion, but there was no time to explain. And even if there were, what could she say? *Your aunt is a murderer, and I fear for your safety?* No, it was best for now simply to remove him from danger. Nor could she walk around with the journal in her hand.

"Christopher?" she prompted.

"Yes, ma'am," he said, and nodded.

"If your aunt Ruth calls for you, you are *not* to come! Understand?"

He nodded again, and Sarah turned around, surveying the mess on the floor. She had to clean it before Ruth discovered it. She left Christopher on the bed as she hurriedly picked up the items he had strewn on the floor and returned them to their little corner of the wardrobe, shutting the door after them. That done, she turned to Christopher, lifting him into her arms, deciding to take him to Peter's room. She needed to see to his safety herself.

"I'm going to take you there," she said, as he lifted his arms around her neck. The sickeningly sweet floral scent of the journal filled her lungs, making her stomach roll and her heart beat faster.

She had to find Peter.

Peter would know what to do.

Chapter 33

Sarah settled Christopher within his father's room and left him at once, not wanting to draw attention to his presence there. She loathed having to abandon him and knew he was likely to be frightened, but it couldn't be helped. Something in her gut told her he would be safer there than he would be with her.

And if something should happen to her before she was able to speak with Peter, then Christopher at least had the journal to give him as proof. She had left him with specific instructions to give the diary to his father as soon as he came into the room, and not to reveal himself until she returned for him or until he heard his father's voice.

And thank God she left when she did, because no sooner had she closed Peter's bedroom door than Ruth's voice startled her in the corridor.

"Sarah," she said, in a tone that was warmer than Sarah had ever heard her use before.

Prickles bolted down her spine at the unnatural

sound of it, and the hair on her nape stood on end.

Swallowing, Sarah turned to face her cousin's murderer—no, perhaps she hadn't committed the deed with her own two hands, but it was obvious enough from her entries that she'd had a deciding role in Mary's death.

Sarah forced a smile. "Ruth," she said in greeting, and her stomach knotted.

Ruth tilted her a sweet look that made gooseflesh erupt on her body. "Dear Sarah," she said, "I know you've suffered much these last days . . . I only wished to extend my sympathies over your friend's death. This house has seen so much tragedy," she lamented, and shook her head, with a genuine look of sorrow.

Sarah's heart began to thump wildly and her hands trembled, but she kept her composure. How could Ruth be so casual after all that she had committed? How could it not be evident in her eyes? Did she have no conscience? No heart? Feel no shame? Did she even recall the things she had written? The things she had done?

More than anything, she needed to draw Ruth away from Peter's room, away from Christopher. Taking a deep breath, Sarah began to walk away from the room, hoping Ruth would follow.

She did.

Sarah breathed a sigh of relief. She didn't want her anywhere near Christopher.

"Thank you," Sarah said, and then asked, "Have you seen Peter, perchance?"

Ruth caught up with her quick strides and walked

beside her down the hall. Had Ruth sought her out, then? And what did she want?

She was up to something, Sarah sensed.

"I'm afraid not," Ruth answered.

An uneasy silence fell between them.

Sarah picked up her pace, hurrying farther away from Christopher, toward Peter's office. She prayed he would be there. Fear began to take shape within her breast, a tangible lump that stole her breath away.

"Actually," Ruth disclosed then, "I was looking for you. I hoped you would have just a few moments this morning," she said much too sweetly.

Sarah's heart tripped. "Me? You were looking for me?"

Ruth smiled. "Yes. I'm afraid we've not had the opportunity to get to know one another as perhaps we should, and it seems to me my brother has grown quite fond of you. I thought it might be rather nice for the two of us to chat a bit while Peter is out. Don't you think so?"

"Peter is out?" Sarah's heart sounded like thunder in her ears. "I thought you said you'd not seen him?" She halted at his office and peered within. Her heart lurched at finding it empty. He wasn't there. She turned to face Ruth, her stomach rolling.

Ruth gave her a sweet smile. "Well . . . I haven't, you see, but I was told that he is off to a meeting this morning—business, I suppose. He always did work entirely too much, that brother of mine," she disclosed with a sigh. "That was part of the problem, I think, between him and Mary. Poor Mary," she said, and added, "Cile always was quite insistent, I'm afraid."

Sarah nodded. "Cile?"

Ruth smiled benevolently. "Yes, of course. The two of them have long been inseparable."

Was that why Mary had doubted Peter? Had Ruth filled her mind with half-truths and innuendos?

"Have you a few minutes, Sarah?" she persisted.

Sarah stared at Ruth without answering, uncertain how to respond. She reminded herself that Ruth couldn't possibly know about the journal so soon, that she'd discovered it—or could she?

She shuddered, and nodded, swallowing the knot that rose in her throat. "Certainly."

"Wonderful!" Ruth exclaimed, and added, clapping her hands in an expression of delight, "I've taken the liberty of ordering some tea and biscuits to be served in the parlor." She smiled brilliantly. "This shall be quite nice, I think, and long overdue!" And she turned to walk away, clearly expecting Sarah to follow.

Sarah had to force her feet to move.

She took a deep breath and followed down the corridor.

Ruth was certainly up to something. She was behaving so strangely. She'd not once spoken to Sarah so cordially in all the time Sarah had been in Peter's home.

Alarms sounded in her head, blaring in her ears.

The sweet scent of chamomile tea filled her lungs as she entered the parlor.

She froze in the doorway, not quite able to enter the room.

"Oh, good!" Ruth said, and went directly to the small table where the teacups and biscuits were laid out so neatly for them. "It's already been served, I see. How proficient of Caitlin!" She turned to face Sarah. "Do come in," she urged, seating herself upon the chair facing the door.

The curtains were open wide to University Place. Only a thin veil of lace shielded them from view. Anyone might see them within this room. Sarah assured herself that even a madwoman would not attempt murder in such a public place. She entered the room at Ruth's beckon, though hesitantly. Her stomach turning and her heart racing, she made her way to the chair facing Ruth.

"I must say, Sarah," she said in an admonishing tone, "that I was quite taken aback to discover your ruse with Peter, and I cannot say as I approve . . ." She rose from her chair once Sarah was seated, smiling softly. "However . . . excuse me, but I think I shall close this door," she said, changing the subject suddenly.

Sarah's heart tripped. She rose from the chair at once. "Oh, no!" she exclaimed, but Ruth had already reached the doors and was closing them.

Ruth turned to face her. "Much better," she said. "We don't wish to spill our dirty laundry to the servants, now do we?"

Sarah shook her head helplessly, feeling a bit out of control. Her thoughts began to race.

Her gaze fell to the table, to the neat setting of

cups and saucers laid out for them ... both cups empty as yet. Between their cups sat a steaming kettle of tea, and the usual accompaniments ... sugar ... cream ... A small tray of biscuits sat to one side. The combined scents of tea and fresh biscuits wafted to her nose, deliciously sweet ...

Inviting.

Much too ...

"Sit," Ruth demanded of her, and waited for Sarah to comply.

Sarah did, frowning. She would be bloody damned if Ruth thought she was going to put a single morsel of biscuit or a drop of tea to her lips.

She was hardly stupid.

But then ... Ruth didn't know she'd discovered her journal.

In truth, Sarah might otherwise have been completely oblivious ... had she not stumbled upon the diary ... but she had ...

Stay calm, she demanded of herself.

Stay calm.

She didn't have to eat or drink.

Ruth couldn't make her.

All she needed to do was stall until Peter arrived.

It wasn't as though Ruth had dragged her away to some dark cellar; they were both seated in the broad light of day and in hearing distance should Sarah feel the need to shout for help.

And still Sarah's heart hammered as she sat once more within the chair facing Peter's sister.

"There now," Ruth said, smiling once more, and sat again as well. She didn't move toward the tea at once, rather she sat back within the chair and studied Sarah a moment. "You really are quite lovely," she pointed out. "I can certainly see why Peter is enamored with you." She shook her head and laughed softly. "It was the same with your lovely cousin, too. Mary was such a darling."

Sarah nodded, uncertain what to say. "She was," she agreed, and peered out the window, hoping Peter would pass by, hoping *somebody* would, anybody. She breathed a little easier when a young couple strolled slowly by, and returned her attention to the table between them.

She stared at the kettle of tea. It was a beautiful porcelain set with tiny pink roses painted over blue flowing ribbon. Steam drifted out from the delicate spout, fragrant and sweet.

"As I was saying," Ruth continued. "I cannot say as I approve of your methods. I certainly wish you might have revealed yourself from the first, though I do understand your silence. I might have done the same," she said. "Perhaps . . ."

Sarah nodded and smiled. Her brows lifted. She took a deep breath and tilted her head, not quite certain how to respond.

Ruth reached out and poured herself a cup of tea. She filled Sarah's cup afterward . . . from the same kettle.

Perhaps Sarah was being a bit melodramatic, but she refused to take a single sip until Ruth did. She didn't trust the woman. Someone had drugged her tea once before, and she had been completely oblivious to it.

Not this time.

Ruth lifted the cup to her lips and then paused, lowering it and settling it once more within its saucer. Sarah's gaze focused on her cup. "Would you care for sugar?" she asked Sarah. "How remiss of me! One lump or two?"

"One," Sarah answered, placating her. She blinked, lifting her gaze to Ruth's face. Her eyes revealed nothing—nothing at all.

"I take mine without," Ruth disclosed. "So I completely forgot to ask. Forgive me."

"Not at all," Sarah replied, and turned again to peer out the window. The street was much too empty for her comfort. Someone passed by the window every so often, but not nearly often enough to give Sarah any sense of ease.

Ruth's smile faded a bit. "You seem nervous," she remarked, watching her, and Sarah sucked in a breath.

"Not at all," she lied.

Ruth smiled. "Good!" And she pushed Sarah's cup and saucer nearer to her. "But you should drink anyway," she demanded. "It's a special blend to soothe the nerves."

Sarah reached out to pull the saucer closer, her hands trembling.

"It will do you good, I think . . . You have been through so very much, my dear."

Sarah lifted a spoon to stir her tea, stalling. She didn't have to drink.

She wasn't going to.

Ruth couldn't force her.

But this was a dangerous woman, with blood already on her hands, and Sarah's fingers trembled as she stirred. The chink of silver against porcelain rang like a death knoll in her ears.

Peter entered through the Twelfth Street entrance and hurried toward his bedroom, hoping to find Sarah there.

Once he was certain she was safe, and his son as well, he intended to confront Ruth with the message she had given him. She had to recall who delivered it. It was imperative he discover who had sent it. His gut told him that whoever had penned that message had malicious intent, and he was going to find the bastard if it was the last thing he did.

The police may have closed the investigation, but he didn't believe their conclusions for an instant. Two murders in one home in the space of six years was entirely too much of a coincidence. Perhaps it didn't matter to the New York police that two innocent women were dead now, but it damned well mattered to Peter—particularly when the first had been his wife and the mother of his child, and the second intended to be the woman he loved.

He loved her, dammit—knew it without a doubt. He couldn't stop thinking about her, couldn't get her out of his mind. And the possibility that she might be harmed frightened him as much as it might to lose his son.

Opening his door, he found his room empty. Desperation made him call out her name.

"Sarah?"

He burst through the door and walked through his room, toward the adjoining room, calling her name once more.

"Daddy!" a little voice called out.

Peter froze. "Christopher?" His gaze scanned the room, searching for his son. "Christopher?"

"Daddy!" he called out again, sounding frightened. His voice was coming from beneath the bed, Peter realized suddenly, and fell at once to his knees.

"Christopher!" He crawled toward the bed, reaching under to drag him out. His son's expression was filled with confusion and fright. "What the devil are you doing under there?"

"Miss Sarah told me to stay there!" Christopher said at once. Peter seized him by the arm, pulling him out. He came willingly, dragging a small book with him.

Peter was confused. What was he doing under the bed? And why would Sarah ask him to hide there? And why would she leave him alone? Where was she?

"Why did she tell you to stay there?" Peter demanded at once. "And what is that in your hand, son?" he asked, reaching for the book.

"It's the boogeyman's, Daddy!" Christopher exclaimed, releasing it to him. "I showed it to Miss Sarah and she made me hide it under the bed. She said I hadda show it to you when you came, and told me not to come out from under the bed 'cept if you came."

Prickles of fear shot down Peter's spine. "What are you talking about, Christopher?" He took Christopher into his arms and sat on the bed with him, examining the book. He opened it.

June 10, 1879

He's going to marry the bitch!

His brows lifted. Good God! Whose words were these? Though he sensed he knew. He closed the journal, searching for a name on the binding. There was none to be found. Who was going to marry what bitch?

"Where did you find this, Christopher?"

Christopher launched into a frenzied explanation of his and Sarah's morning discussion and his nightly visitor, and of the smelly book he had discovered deep within his wardrobe.

Peter listened with a growing sense of unease. He lifted the book to his nostrils, breathing in its strong floral scent, and then flipped the book open once more, turning pages. Frowning, he stopped at a recent date . . .

March 20, 1886

I was right! I knew it!

I saw them returning today from their walk . . . Peter might deny his interest in that woman, but the flowers in her hand prove otherwise. Men are such pigs! How can he so easily find himself swayed by a stranger with a pretty face? God, he does not even seem to care that she is blind!

I will not be discarded!

I will not be abandoned!

And yet I know he will, and so easily. Just like his father!

No! I must not allow her to wheedle her way into this home.

There must be a way to be rid of her. I did not work so hard all these years to lose everything now. Nor did I bloody my hands with Mary's death to see it all wasted.

There must be a way, and I shall find it . . .

The hair on his nape stood on end as he read, and his heart began to hammer. Just like his father . . . Mary's death . . . Whose words were these? A sense of urgency forced him to flip to another page and read.

March 23, 1886

I don't know what to do! Everything seems lost.

The fire didn't work! The drug was supposed to keep her asleep until morning . . . How did she smell the smoke? She's wheedling her way into his graces—don't seem to know how to stop it. There must be some way! I won't lose everything—won't!

I know someone who might help—he did

once before . . . greedy little hoodlum.

Tomorrow I'll search him out . . . There must be some way to be rid of Sarah Hopkins!

Peter swallowed convulsively. His head registered what he was reading, making sense of the words. His heart refused to believe it . . . the fire . . .

April 3, 1886, was the next entry . . .

Nothing works!

God! She has the lives of a wretched cat!

Today's accident was almost too much—I am running out of opportunities. And Peter is growing suspicious. She gets closer and closer and there is nothing I can do. Nothing! That shameless harlot is a danger to all I have built. Peter would have had nothing were it not for me! They say it was Mary's money that saved him, but the stupid fool would never touch Christopher's funds—all the more for me! What bloody good is money to a boy who cannot see! Peter would have ended with nothing but the clothes upon his back were it not for contacts I have given him. Me! Without me, Peter would have nothing!

He bloody well owes me. And he owes me everything! I will not stand by and watch him give it all to some witch with a pretty face.

I will not lose everything!

This time I'll not leave it in somebody else's hands.

Peter thought he was going to be ill. The carriage accident . . . Ruth? Were these Ruth's words? How was it he had never seen her hatred before now? What had he ever done to incur it? She had always been distant, never sharing much of her thoughts or her time with him, but she had given so much to Christopher. He had never guessed at the fury she hid behind the emptiness of her eyes—had always believed she'd simply lacked a passion for life.

How wrong he was . . .

Her next entry seemed confused . . . fragmented thoughts . . . angry and yet subdued . . . The laudanum, he thought . . .

What is today's date?

My head is killing me.

One day has passed since that night. One day and another . . . half. Is that right?

My last entry is marked the 3rd. So it must be the 5th. April 5, 1886. How ironic that it should be nearly six years to the date since Mary's death.

God, I can't believe it. Everything I have tried has failed. If I don't do something, I will lose everything. How unfair to be in this position—why me? Why?

Damn the unfairness of it all!

Damn Sarah Hopkins—Woodard—or whatever the hell her bloody name is!

Peter already suspects—yet I cannot kill him. No, can't kill Peter. They will put him away...

Sarah should be the one dead. Not Mel. Little liar! She wasn't blind! God, she isn't even blind, and Peter seems not to care that she lied her way into this house!

How much did she see the night of the fire? How much does she know? I must find out tomorrow. Over tea. I'll talk to her. Find out. Tea would be good. Can't fail.

If I fail, it will be the end.

I refuse to fail.

Scratched into the bottom of the page with such force it made Peter's gut twist was . . .

Die, Sarah! Die!

Peter's reaction was physical. He felt it like a punch to his gut. All these years he had harbored his wife's murderer. She was his goddamned sister!

How had he been so blind?

His hands shook as he set down the journal, and his heart pounded as he looked at his son.

"Christopher," he said sternly, taking him by the shoulder and gripping him firmly, "this is very important, son."

Christopher nodded.

"Everything will be all right, but I want you to stay here in this room. Can you do that for me?"

"Yes, sir," he said, and Peter rose from the bed, retrieving the journal.

"Stay here," he directed, and went in search of his sister and the woman he loved.

Instinctively he knew that where he found one, he would find the other.

His sister needed help. He intended to give it to her.

He only hoped he wasn't too late.

God, for Sarah's sake, for his sake, for Christopher's sake, he prayed it wasn't too late! He didn't want to live without Sarah—didn't think he could bear losing her, too.

He heard their voices at the end of the corridor, and with his heart tripping in relief and clutching the journal in his hand, he rushed to the parlor.

He thrust open the doors to find them seated cozily before a small table set with tea for two. It was a picture-perfect image, tarnished only by the knowledge of what he had read within the journal he held in his hand.

"Peter!" Sarah exclaimed, and rose at once, dropping her cup on the saucer. The fine porcelain shattered, spilling hot tea on the table. It soaked into the cloth and trickled to the floor. She ran to his side, her face ashen.

His sister sat there, quite serenely, hardly fazed by the sound of breaking glass . . . except when he looked into her eyes. They were filled with something like defeat in that instant. Her gaze centered upon the book he held in his hand, and he thought she might faint where she sat. Her eyes rolled back and her head lolled backward a bit, but she sat straight once more and faced him squarely.

He drew Sarah into his arms, clutching her to him, embracing her with a hand at her back, relief and too many other emotions warring within him. He wanted to tell his sister that he would help her. Wanted to see her rot in jail for taking Mary's life. He didn't know what the hell to do, what to say, what to feel—except relief that Sarah was unharmed.

Ruth's gaze never left them.

Her expression wavered between sadness and fright and anger and confusion. "I never had a chance, Peter," she said calmly, and then reached out to lift up the full cup of tea that sat untouched before her.

Peter watched her with a sense of numbness, as though he were standing in the middle of a dream he did not quite comprehend. Somewhere deep within he understood what his brain would not register. He held Sarah close as he watched his sister rise to her feet.

Sarah turned as Ruth lifted the cup to her lips. "Oh God!" she cried out, and her knees buckled. Peter caught her, though still he did not quite comprehend.

"I never had a chance," Ruth said once more, sadly, and drank down the entire cup of tea. She poured herself another and drank it down as well, and it was in that instant as she guzzled the last of it that Peter fully understood what she had done.

He watched in stunned disbelief as she wobbled

on her feet and then crumpled with a thump to the floor. Sarah cried out at the sound and buried her head against his chest, clutching his shirt in horror. She began to sob and he pressed her against him, dropping the journal at their feet and holding her with both arms.

His mind reeled as he stared at his sister's body lying so limp on the floor.

It was over—over before he had even begun to comprehend what had happened—and he was, for an instant, too stunned even to blink.

Chapter 34

Ruth's funeral had been as quiet an affair as was possible, considering that there had been three deaths at the Holland estate in the last six years, with two of them occurring in the past week.

It was difficult to feel any sense of justice after reading Ruth's journals in their entirety. Ruth had been a desperate woman who had felt herself a victim at the hands of men. Sarah and Mary both were representative of all that Ruth had been denied in her life. And more, both of them had stood in the way—or so Ruth had thought—of all that she had felt should have been hers. It was difficult to blame Ruth entirely. Sarah blamed society in part for making women feel so helpless that they should resort to such desperate measures.

And yet Sarah had known many women in similar situations as Ruth—Mel, for example. Mel had found a way to survive and to do it with zest and pride and joy.

Some women were born victims, it seemed.

Sarah only thanked God Christopher was safe. She had accomplished what she had set out to do—uncover Mary's murderer and safeguard her son. Only she'd done something more in the process . . . something she'd only realized without a doubt as she'd watched them lower Ruth's casket into the ground.

She'd fallen in love with Peter Holland.

She kept her silence even after they left the cemetery and were safely away from the prying eyes of the press. She sat within the carriage, Christopher beside her, holding his little hand. His father sat before them, staring out the window.

Sarah watched him, admiring his beautiful face, wanting nothing more than to take that face in her hands and whisper *I love you* against his mouth.

She did love him, and her heart ached to hold him.

She couldn't bear the thought of leaving him.

Swallowing, she turned again to stare out the window, watching the streets pass by.

''Sarah,'' he called softly, and his voice was like a whisper to her heart.

Sarah blinked, and turned to him as he drew something from his coat. Without another word, he reached out to place the item on her lap.

It was a book.

Mary's?

''Is it . . .''

''Mary's journal,'' he affirmed. ''I thought you might like to read it.''

Sarah stared at the tiny book he'd presented to her, thinking how ironic it was that she'd searched so diligently for it as evidence, only to find Ruth's diary, instead. She met Peter's gaze.

He was watching her, frowning. "I'm sorry," he offered with a sad shake of his head. "I know she was dear to you."

Sarah nodded, and reached out almost reverently to lift the book into her hands, inspecting it.

It was small—deep red leather, embossed with Mary's name at the bottom right corner in delicate print. Sarah smoothed her finger over the gold lettering, trying to find the courage to open it and read Mary's last recorded words.

She turned the book and found it locked, and peered up at Peter in surprise. "You never opened it?"

He shrugged. "I didn't find it until some time after the investigation," he told her. "As I said . . . I think I was afraid to know what she had to say."

Sarah thought she understood. She was afraid as well, and yet for her, at least, it was time to face her cousin.

"I never found the key," he said.

Examining the delicate lock, she remembered the tiny charm she'd found in the first room she'd slept in. She wondered if it had survived the fire, wondered, too, if it might possibly be the key to Mary's final journal. She hadn't been in that room at all since the night of the fire, hadn't had any reason to go back, as she'd inspected both that room and the nursery quite thoroughly and to no avail.

"Where did you find it?" she asked, still scrutinizing the fine gold lock.

"In the nursery," he told her.

Sarah nodded. It made sense, then, that she would have kept the key in her room.

Her throat felt suddenly too tight to speak. Gratitude overwhelmed her. She knew it couldn't be easy for him to hand her a record of his past mistakes. "Thank you, Peter," she whispered, and looked up into his eyes.

She caught a glitter as he nodded and turned away.

Mary's last entry was dated the eve of April 15, 1880.

Through the entire journal there was nothing revealed that might have shed light upon her murder, and yet Mary had unknowingly left Sarah with so much insight into her and Peter's relationship.

It seemed quite clear to Sarah what had happened between them—at least from Mary's point of view.

She just didn't know Peter's.

It seemed to her that Mary had never been certain of Peter's love—his affection, yes, but never his love. In her own words she had tried so desperately to win him, but Peter had never given his heart and then finally had withdrawn from her completely.

Toward the end of her life, however, the last few entries in particular, Mary had begun to realize she'd handled her marriage terribly, that she had perhaps reacted to his withdrawal from a point of pain and not logically at all. She had begun to realize that her fears were simply that, *her fears,* and that if his eyes had wandered, then it had been because she had abandoned him so completely. She'd seemed pretty certain, however, that he had not, because she'd confronted his friend Cile directly about their relationship, and Cile had answered honestly—that yes, she did love Peter, but that Peter had never returned her feelings, that she'd respected his vows.

Apparently, however, Peter had confided in Cile, because Cile had also revealed to Mary the depths of Peter's disappointment over their failing marriage. It seemed Peter blamed himself for Mary's withdrawal—for not reassuring her when she'd needed it most. And perhaps that was true, but Mary and Peter had been so young, and these things were so much easier to see in hindsight.

And yet, according to the journal, Mary had begun to understand the mistakes they had made, had nearly decided to move back into her own room— nearly, though not quite . . .

As it turned out, she never had.

Pride had kept her from it.

Pride was a thief of time.

The two of them might have been happy together, but pride had kept Mary from going back to her husband, and pride had kept him from going to her.

Pride had kept Sarah and Mary apart, as well.

It wasn't until she turned the final page that she found the lock of hair—hair the color of Christopher's, though it was much too thick a lock to belong to a six-month-old child. It was secured to the back inside cover with a single phrase written beneath it: *I'm sorry, my dear Sarah.*

Sarah's heart jolted as she realized what it was.

Mary's hair.

Emotions choked her as she stared at her cousin's lock of hair, blinking away tears as she remembered a time so very long ago when they'd made each other vows. How old had they been? Sixteen? Seventeen? She had almost forgotten that day. But Mary hadn't, and the apology choked her breath away.

Swallowing the knot in her throat, she closed the journal and laid her head back against the chair in Mary's room, trying not to weep over so much regret.

She stared at the bed where Mellie had died and where Mary had once slept and wondered why she had subconsciously chosen this room to read Mary's last words.

Not to punish herself, perhaps, but as a reminder that all that had passed before need not pass in vain.

It *was* possible to learn from past mistakes.

Though Mary had never written Sarah to say so, it was apparent that she had begun to soften toward her, and at the point of Mary's death it had become more a matter of pride than anything else—pride alone had kept her from breaching the silence between them. As Mary had pointed out in her journal, Sarah had been as capable of breaking the silence as Mary had been, and Mary had felt Sarah responsible for making the first attempt.

And perhaps rightly so.

It was true . . . Sarah could have . . . and probably *should* have been the one to raise the white flag. It had been her own ultimatum that had damaged their relationship to begin with. That she had not relented was something Sarah would have to live with for the rest of her life.

And yet, must she punish herself forever simply because she had not had the insight and fortitude to make the right decision all those years ago?

Was it right for Peter to continue to blame himself for his mistakes with Mary?

The answer was no.

And Mary hadn't continued to blame her, either—nor Peter. She had long forgiven Sarah, except for her stubbornness. It had saddened and angered Mary that Sarah had gone so very long without apologizing. And it had hurt her immensely that she'd felt Sarah hadn't cared enough.

If Mary had only known.

If she'd only realized how often Sarah had berated herself for her own stubborn youthful pride . . . Why couldn't she have let it go long enough to right the wrongs between them?

Such foolishness.

But what was done was done, and Sarah could hardly undo the damage now.

The question now was . . .

Could she walk away from Peter?

Could she simply pack her bags and go?

And the answer was no.

She lifted a brow as she thought about Peter's proposal, and then Christopher's, and smiled.

It was a bold thing to do, but she wasn't the sort to wait about for things to happen. Her uncle had always taught her that if she wanted something badly enough, she need only pursue it.

Why should it be a man's right to ask a woman to wed?

She had as much right as he, did she not?

She only prayed Christopher had been speaking for his father when he had asked her to marry them, because she would die if Peter should say no now, if he should laugh in her face.

And with that in mind, she rose determinedly from her chair, took a deep breath, and marched toward Peter's office.

She found him sitting at his desk, sifting through his papers, but it was obvious to Sarah that his mind was not on his work. His sister's death, no matter that they were not close, had left him in a state of shock.

She wanted to hold him in that instant.

She wanted to make love to him . . . for the rest of her life.

"Peter," she began. He peered up at her, his eyes full of sorrow. Now was not the time to speak of Ruth; perhaps later when the wound was not so fresh. There was nothing he might have done differently; he couldn't have known. Looking back on it, the signs were there, but there was nothing in Ruth's demeanor that might have led them to such a horrifying conclusion. Sarah was going to make him understand that—wouldn't let him blame himself.

He'd been blaming himself for far too much far too long.

"I have been thinking," Sarah continued, and

took a deep breath, trying not to smile at what she was about to say.

"Forgive me for bringing this up at such a terrible time," she said, marching into his office and standing before his desk, "but I have been ignoring the matter of my reputation far too long, you see . . . I cannot remain oblivious to it now that my task here is done."

He stared at her, unblinking, and she began to ramble.

"A reputation is such a delicate thing, you realize . . . and I must do what I can to save it . . ."

Peter swallowed as he listened to the woman he loved.

She was going to leave him now, he sensed it.

The drama was over, and Christopher was safe.

No reason for her to stay.

He'd been sitting here, trying to work up the courage to ask her once more to stay, to beg even if that was what it took. God, he loved her.

She was going to leave him.

He nodded, not quite able to face Sarah as she spoke. Staring at his papers, he tried not to choke on his grief over what she was about to do.

He wouldn't stop her.

He had no right to.

"I think it's only right you should marry me," she blurted, and Peter lifted his gaze to her in stunned surprise.

Her chin lifted defiantly, and her expression was perfectly sober.

His brows twitched and he shook his head, not

quite believing what had come from her lips.

It was the most arrogant proposal any man had ever imposed, and to hear it from the lips of a woman—not just any woman, but the woman he loved—made him grin.

"You think I should marry you?" he asked her.

Her chin lifted higher. "I do!"

He threw his head back and laughed out loud, his heart bursting with joy. He rose from his chair at once and came around his desk.

"I don't see what is so blessed funny!" Sarah exclaimed, quite in a huff at his reaction.

"You don't?" he asked her, and pulled her into his arms.

"No, I bloody well don't!" she exclaimed, and struggled against his embrace as he tried to hold her.

"I do," he replied, laughing still. "You're an arrogant, demanding woman, and I love you madly! Ask me again," he demanded, "so there is no mistake."

"Why are you laughing?" she asked quite indignantly, ignoring his request, but his joy must have been infectious because he felt her laughter as he tightened his embrace, wanting to draw her into his very soul.

He buried his face in the hair that spilled against her throat. "Ask me again," he demanded of her once more.

"I will not!" she swore, and he drew back to watch the flush rise into her cheeks. God, but she was beautiful.

He kissed her on the bridge of her nose, a gentle

peck. "Just once more, Sarah . . . I love you."

He gave her a nudge and she threw her arms about him, hugging his neck, smiling up at him. "Very well," she relented, and dared to repeat, "Will you marry me, Peter Holland?"

"Only if you'll return the favor," he answered with a wink, and drew her into a more intimate embrace. She laughed and he kissed her lips and whispered, "I love you, Sarah Woodard . . . I love you with every beat of my heart."

"And I love you, Peter Holland," she whispered back, "And I'm going to love you the rest of my life!"

"Are you now?" he asked her, and deepened the kiss, teasing her with his tongue and his lips.

"Shall I prove it?" she returned softly, and moaned against his mouth.

The sound of it hardened him instantly and heated his blood; she never ceased to arouse him. "Certainly," he replied. "Every day for the rest of our lives. Beginning now," he murmured, and sealed the proposal with a kiss.

Epilogue

A glance inside the parlor window at University Place and Twelfth Street revealed a festive and familial air. An eleven-foot Christmas tree dominated one corner, its tip barely clearing the ceiling. The angel at its helm was bent forward, as though peering down at the scene below.

Christopher Holland sat with his two sisters, Melissa and Laura, at the foot of the newly decorated tree, Christopher with a Braille-embossed book in his lap. Laura lay on her belly listening to her brother read to them from *The Christmas Story* while she drew on paper. Three-year-old Melissa was much too engrossed with her brother's tale to draw, though she had her own sheet laid out on the floor beside her.

"And while they were there, the days of her confinement were complete," he read aloud, though he'd long ago memorized the tale, "and she gave birth to her firstborn *son*." He paused in his reading and waited, listening to his father and Sarah. The two of them spoke in low tones, thinking probably that no one could hear them, but Christopher could.

"I think that was a hint," his father said with a trace of laughter in his voice. "Too coincidental that he should stop there."

Sarah laughed, and whispered, "He wants a baby brother something terrible, Peter."

"I know, and it's going to be a boy this time," his father whispered in return, determined that it was to be so.

"You shouldn't make promises we cannot keep," Sarah chided him. "You said that very thing the last two times, and look!"

"I see a very happy boy who loves his two little sisters," Peter countered. "He'll love this child no matter what . . . just like his father will."

Christopher could feel his mother's smile where he sat. His father had been wrong all those years ago. Sarah had not been black . . . but yellow. She was that light Peter had spoken of. She had changed their lives forever the day she had come into their lives. His father no longer sat alone with his untouched glass of port in his office—a scent Christopher would always associate with unhappiness.

It was their sixth Christmas together, and he had never been happier in all his life. Merriment sang throughout the Holland house like joyful carolers.

"She wrapped him in swaddling clothes," Christopher continued, "and laid him in a manger . . ."

"What is swaddling clothes?" Laura asked her brother.

"Baby blankets," Christopher told her.

"Whassa manger?" Melissa asked, scooting closer to him. She craned her neck to look into his face. Though Christopher couldn't see her, he sensed her scrutiny nonetheless.

But it wasn't his face she was preoccupied with . . .

"A manger is a trough where they put feed for animals to eat," Christopher explained. Melissa snuck a cane from the tree beside his head, but Christopher smelled it and seized it from her.

Melissa giggled. "Whassa trough?" she asked, unfazed.

Christopher hung the cane once more upon the tree. "You'll spoil your supper," he chided her.

"A trough is like a dinner plate," Peter interjected, grinning as he watched his children. He put his arms around his wife and drew her against him, rubbing her belly.

She was carrying his child, yet another—three children in six years, but they couldn't seem to help it. He wanted her just as much today as he had that first night. He craved her more in fact, than ever, and if she weren't so pregnant with his fourth child, he would carry her back to their room and make love to her once again. As it was, he was afraid she might not make it through the unwrapping of the gifts. She placed her hand over his on her belly, and he smiled and sighed contentedly.

"I love you, Sarah Holland," he whispered, and kissed the back of her neck, relishing the feel of her in his arms. He hugged her gently.

She tilted her head just a little, enjoying his kisses. "And I love you," she said in return.

And both of them settled back upon the divan to watch their children together . . .

Dear Reader,

Heat up your summer with some sizzling June romance reading from Avon Books, beginning with Judith Ivory's Avon Romantic Treasure SLEEPING BEAUTY. This unique twist on the popular fairy tale is lushly sensuous. And the romance between Sir James Stoker and the delectable Coco Wild is unforgettable!

If you love Regency-set romance, don't miss ONLY IN MY DREAMS by Eve Byron. Eve's love stories are filled with passion, humor and a touch of intrigue. Here, Lorelei Wildewood had been forced into a marriage of convenience with Adrian Winters—a man she barely knew. Adrian promptly went off to sea, but now he's back, and his fiery kisses make Lorelei think that marriage might not be so bad after all...

Western settings are a favorite of mine, and Kit Dee's ARIZONA RENEGADE has everything western fans could ask for—a wild, beautiful setting, a sexy U.S. Secret Service agent...and an innocent temptress. Strong romantic tension, complex characters and a memorable love story all combine to make ARIZONA RENEGADE a book for your keeper shelf!

Fans of Contemporary romance won't want to miss Eboni Snoe's TELL ME I'M DREAMIN'. Nadine Clayton has had it with being a workaholic! So she sheds her business suits and takes off for the sunny Caribbean...where she meets a mysterious man she simply can't resist. This is the perfect love story to take to the beach!

Happy Reading!

Lucia Macro

Lucia Macro
Senior Editor

AEL 0698

Avon Romantic Treasures

*Unforgettable, enthralling love stories,
sparkling with passion and adventure
from Romance's bestselling authors*

❀❀❀❀❀❀❀❀❀❀❀❀❀❀❀❀❀❀❀❀❀❀❀❀❀❀❀❀❀❀

WALTZ IN TIME *by Eugenia Riley*
78910-8/$5.99 US/$7.99 Can

BRIGHTER THAN THE SUN *by Julia Quinn*
78934-5/$5.99 US/$7.99 Can

AFTER THE THUNDER *by Genell Dellin*
78603-6/$5.99 US/$7.99 Can

MY WICKED FANTASY *by Karen Ranney*
79581-7/$5.99 US/$7.99 Can

DEVIL'S BRIDE *by Stephanie Laurens*
79456-x/$5.99 US/$7.99 /Can

THE LAST HELLION *by Loretta Chase*
77617-0/$5.99 US/$7.99 Can

PERFECT IN MY SIGHT *by Tanya Anne Crosby*
78572-2/$5.99 US/$7.99 Can

SLEEPING BEAUTY *by Judith Ivory*
78645-1/$5.99 US/$7.99 Can

Avon Romances—
the best in exceptional authors and unforgettable novels!

Discover Contemporary Romances at Their Sizzling Hot Best from Avon Books

TILL THE END OF TIME *by Patti Berg*
78339-8/$5.99 US/$7.99 Can

FLY WITH THE EAGLE *by Kathleen Harrington*
77836-X/$5.99 US/$7.99 Can

WHEN NICK RETURNS *by Dee Holmes*
79161-7/$5.99 US/$7.99 Can

HEAVEN LOVES A HERO *by Nikki Holiday*
78798-9/$5.99 US/$7.99 Can

ANNIE'S HERO *by Maggie Shayne*
78747-4/$5.99 US/$7.99 Can

TWICE UPON A TIME *by Emilie Richards*
78364-9/$5.99 US/$7.99 Can

WHEN LIGHTNING STRIKES TWICE *by Barbara Boswell*
72744-7/$5.99 US/$7.99 Can